# MAD HOPE

*stories by*

HEATHER BIRRELL

Coach House Books, Toronto

first edition

Canada Council for the Arts Conseil des Arts du Canada ONTARIO ARTS COUNCIL CONSEIL DES ARTS DE L'ONTARIO Canada

Published with the generous assistance of the Canada Council for the Arts and the Ontario Arts Council. Coach House Books also acknowledges the support of the Government of Canada through the Canada Book Fund and the Government of Ontario through the Ontario Book Publishing Tax Credit.



LIBRARY AND ARCHIVES CANADA CATALOGUING IN PUBLICATION

Birrell, Heather
Mad hope / Heather Birrell.

Short stories.
ISBN 978-1-55245-258-5

I. Title.

PS8553.I792I56 2004 C813'.54 C2012-900238-0

*Mad Hope* is available as an ebook: ISBN 978 1 77056 315 5.

*For Joan Firmin, a.k.a. Nanny,*
*a.k.a. Mrs. Lady, 1917–2011*

## The Frog

What a wonderful bird the frog are!
When he stand he sit almost;
When he hop he fly almost.
He ain't got no sense hardly;
He ain't got no tail hardly either.
When he sit, he sit on what he ain't got almost.

– Anonymous

# Table of Contents

# BriannaSusannaAlana

AT THE TOP OF THE STREET where Brianna, Susanna and Alana lived was a parkette in the form of a teardrop turned sideways. The parkette had a slide, two sets of swings (one for babies and one for big kids) and a climbing frame in the shape of a rocket ship. Brianna, at six, was not a baby, but still gave the big-kid swings the respect they deserved. Susanna, at ten, loved the big-kid swings, and had the soar-and-smash scars to prove it. Alana, at nearly thirteen, was *so* over swings of any kind.

Just above the parkette was a used-car lot, and next to that, an apartment parking lot, and next to that the apartment building itself, a brownstone of moderate proportions. Surrounding the brownstone was a well-manicured lawn that had been sectioned off in the northwest corner by yellow police tape. The police tape had been there for eight days and now appeared slack in places, fatigued.

From the observation pod at the top of the rocketship, Susanna had a good view of the goings-on around and inside the police tape. She observed, then reported her findings in urgent bulletins to Brianna and Alana. The former received these bulletins eagerly, if indiscriminately, jumping up and down below the pod, while the latter sat on one of the rungs of the slide yawning and peeling back the petals of skin around her fingernails. Still, whatever Susanna could tell them could not in any significant way diminish or augment what they already knew. The reason for the police tape was that somebody had been murdered.

'I think,' Susanna said, lifting and twisting her chin with what she imagined was authority, 'we should all think back to what we were doing the day of the murder.'

'Whatever,' said Alana.

'Two, four, six, eight,' called Brianna, still jumping.

'There's a cardinal,' said Susanna, pointing to the top branches of a tall spruce across the street.

'Not a clue,' said Alana. 'Not a clue about the murder.' She stood up, climbed to the top of the ladder and sat down on the platform.

## Alana

Alana had been walking home that day with her friend Zoe when three boys they did not recognize slouched out from behind a parked car.

'Hey,' said one, and hiked up his pants, 'my friend wants to do you bitches hard and anal.'

Zoe turned to Alana, giggling. 'What should I say?'

Alana shrugged. She liked the look of one of the boys, his half-up, half-down mouth and red Nike jacket. He sucked his teeth at her, eyed her chest.

'What should I *say*?' Zoe hissed.

Alana shook her head.

So they did not say anything, but let two of the boys follow them to a nearby Starbucks, where the girls bought chai lattes and sat down to sip at the foam. Two tables over, the boys lounged with their knees akimbo, flicking sugar packets at each other.

Alana and Zoe began a conversation that required them to laugh and twirl their hair. They pretended they knew what they were talking about.

*Dialogue*, thought Alana. We're doing *dialogue*.

When one of the boys got up and began walking towards them, they leaned in across the table so their foreheads almost touched. They smiled at each other.

The boy pulled up a chair. 'Hey,' he said. It was not Alana's boy.

'Hey,' said Zoe.

'Me and my boys're going to the ravine. Catch fish or somethin'.'

'Yeah,' said Alana's boy, now standing behind the first boy. 'Or somethin'.' He pinched his fingers together, drew deeply on an invisible joint.

'Cool,' said Zoe to the first boy. 'What's your name?'

'I'm Darryl.' He looked for a green moment as though he might have said the wrong thing.

Alana opened her eyes wide because she knew she could appear almost Chinese if she relaxed and was not careful. And because some part of her felt more alert.

'And this is Jordan,' said Darryl.

'Cool,' said Zoe again.

The boys sat down and pulled more sugar packets from their pockets.

## Susanna

Susanna could not remember the day of the murder, nor could she invent it (although she cast mightily back into her mind). This was bizarre, since memories – their particular bents and textures – were usually her strong suit. At home they didn't really talk about it. *In our own backyard,* she heard her mother say on the phone. *Your friends and neighbours,* her father sighed to himself over the headlines. The problem with the mystery, in Susanna's view, was that the most pressing W questions (Who, What, Where, When) had already been answered. The criminal had been caught. The only leftover was Why. And finding Why after the death, after the arrest, was a problem. How did you dig up the clues that led deep into people's brains? The Motive, that's what Susanna was looking for.

What Susanna did remember was an afternoon two days *after* the murder, walking home by herself, thinking about the

Motive and the Concept of Evolution. She knew that sometimes ideas in books that had nothing to do with the mystery at hand could loop you back towards a solution. There was a book she was reading now, one of her mother's, a science book about the origins of the human race. She didn't understand most of it, just read the words like a robot when she wanted to relax. But there were a few pages that had stuck with her, a section explaining our ancestry, way back before kings and queens and ancient castles. It was about chimpanzees, apes and humans, mothers all holding hands with their children around the entire earth – as if the earth were time, the distance years – then turning to face each other as cousins, as relations. What the author was trying to show was that blood and time could not really separate us from the animals we were and always had been. What it meant was that we were *actually* animals. But animals who could write books about how we are actually animals. Animals who murdered for complicated reasons. This was confusing in the best kind of way. She liked it when she had to fight to keep things straight.

There were lots of leaves on the streets, but rain had clumped them up with mud and pollution. Even so, Susanna dragged her feet through the gutters happily. When she got home she would have the entire house to herself. Alana was at piano and Brianna had playgroup. On Wednesdays Susanna was a latchkey kid.

### Brianna

The day of the murder Brianna hid behind her favourite tree in the schoolyard at pickup time. She watched her teacher, Ms. Sawchuk, talking to her babysitter, Frances, who nodded, then shifted her shoulders up and down quickly. Then she saw Caroline – a fat, wily, lively girl from Grade 2 – skip up to the two grown-ups and point towards the tree. Brianna pressed her cheek hard into the bark. She turned her face and kissed the trunk with all the tenderness she could muster. 'Goodbye, friend,' she said. Then Frances hauled her out and pulled her towards the car, which was a modern station wagon named Saturn.

'That was very naughty,' said Frances, once belted in. She turned the key in the ignition and the car roared to life. 'I was so worried.'

'Hello, Saturn,' Brianna called from the back seat.

Alana

Outside the coffee shop, the light had begun to dim. Alana loved fall; it made her so sleepy and willing. She watched an old man on the sidewalk clutch his hat to his head, railing against the wind like something from a movie. Darryl and Jordan were still there, telling stories involving lockers and basements and cops. From the stories, Zoe and Alana understood the boys were from the high school. The girls, who were not from the high school, didn't tell many stories, unless they were about TV shows.

'We gotta split soon,' said Jordan. 'You wanna come?'

'Mmm,' said Zoe. 'Just let me consult with my girl.' She tugged on Alana's sleeve and jerked her head towards the washrooms.

The women's washroom was a single, large and harshly lit, with metal bars on the walls for the disabled. Zoe looped her purse over one of the bars, and shimmied her jeans down her hips. Alana looked in the mirror. She was happy with the way her hair was falling in a smooth curtain down her cheek, but above her left eyebrow was the small rosy swell of a blemish.

'Undergrounder,' she said to Zoe, tapping at the spot.

'Do you wanna go with them?' said Zoe, standing up. She bounced twice to ease her jeans back in place.

'Sure,' said Alana, because she really did.

But Darryl and Jordan were not back at the table. Alana looked out the window and spotted them climbing on a parking meter outside.

'Coupla monkeys,' said Zoe, smiling.

On the street they paired off. Jordan asked Alana what kind of shit she was into, and she had no idea. Then he pointed to the earphones dangling from behind his ears.

'Music,' he said. 'What do you like?'

'Oh,' said Alana. She liked her parents' old cassettes from the eighties and soft-rock stations that played people singing about love over mild-mannered saxophones. 'Some old school, sometimes pop, you know.'

'Cool,' said Jordan.

Alana wished he would plug in the earphones so they could just walk. 'Yeah,' she said. She focused on Jordan's gait; it was purposeful and lopsided. His hip dipped and his arm swung like a creature who had chosen – righteously – to remain less evolved. His hair – jagged at the nape – had been dyed blond recently; there was a laissez-faire brown crop circle at the crown. Her cellphone began to bleat softly, rhythmically, from her coat pocket. She cherished the phone, its sleekness and weight in her hand, the flutter in her gut when she saw she had messages waiting. She flipped it open, pressed a keypad.

'H'lo.'

It was Frances, the babysitter. Alana was overdue at home. Brianna was waiting. They were both waiting. Alana thought about Brianna. She was twice the age and twice the size of her little sister. If she were a fish in a pond she would eat her, chomp, just like that. She closed the phone and slid it back into her pocket.

Zoe, who had seen the whole thing, tugged at Alana's sleeve. 'What?' she said, then clenched her teeth together.

'Gotta go get my sister.'

'Lame,' said Zoe. She spat into the gutter and looked over at Darryl.

Alana began to walk away, then stopped, turned around and sidled up to Jordan. 'Meet me later,' she said, and brought her lips close to one of the headphones. She whispered instructions. He nodded and snaked his hand up under her shirt, brushed his fingers against the skin above her belt.

'Bye,' she said.

## Susanna

'Hel-*lo*, Sunny!' shouted Susanna, as she pushed open the door. 'I'm home! Susanna's home!'

*Oh yes,* Sunny barked, skittering on the smooth floor of the hallway. *Oh yes, you are!*

Susanna stroked Sunny madly behind his ears, then slapped his belly when he rolled over for more. 'C'mere, you old mutt,' she said like a pro, then reached for his paws, holding them up in the air so he could dance, his legs splayed, the tender flesh of his underside and the nubs of his groin exposed. 'Do you know the way to San José?' she sang, but he didn't like it, didn't even look at her. 'Not so good on the old hind legs, eh, Sun?'

This was another thing that made humans different from animals: language. Not only our big brains, but also our breathing patterns – the ability and anatomy to walk and talk at the same time – made us what we are today. Sunny might be able to help Susanna with some aspects of the investigation – his nose, for example, was invaluable – but in the end, the human brain would prevail.

At school, news of the murder was passed around like an amulet; it was both excruciating and propitious to give it up to someone else. What they knew for certain was that the victim was the murderer's mother, an old lady who once baked carrot muffins for her neighbours in 3F. He had buried her in the small garden adjoining the apartment building. Plus, one night about three months ago, someone had overheard the killer – a quiet man who wore his salt and pepper hair army-short and drove a red Ford pickup – shouting the questions, 'Why?' and 'Do you think Dad ever really loved me?' in a choked, anguished voice. It was assumed he was drunk. There were rumours that a reward was being offered for more information that could, in the words of Jill Nelson, 'really nail the guy.' The culprit, according to Jill, was a part-time plumber. 'He only did a few jobs here and there,' she said to Susanna outside the gym doors. 'He was, like, a temp worker,' she added, in a tone that suggested her father worked at a job distinctly full-time, professional and non-plumber. 'They should lock him up and throw away the key.'

Susanna nodded. She had no choice; while you were within her range, Jill Nelson's proclamations were indelible. But when Jill was gone, Susanna wondered. Even the dog, who was now blinking up at her lovingly, divined things the rest of them couldn't, despite their big brains. For instance, when Brianna had her petit mals, Sunny predicted them. Susanna had seen him doing a panicked prance around her sister's feet just before Brianna's eyes pinwheeled back into her head. She had read that some dogs would go further for their epileptic owners: lapping urgently at their faces, pushing them with careful snouts into soft chairs, positioning their bodies in the paths of their falls. That was Love. Or else a Survival Mechanism. Too bad the dead woman didn't have a dog like that. 'Loyalty,' said Susanna to Sunny, 'that's what's missing in Today's Crazy World.'

Yes, science could offer some answers, but there were phenomena you smelled without realizing, situations you simply absorbed through your very pores. *I went to the University of Life*, Susanna once heard her father say. She had filed this away, along with, That's Life in the Big City, and You Can't Always Get What You Want. In the schoolyard, Susanna kept quiet throughout much of the speculation, but in her heart she knew *she* would be the one to finally, glamorously dig up some obscure, invaluable piece of evidence. What she had was good instinct.

In fact, there were already clever life things she was learning to do, secretly. That very lunchtime, Susanna had dropped her knapsack in the school toilet by mistake, right down there into the pee.

It didn't matter that she rescued it quickly, it was still dripping. It would smell. Jill was there too, and called in to her, 'Are you okay?' But Susanna did not panic. 'I'm okay,' she called back. 'out in a minute. You go ahead.' She stayed calm and used her head, reasoned it out, quickly flushing, then waiting for the tank to fill before she pressed the lever again and dunked the bag into the clean second swirl. Outside of the stall, she clicked the hand dryer on, allowed it to fill her head with its heat and noise. She held the bag up to the nozzle until it was dry.

## Brianna

Once home, Brianna helped Frances make cookies – there was some bother with a plastic measuring cup whose lines had worn away, but Frances had a feel for ingredients and quantities, and in this regard Brianna trusted her – then she went to her playroom to tell stories to her dolls.

She sat down on the floor and surveyed the set-up. Her dolls were piled in a heap on an old plastic serving tray her mother had given her, and she had arranged her racing cars in the form of a flower directly opposite the tray. The cars looked like humped metallic insects waiting for something exciting to happen. Something exciting *would* happen. World Creation. She picked out two of the dolls, laid them out before her, stripped off their clothes and pushed them down, squashing the soft plastic of their tummies.

'You are now part of the earth,' she said. Then she scrabbled them up out of the soil, blew on them two times each. 'Out of thin air,' she said. 'Man and woman.' They began to stir and come to life, pushing their limbs out, yawning excitedly. Then the girl doll walked over to the racing cars/insects and woke them up with a wave of her hand. But next to the racing cars was a flying spindle that sprung up and pricked the girl doll's palms.

'Help,' said the girl doll weakly, 'I'm bleeding.'

'We will have to hang you up on the cross,' said the boy doll. 'You are a sacrifice. Sorry.'

'I don't think so,' said the girl doll.

'It doesn't matter what you *think*,' said the boy doll.

The girl doll whistled and a silver pony came galloping in from the hinterlands.

'We have not yet created ponies,' said the boy doll.

'I don't care,' said the girl doll, and when she touched the pony with her palms her wounds healed and the pony whispered he would hide her at the top of the CN Tower.

'Goodbye!' called the girl doll.

'You can't leave,' said the boy doll.

'You better believe I can,' said the girl doll.

Then the boy doll got very angry and said he would punch her in the vagina.

'BE QUIET OR I WILL PUNCH YOU IN THE VAGINA!' Brianna shouted.

And then there was Frances, her face gathering force in the doorway like a thundercloud. '*What* did you say?'

'Sorry,' said Brianna, because sometimes saying sorry got people to stay quiet and smile with their lips closed.

'Well,' said Frances. 'Watch your tongue.' She picked up one of the racing cars and turned it over carefully in her hand. Then she looked at her watch. 'Where's that sister of yours?'

## Alana

Alana took her sister Brianna to the park, their fingers interlaced in a kind of lock.

'We're trying the big-kid swings today, whether you like it or not.'

'Not,' said Brianna, and Alana looked at her, impressed, but still hoisted her up onto the black rubber band and gave a tiny push.

'Too scary,' Brianna whispered, her voice stolen by the sensation of so much wind whooshing around her midsection.

'Okay,' said Alana. 'Corkscrew, then.' She began to twist the chains of the swings together. Brianna was silent, holding on.

Alana looked around. Where this afternoon there had been only fall – trees all lacy with leaves, the night creeping in with the cold, Zoe shifting from foot to foot in her miniskirt, cursing September – there was now something else. He would come, she thought. It was like fate, or, again, a movie. Or he would not come, but only because his mother was sick, or he'd been hit by a car. Then she would help him, be his one and only helper. They would maybe go on a trip together – somewhere with a desert and strange mounded homes. But then she remembered his hand on her skin. She was not skinny. If he'd noticed? Put a little pressure on the pudginess there?

Brianna looked small, all wound up in there. It didn't seem so long ago she was a baby, feet curled into themselves like little crullers. She was so easy to love then. There was something about smallness. Even today in homeroom Alana had slipped into a daze at the sight of Zoe's box of mini butterfly clamps. She found she could not stop staring into their tiny, shiny maws, flapping their metal wings back and forth, squeezing to feel the built-in resistance. What it did – playing with small things – was make you feel like a god.

'Ready, Freddy?'

'Not Freddy,' Brianna mumbled, hunched over under the chains.

'I'm letting go.'

''Kay.'

It was always super slow, the initial unwinding, then there was a moment where the momentum took over, and, voila!, you were out of it, free, listing lazily in the other direction. Brianna looked like she might puke.

'Again,' she said.

Alana began to twist, but then she noticed something at the periphery. A flash of red near the fence, rounding the corner. She turned her head quickly to make sure.

'Don't stop twisting, 'Lana.'

'Rocket-pod time, Brianna. One small step for man, a giant step for girls like you.' Alana grabbed Brianna under the arms so she had no choice but to cling like an orangutan.

'I need you to stay here, in the pod, and be on lookout duty.' Alana had secured her inside the bars of the small dome. Brianna was sitting with her knees drawn up, face blanched. 'Don't be scared. Maybe one day you'll be an astronaut. You could be that, you know. You could be anything in the world.'

'Not an armadillo,' said Brianna, and Alana knew she was off the hook.

'See you later, armadillo.'

Jordan was right there, near the swings, fiddling with an unlit cigarette, waiting for her. He looked good, better than before, away from the street, away from the others. She had forgotten how tall he was, how his hazel eyes darted and understood.

'Can we go somewhere to talk?' he said, and Alana was amazed. She showed him how to scale the aluminum siding that bordered the car lot and they wandered amidst the cars, thumping them insolently with their open hands. On the border between the car lot and the parking lot someone had planted some overgrown shrubbery and two spindly trees and dragged a small picnic table into the patchy shade. When they sat down, the picnic table rocked over the uneven ground like a tugboat. They kissed. Jordan pushed his hand under Alana's shirt, and she let him. He kissed her neck behind her ear, and slid his fingers under her thin bra. Alana felt worried. How to reciprocate? Under his shirt was flat and uninteresting. He pushed her hand downwards. She unzipped.

They kissed and kissed, slackening their jaws, using tongues. Then Jordan bent her head so she could see exactly what he had below. She kneeled on the ground in front of him. There was a Mars bar wrapper under the picnic table, and some pine needles, which was peculiar, since there were no pines nearby. Jordan took off his jacket, then draped it over Alana's head and shoulders and his poked-out penis. It was the beginnings of a puppet show. His T-shirt was bunched up under his arms. Above Jordan's belt were two long muscular indents, as if he were made of smooth clay and someone had picked him up carefully by his hip bones. The indents ran on either side of a trail of small black downy hairs. But Alana could not see where the hair led; the trail was obscured by white boxers that puffed out of the fly of his jeans like Kleenex. She touched one of the indents with her fingers and her heart began to beat between her legs. The skin was so soft and tight! Jordan made a sound, and Alana understood. She put her lips around his penis, then worked them down so that her mouth was full. She did this several times – up and down, trying not to let her teeth get in the way. Jordan placed his hand on her head and made another sound that was almost a word. Jordan's whole body shook. Alana gagged, then swallowed.

Then it was over, and the thing itself – the lovely indents, her migratory heart and the almost-word – was gone, shoved down into the deepest drawer of her self, but Alana had already trapped and tidied the *story* of it in her head thousands of times. There was an unstated currency in these happenings; the value would be in the timing of the revelation, the payoff would be in the exact spin she put on the thing.

### Susanna

In order to find all the pertinent information, Susanna knew it would be necessary to return to the scene of the crime. 'The Return,' she said to Sunny, who licked her wrist. She decided to take the dog with her for protection. It could be the murderer had an accomplice, lurking. She gathered some supplies: a magnifying glass from her science set, a plastic bag to collect evidence, an apple for provisions, another plastic bag for Sunny's poop. Then she hooked the dog on to his leash, closed and locked the front door with her key, and began to walk up the street, stopping to let Sunny sniff and snoop in other people's gardens. Susanna recognized the shape of each fading flower bed, the particular means the cracks in the sidewalk had for accommodating crabgrass and dandelions.

It was strange how well she knew her way around here, how everything came to her automatically, like her heart knowing how to pump, and when. It was a kind of memory, she thought, like the monarch's. Monarchs, who flitted around in the backyard in August, settling on blossoms to feed, then swooping and flirting. They were better than a whole circus. But this was not the most amazing thing. When it was time – how did they know? – the whole lot of them began a journey south, across the border, through the States, alighting on a few hilltops in Mexico. There, masses of them bent tree boughs with their weight. It took a long time, months, for them to get there, surfing updrafts of warm air, but if they got tired and died, it didn't matter, their sons and daughters had the maps in their minds' eyes; it was a memory that was inherited. Susanna has seen pictures of them clustered around Mexican tree trunks. This was all it took – one giant flapping, delicate creature – to prove how very little we know of the world. And if whole troops of scientists could not solve the mystery of the monarch, how could Susanna discover the depths of a stranger's soul?

What would ever make you so angry you'd want to kill your very own mother? 'Your own flesh and blood!' she said, then pinched some skin on her forearm to reinforce the idea. Monarchs could avoid most predators because of a poison in their bodies that birds and frogs, animals with backbones, could not stomach – cardiac glycosides. People were not always so lucky.

Sunny began to pull at his leash. *Squirrels,* he barked. They had reached the park's outer edge, and he wanted to run. But Susanna had other plans. 'C'mon, Sunny,' she said, 'we're going to check out the makeshift grave.' She tugged him gently. But then something stopped her; when she considered the grave, the thud as the body fell, all her objectivity was supplanted by a terrible billowing sensation in her chest. It was as if her breath had lost its way, as though everything her body ever knew had evaporated. She cut through the parking lot and spotted an old picnic table next to some bushes. 'I think we need to sit down,' she said to Sunny, who didn't agree, but was beholden. Seated, she bent over and put her head between her knees. Under the bench was a Mars bar wrapper and some pine needles, which was peculiar, since there were no pine trees nearby. Susanna sighed. Then she noticed one of the pine needles was moving. An ant was carrying it! The source of the pine needles was metres away, but the ants were determined to make a nest here, under the table. Incredible!

She remembered something then, from the day in question, although it would not be worth any reward. It was her mother's voice. (Then the three of them *had* been at the park. Curious!)

'BriannaSusannaAlana!' her mother had called. 'Don't make me send your father up there!'

Why not, Susanna wondered, and it was a credit to her innocence and her father's oblivious, kindly nature that she honestly could not imagine the answer to this question.

**Brianna**

Brianna opened and closed her eyes rapidly, and swivelled her head around. This was called Taking Snapshots. In this way she didn't have to see it all – the whole world – at once. She was very frightened. There was no climbing down from the pod. When she looked down at the patch of gravelly ground below, she realized what had happened. The pony had succeeded. But where was he now?

'Tallest free-standing structure in the world,' she said wistfully. It was likely she would be here for a few days, with no food or water, and wild animals pawing at the dirt, their teeth aglow. She didn't mind raccoons so much, but squirrels were dishonest, and there were certain birds whose long beaks made their eyes appear smaller, like cruel glass beads. Maybe she could escape. What was it Alana had said? *You could be anything in the world.* She let go of the bar nearest her and extended one of her arms out, into the atmosphere. It was not so bad. She brought her arm in again, then dangled one leg down, swung it back and forth. But the actual means of escape confounded her; there was too much space between her body and the ground, too much room for disaster.

She felt cold and hungry. She wanted her mother. She wriggled around and felt in her coat pocket. There were some crispy bits of something! Chips? No, old tangerine rinds dried to hard shards. She took them out, sniffed them, then placed them in her mouth experimentally. She would put the moisture back in with her tongue. But it didn't work at all. It was a bit like the sign for the store called the Bay at the mall, with its large, strange symbol that meant B, but looked nothing like a B at all. Why did they have to do that? Make the connections so odd and tattered? She hated the not-B of the Bay with all her heart. She concentrated on this – hating the B – until there was a noise from overhead, flapping and throat-clearing. A crow landed over near the slide. It had come to keep her company. Or to peck at her head. Brianna began to search for her sisters.

There they were – up near the apartment building, talking to a man with a shovel. Alana seemed to be yelling, and the man was bowing his head. Alana was getting the man in trouble! Or maybe the man was saying a prayer. 'Our father,' said Brianna, 'who art in heaven, howled be thy name. Thy kingdom come, thy will be done, on earth as it is in heaven.' What was it like in heaven? Lime popsicles, Brianna thought. Kind-hearted wolves and old men with moustaches who were gods and angels. A few ladies with big skirts and kittens. All of them floating around howling and humming the songs that were the earth people's lives. And if they stopped humming? Thy will be done. She held tightly to the bars.

Whoopsy-daisy, she thought, and the world wrestled her down.

It was the first time she had woken from an absence by herself, without the wild-eyed faces – of her parents, her sisters, Frances – glistening down at her. She was completely alone, up in the rocket pod, and she had come back. It came as a swift, welcome shock to her that she could do it; she could exist without them.

Down on the ground, the crow was showing off, walking in wide circles around a pile of twigs and dog poo. Brianna could hear her mother striding up the street, calling out. She would be rescued soon. She realized she didn't want to be rescued. *Brianna*, her father once said to her, *you're the kind of girl who Turns on a Dime, aren't you?* She wasn't sure what he meant, but she thought she was doing it now, Turning on a Dime.

All of a sudden something occurred to Brianna: a historical person from a poster at school. She liked the sound of the name; it reminded her of someone old-fashioned, raw-faced and strong, a washerwoman from a fairy tale.

'Nellie McClung,' she said to the crow, who cocked its head as if irked, 'the first woman to get the vote.'

### Alana

Jordan reached into his backpack and pulled out a bottle of water.

'Want?' he said, after he'd swigged some.

She nodded, lifted the bottle to her lips and felt traces of his very self slide down her throat as she rinsed her mouth clean. There seemed very little left to do. Still, Jordan picked up her hand, released it onto the bench, then placed his own hand overtop of it.

'Your hand's so small,' he said.

Alana looked for her hand and could not find it, so she looked out into the evening, which was darkening, the whole sky shuddering with reds. Then she looked for her sisters.

Brianna was still sequestered in the rocket pod, and now she could see her other sister, talking to a man with a shovel, a gardener maybe, over near the apartment building. Would it always be like this, the three of them linked like points of light in a lopsided constellation? Susanna was laughing at something the man had said, and he was leaning down to pat her shoulder, like they were in cahoots. That was the last thing Alana needed, for her sister to hook up with some old pervert in a granddad sweater. When they were younger they had played a game called Disappear, designed so that Alana could get some peace. But it was not long before Susanna and Brianna caught on, came blundering in to whatever cocoon Alana had spun for herself, casting off their small squeals and powdery smells, convinced they had won something fantastic. It struck Alana that, of the three of them, she was the only one who truly understood the way things were, and she was overcome by an arrogant upswell of love for her sisters.

Jordan had removed his hand from hers to root around in his knapsack. He hooked a wire and plugged up the ear closest to her, then held up the other earphone by its lead so it swayed in the air between them. 'Want?' he said again.

'Sure.' They sat there listening. Traffic surging and surrendering up on the main street, Drake doing his thing, Canada geese honking their way to some sunshiny shore. Alana felt something like happiness, but rougher. She could not be happy; she was alive, with tomorrows prickling up the back of her neck. On the hill, Susanna was still talking to the man with the shovel. She had pulled a notebook from her bag and was showing him something. Jesus, *her homework*? Alana could hear her mother's voice soaring through the twilight.

'Who's that?' said Jordan, jerking the earphones away. 'Holy shit. That's not your mother, is it? God, how old *are* you, anyway? She's not coming up here, is she?'

Alana shrugged. *Of course.* But she knew this first call was only a warning; there would be others, there were always others.

'Fuck, bitch, are you even, like, listening to me?'

Alana stood up on the picnic table to get a better view of Susanna's pervert. He was bending down, gesturing towards something bunched at his feet. It was a bag of dry leaves. No, a sleeping bag made of plastic. He pulled the bag closer to where Susanna was standing. The bag was heavy – there must be rocks or tools inside. Or a body. Then the man tried to show Susanna what was in the bag, and it could be that Susanna *saw.*

'I'm outta here,' Jordan said, and shouldered his knapsack. And Alana ran. She zipped like a cursor between a row of gleaming parked cars, skirted the apartment building, came up over the crest of the lawn and lunged for Susanna. She pulled her away from the man, down the street towards home. When she was sure they were safe, she stopped and clamped her sister's head hard into her soft tummy, saying, 'It's okay.' And, 'You're *okay.*' What Alana meant by this was something akin to what her father told her when she used to regale him with her schoolgirl sorrows and grazed knees, before she started curling her eyelashes and carrying tampons like switchblades in her back pocket. What she meant by this was: Buck Up, Kid. This Is Only the Beginning.

# My Friend Taisie

'IN MY NEXT LIFE,' I tell Taisie, who is drying a glass pitcher with a tea towel covered in tiny Eiffel Towers, 'I will come back as a dancer.'

'Thomas,' she says, 'you *are* a dancer.'

'Exactly,' I reply, flexing and pointing one exquisite foot. 'I am already a dancer.' And I am thinking, that's how good it feels, that's how unlucky you are, all of you who have never danced. It is smug and mean of me to have these thoughts, but it is also the truth, and I believe that the truth, while not always possible to speak, is essential to the evolution of the spirit. Joe always said that if you can't say something out loud, you can say it to your Self and if you are lucky, your Self will listen, head cocked, eyes heavy-lidded and entranced.

Taisie picks up a sticky note from the counter. 'I have to remind myself of things these days,' she says. The note says, *Register yourself at Sears, 6th floor Help Desk.*

Joe used to leave me notes around the house. Like: *What, according to you, is the funniest thing ever?*

'Let's go and get me registered,' Taisie says, turning, one hand tucking a piece of blond hair behind her ear, the other cupped under her hard, distended belly. 'You get Anton.'

A few things you need to know: 1) Anton is six years old and black. Taisie, who is white, recently single and pregnant, adopted him officially last year after his parents died. Taisie likes having me here because my mother was black. I am a role model. My father was white and a class-A asshole, so I'm not sure what that says for white parents and black children, but this is something I keep to my Self as opposed to sharing with Taisie, who is my friend and should therefore be supported. 2) The problem with Anton is he sees Truth everywhere, and hasn't yet learned how to tell it to his Self in confidence. This truth-telling thing is a problem with most kids who live in housing projects; they don't yet know how the rest of the world tamps down reality with dreams of condo furniture and vacations in Belize. 3) I am here with my friend Taisie in Toronto because Joe is dead. He jumped off the Capilano bridge almost six months ago. They found him in a heap at the bottom, water flowing around and over him like he was just another weird-sized boulder plunked down by God.

I hold Anton's hand on the escalator to the baby department in Sears, the two of us following our reflections in the panels of mirrors as we go up. It is surprising, always, to see myself like this, even though I am accustomed to tracking my likeness in dance studios, assessing and appraising, stalking and chiding my wayward feet, correcting my one drooping shoulder. But here is my static self, moving, but not *movement*, mired instead in the terrain of splendour and surface. It's shocking the way my profile – the high, rounded forehead, the dark, fierce eyebrows and full protruding lips – tails me, less like a shadow than a spy, daring me to smile or to age or to duck suddenly from view.

'Look,' says Anton, touching his own face in the reflection. 'I'm on the move, like a motorbike man.' He presses his fingers into the mirror the whole way up.

Taisie leads like the proud prow of a ship, belly first. We follow her to a computerized kiosk whose inset screen asks questions when you touch it.

'Is this how you register?' I ask, encouraged by the apparent efficiency of the operation.

'Yes,' she says. 'Do I want a message to appear on the registry printout?'

'You mean like *Save the whales*?' I say. 'Or, *Help, I'm pregnant and my shoelaces are undone*?'

'No,' she says. 'Not like that.'

Once joyful and quick to laugh, Taisie is now prone to bouts of humourless intensity when her attention is not flitting like a debutante between topics. It's the hormones, I know, but it can make things a drag or a crapshoot.

'What does this say?' says Anton, pointing to an onscreen option.

'*Thank you for your generosity*,' says Taisie. 'You're right, that's a good one.'

The machine stutters out a printed page with instructions and a password.

'Are we done here,' I say. I sound like a police officer or a patriarch and for some reason this pleases me.

'No,' says Taisie, patient in an angry way. 'Now we choose. But first we need to go to that counter and get a registry gun.' She points in the direction of a large sign that reads, *One Day Clearance Now Extended*, and embarks on her mission with the kind of determination only the very pregnant can muster.

If Anton is at all alarmed by this, he does not say. He takes my hand again and we set off after her.

The woman behind the counter is interested in names. 'If it's a girl?' she says.

'It's a boy,' says Taisie. 'We already know.'

'You can never know,' says the woman at the Help Desk. 'You can never know for sure. My nieces are Celine and Connie, pretty names and original. You can almost be certain they'll be famous when they grow up.'

'Yes,' says Taisie. 'But you can never know for sure. Where do I get my gun?'

The woman frowns and points, then busies herself cleaning out a small plastic receptacle used for receipts. Under the receptacle is a stack of shiny magazines with pictures of smiling, sordid people. She is obviously dazzled by creepy celebrity, this Help Desk woman, but she has a point. For example, my Joe was the kind of guy you were glad they named Joe. It's a short, friendly sort of name, simple, with no awkward dangling bits. It has a kind of happiness and stability built in. You don't expect a person like Joe to die because there's no particular reason for it. Other people you can imagine it, although you might not wish it on them: the piano teetering on the balcony before sailing in cinema slo-mo down onto Sarah's unwitting form, or the ice working its way free from the overhang to deal its glancing sidelong blow to Luke – someone tall with a shaved head. The cancer nosing its diligent, mutant way through Alison, with its inception … where? They never really know, do they, and when they know, they still shake their heads or slap their notebooks shut and sit there close-mouthed and wide-eyed. Or the plane that panics mid-air: a banana up the exhaust pipe or a disgruntled man to blame. The man is unhappy because someone he knows, perhaps someone named Joe, has died, or been made president, chief, prime minister, leader of the pack. Or not been made president, chief, prime minister, leader of the pack. He's upset, so he brings a bomb, or snips a wire, or points a gun at the pilot's temple.

And then all those people in the plane's belly have a moment, or three, or maybe even a whole half-hour, just to weigh things up. And I imagine it's a bit like those times when you look up in the middle of an exam, in the midst of all those pens scratching furiously, everyone so intent on Lear's crappy decision or how to deal with the remainder in the long-division question, or the nature of a world where so many men feel the need to point their guns at pilots' temples, and you wonder, unhurriedly, what brought you to this particular moment in your life. And maybe you ask yourself why your name is Aline and not Oxana or why you were born human and not, say, salamander. Joe shouldn't be dead because his name's Joe, and he was a soft walker was Joe, a soft, soft walker.

Anton tugs at my hand.

'Look, Anton,' I say. 'I think that's the stroller with the ejectable seat.'

He eyes me warily. I do a little merengue move to mollify him. 'Let's go check it out,' I say. 'Please.'

He drops my hand, but saunters his way towards the display. 'We'll be over there,' I say to Taisie.

'Okay,' she says, with some small hate in her voice. 'But I'll need you later to pick out outfits.'

'I am nothing,' I say to Anton, as we clip and unclip various stroller accoutrements, 'if not good at picking out outfits.'

'Okay,' he says. 'I'm gonna sit in one.'

'I think you're too big, honey,' I say.

'I am not too big,' says Anton, climbing gracelessly into a jogging contraption *on sale* for *one thousand dollars.* He perches himself on the seat and initiates a quite passable shimmy in the hopes of getting his bum to fit. 'I'm a baby,' he says, clenching his teeth, still wiggling.

'You're not,' I say. 'You're a little man.'

'I'm a baby,' Anton says. 'You need to know that I am a baby.'

'Anton,' I say, detesting myself for the low, measured voice I have adopted, for the parent who possesses me. 'You are going to hurt yourself, and probably me, and break that ridiculous *chariot,* and I will have to give up dancing and get a day job with medical insurance in order to pay for the painkillers and the department store will never, ever let us shop here again.'

He looks nonplussed and somewhat regal, silent and oversized.

'Or ride the escalators,' I add.

'Okay,' he whispers. 'But I'm still a baby.' He rolls defiantly out of the stroller.

We find Taisie staring at a shelf full of pastel-hued receiving blankets, shaking her head. She turns to us, exhausted, panic playing across her face. 'I can't decide,' she says.

'That one,' says Anton, pointing to a green and yellow package called Blankies.

'Yes,' I say. 'Blankies.'

'Okay,' says Taisie. 'I need to use my gun.' She waves the contraption at the price tag, but nothing happens. 'Stupid gun,' she says, shaking it.

'Stop calling it a gun,' I say. 'It's a wand.'

'I think it's a gun,' she says, examining it. 'I think they call it a gun. Here, you try.'

I take the wand from Taisie and aim it carefully at the bar code. The end of the wand flashes red like a dragon's eye and bleeps.

'Magic,' I say to Anton. 'Sears-style. Where's Taisie?'

Taisie is examining a shelf full of baby bottles and breast pumps.

'I cannot believe there are no glass bottles,' she says.

'Aren't they too heavy?' I ask.

'Yes, but no. I mean, they are but plastic is very dangerous. It can lead to cancer and developmental delays and birth defects. There's a hormone that leeches out into the liquid. Very bad news.' She reaches for a box, reads the back, then shakes her head. 'Plastic is bad. Bad plastic.' She slams the box back down on the shelf and waddles purposefully over to the Help Desk.

I look at Anton. He looks back at me in a way that suggests he knows what I am thinking: *Plastics don't kill people, people kill people.*

On the way home Anton falls asleep in the car, propped up against an overturned, second-hand bassinet.

'Maybe we need a pet,' says Taisie, changing lanes. 'Now that we're like a family. A dog?'

'Fish, maybe,' I say. 'It's good to start small. We had two fish when I was little. Names: Rhubarb and Custard.'

'Why?'

'We had no idea at the time – just heard the names on a British TV program and thought they sounded exotic. But our cat understood.'

'What? Oh.'

We are stopped at a light, two lanes of traffic to either side, parking lots and scraggly trees beyond them. It's funny: when I am in the west of this country, I miss the east, or the centre-south-east, I guess I should say, in deference to Maritimers, who are tetchy when it comes to geography although magnanimous in almost every other respect. Then once I'm back in Toronto I feel sort of sad and full, like I've just eaten too much dinner I didn't deserve. It's the simplicity of this landscape, the comforting stodginess of ill-used space on the fringe of the city. In the fall especially, it feels like home; too chilly to walk to the mall and who would want to anyway? Joe. Joe would want to.

'Did you bury them?' Taisie taps my leg.

'What?' I say. 'You don't bury fish.'

'I don't want a pet,' says Anton from the back seat. 'Please don't buy a pet.'

I turn around to check on him. 'You okay, buddy?'

'I don't want a pet,' he says.

'Let's have pizza tonight, eh, boys?' Taisie says brightly. And to me, whispering, 'With hot peppers. They say spicy food and sex.'

'Spicy food and sex what?' I say, frightened.

'Hurry things up,' she says, rubbing her genie-bottle belly. 'Don't worry, I know. This much T&A must be like total reverse-sexy for you. Just the hot peppers.'

'Green or red?' I say.

'Red,' says Anton from the back. 'I like red.'

On the day of the shower, Taisie puts me in charge of baking miniature frozen quiches and lets Anton vacuum the living room even though the machine keeps sucking up coins and bobby pins and other clanky things even the most technologically advanced Hoover is not designed to digest. I stop her as she dashes by me with a tray of crustless sandwiches.

'Mmm, I love these,' I say, grabbing an egg salad on white from the edge. I observe as she rearranges the remaining sandwiches to close the gap. 'Are you nervous?' I say.

'Why?' she replies gaily. 'Everybody is coming to support me in this new phase of my life. They want me, I mean us … ' She shoots a look over at Anton, instead of down at her belly. 'They want us to do well, to live long and prosper.'

'They think you're crazy, sweet thing.' I grab another egg salad, then put it back when I see the look on her face. The vacuum gurgles, retches and chugs to a halt.

'For a person with a baby on the way you sure have a lot of chokables lying around,' I say.

'I know,' she says. 'It's like you live your life not understanding anything at all and then you find out there's a whole new subset of things you don't understand.' She turns to Anton, who is now standing in the living room doorway looking defeated. 'Anton, that's good, you're such a good helper. Thomas needs help with the quiche.' She looks quickly towards me. 'Don't say it. Real men do, and besides you're essentially just defrosting, not sampling.' She slaps my hand away from the sandwich tray and begins arranging wedges of cheese on a cutting board.

For a long time I believed there was only one type of cheese in the world – it came in a large orange square block with the word *cheddar* printed in capital letters across the middle, and it sat in stacks next to the bags of two percent in the SuperSave. My Self and I agree that it is a very, very good thing that I have been disabused of this notion. Stilton with pineapple slivers, my Self whispers. *Camembert.* Once, while tipsy, I told Joe I could never love a man who didn't love a good cheese. I made him promise that, if we split, he would find someone who appreciated a decent fondue. I sidle up to Taisie and she hands me a slice of Manchego.

'How do you stay so slim?' she says.

I shrug. She's right; they are incompatible passions, cheese and dance, and life is not often fair.

'How many guests?' I say.

'Twenty or so, if they all show,' Taisie says.

'You'll have to sit on a throne.' I pretend-crown her.

'I know, I don't mind.'

I can tell she really doesn't. It's a combination of things – the padding she has created for the wad of new life inside her, and the extra padding all the gifts represent. Anyone who says stuff can't help you feel safe, ward off the creepy-crawlies of the future, anyone who tells you this is only partway right. Stuff can make you feel a lot better, and then turn around like a floozie and make you feel a lot worse. It's a tricky inverse relationship based on the stories you were told as a child, the last time you got laid, how many people admit to loving you and probably the position of the moon, or its glint on the world's rapidly reproducing satellites. Anyway.

'I'll be the greeter,' I tell my starry-eyed friend. 'People need to feel sufficiently greeted these days.'

Anton sits next to me on the bottom step, just inside the door.

'What are we waiting for?' he says.

He seems nervous or tired; it's sometimes hard to tell with kids. With people, for that matter. 'We're waiting for Taisie's friends,' I tell him. 'We're going to dance with them.'

'Really?' He brightens a little.

'Really,' I say. He nods and crosses his ankles officiously. 'If there's one thing I know,' I tell him, 'it's that women love a dancer, especially when they are surrounded by other women.'

He looks like he might be interested, so I press on. 'The thing about west-coast swing is it's always characterized as more *elastic* than regular ballroom,' I explain. 'There's a little more freedom within the constraints of the steps, something less naive and brash about the moves. Impossible, of course, to convey this to a beginner – today is about a tight twirl in the foyer, some impromptu dips and pivots. Something to make us all stand up a little straighter.'

'Let's play a game,' Anton says.

'All right,' I say. I hate games, always have, can't help getting impatient with the conceit, with waiting to take a crack at the trick at the heart of them. Joe liked games, but there was no logic to his games, no real rules to butt up against. He liked to gather things randomly, and it seemed to me there should really be some strategy behind the gathering, a plan.

'I Spy,' says Anton.

'What?' I say.

'That's the game,' he says.

'Okay,' I say, '*what* do you spy?' (And I know I sound angry, but he's being so thick and thrilled and *childish.*)

'I spy with my little eye,' he says, 'something that is … ' He swivels his head around, searching. 'Something that is … '

I witness an idea click firmly into place in his brain.

'Something that is blue!' His gaze has settled on the umbrella stand in the corner next to the radiator. He sits on his hands as if to stop them from pointing out his quarry.

I stand up, execute a half-assed pirouette, then make a show of scanning the zone, peering behind pictures and checking from floor to ceiling for clues. When I get to the umbrella stand I stop, do a quick once-over, then an exaggerated double take. Anton lets out a swift snort and begins to rock back and forth in anticipation. I pull out the umbrellas one by one.

'Don't open them,' Anton whispers. 'Bad luck.'

'Hmm.' I scratch my head and begin to examine the umbrellas individually. There is no blue on these brollies. None. Anton is about to pee, he's so jazzed. I nudge the umbrella stand away from the wall and search its circumference for something, anything – a flicker or a shadow of navy or aquamarine. There is a spot of faded black on the rim of the stand. 'This!' I say, pointing.

'No, no, no,' he says. 'Not blue!'

There is a bluish frame around a black-and-white photo of Taisie and Marco above the radiator. 'This,' I say, getting tired.

'No!' Anton cries, and leaps up from his seat.

'I don't know then,' I say, wishing someone would knock on the door and end all of this frippery.

'It's the umbrellas!' Anton shouts. 'The umbrellas!'

'There is no blue on the umbrellas,' I say, quietly but firmly.

'No,' says Anton, with a modicum of kindly condescension. 'But the umbrellas are closed because the sky is blue. The sky is blue,' he shouts, jumping up and down.

Which is exactly when my prayers are answered and someone knocks on the door then opens it without waiting for a response.

Despite Anton's bewildering notion of the order of things, we become allies for the next hour or so, leading aunts and co-workers through into the living room, ferrying coats and shoes up to Taisie's room, where we pile them into a messy mountain on the bed, which Anton monitors with increasing inquisitiveness.

Back downstairs, I make a production of loving the ladies, baiting them like a bullfighter, enclosing them in my dancer's embrace, arching my eyebrows as I compliment them on their hairdos, laughing wickedly at how they have managed to avoid fashion faux pas, especially – *especially* – if they haven't. Anton watches me, perched on the stairs, staring through the slats. After a while, he adds his own hip-hop moves from the sidelines, gives me little go-girl salutes with his very fine I Spy eyes.

Once the guests have all arrived, he helps me to settle them with drinks, carrying one in each vigilant hand. Taisie is wearing a tight white shift over a pair of hot pink leggings. Not at all wise, but bold, I'll give her that. I know she was thinking *virtuous,* but not *too.* But, well, Taisie is big, even when she's not pregnant, not fat but fleshy – present in the world in a way other women are not. The outfit is not ideal. Martine, one of Taisie's high school friends who carefully retousles her long auburn hair after showering every morning, then hangs vintage forties dresses from her petite, right-angled frame, has cottoned on. She takes a punch glass from Anton, pats his head, then leans over to Jan – a nurse's assistant from Taisie's work with a semi-manageable drug habit – who is sitting on a cushion at her feet.

'Bless her heart,' Martine exclaims loudly. 'Wearing white! And only twelve days before her due date!'

Anton, apparently sensitive to insincerity, whips around to face her, his eyes ablaze with mob-style loyalty. 'Bitch!' he says, and makes like a boxer with his head.

I hear someone whisper, 'Trauma!' into the air, as if it were a shared secret. Which I guess it is; it's hard to sweep a double homicide under the carpet, much as we all (including me, my Self) might try.

'Bitch!' Anton says again, his hands like teapot handles on his hips. I whisk him away in a waltz, but not before he manages one more unintelligible expletive. Once out of the living room, Anton breaks away and escapes up the stairs. I think: Coat Mountain. I think: Go for it, kid.

Back in the centre of things, Taisie is lifting tissue paper gingerly out of a gift bag. That's an issue with this new-style wrapping: you never know if what you pull out next will be the number-one prize or another bunch of decoy decoration. At the bottom of the bag someone has nestled a pair of soft leather booties with ladybugs embroidered on the toes.

'Oh,' says Taisie. She looks up from the boots, and her eyes are full of tears. 'They're really, really beautiful, aren't they? Imagine. My baby will have feet.'

'Oh yes,' say the assembled ladies. They lift their plastic punch glasses in a toast.

Once Joe's note said: *Saddest comic strip character?*

Later that night, Taisie and I watch a show on black-on-black violence in Toronto – black-on-black, it sounds like a new hybrid dance form to me, gumshoe man meets old school hip hop. That, or a hard-hitting investigative news show exposing corporate fraud, how business gangsters avoid taxes to stay out of the red.

'Toronto the Not So Good,' I say.

'Why,' says Taisie, gesturing at the screen, 'does it still feel like they're making a movie about a faraway place?'

'Never mind,' I say. 'Never underestimate the power of the remote.' I press the Mute button. 'How was that?' I say, waving at the pile of loot in the corner.

'Good, it was good,' she says, in a way I know implies the opposite.

On the TV, two men pretending to be computers exchange quips. Then a woman wearing angel wings strokes a man's muscles. They are good muscles, I concede.

'I miss Marco,' says Taisie.

'He'll be here when you have the baby, right?' I say, and it is entirely the wrong thing to say. Taisie and Marco are taking a break after nine years together, three of them married, although not the most recent ones.

'I thought we'd be better married, then I thought it was marriage that wrecked it all, made it all too obvious and bourgeois. But I think we just wore each other out – and I don't mean from fighting, I mean we knew each other until we couldn't know each other anymore. We're like smudged grooves on a record,' she says to me, kneading the cushion next to her.

I give her a look that says she is taking the metaphor too far and she nods sadly. She knows.

'You're courageous,' I say.

'Like fucking hell,' she says.

Strike two. I pick up the TV guide and pretend to be reading. Then I look over at Taisie. 'Anton seems to be doing well,' I say.

'Yeah,' she says. 'I was trying to figure out whether he should be here for the birth. I was, well, I was thinking maybe you could be here with him, and if things get too intense, you guys could, I dunno, go out.'

'Oh,' I say. 'Okay. Will we need to, like, assist with anything or anything?'

'No.' She smiles indulgently and pats me on the knee. 'My midwife will take care of things. Anton was pretty good tonight, no?'

'Yes,' I say.

When the guests were leaving, I found Anton crouched on the stairs. I could tell he was far, far into his Self. Joe was sometimes doing that, sinking down into himself, disappearing. But he was a grown person – so it often occurred to him to walk out the door. Usually he'd leave with a gun in his satchel, rusty, never loaded, an old .22 he found in the back of his uncle's oven. It was odd what he'd come back with: the smallish packs of Cheetos you get in vending machines, antique compacts made of pewter with leaping deer embossed on the front, the powder inside still solid, intact.

Last October, he took off for six days. The night before he left, he sat in the kitchen with his head in his hands. I could see his legs shaking under the table.

'What's wrong?' I wheedled, and hated myself.

'I've got the Chinese Jangles,' he said, smiling.

'Migraine?'

'It's when you think lewd and lascivious thoughts and your shoelaces come undone.'

He kissed me deep and walked out the door.

Joe came back six days later with a tiny, thumbnail-sized basket woven entirely of human hair. He pinched the fishing-wire loop at the top, lifted the lid and showed me the contents, an emptiness that could house a fly.

'For the man who has absolutely nothing,' he said.

Anton managed a few weak goodbyes from his stairway perch, but rallied when he saw Martine buckling her brown Mary Janes. 'Thank you for your generosity,' he said, and I adored him for stumbling upon Irony at such a young, smooth-skinned age. Martine turned for a moment to flick a strand of hair from her eye.

Then she waved at Anton, her lips curving into a small, orderly smile on her pretty, atrocious face.

Taisie shifts around so her legs are draped across my lap. 'Feet,' she says. Then, 'What else is on?'

'Oooh,' I say, flipping through channels with one hand and massaging her instep with another, '*Vain or Insane?*'

'Yes,' she says. 'Yes, yes.'

I've done it, I crow to my Self. I've made her feel better. But my Self just smirks like a mother until I swat him away. On the screen a woman forced to live without mirrors for the two weeks it took to cinch and overhaul her body is about to experience The Reveal. She is wearing a black velvet kerchief around her eyes, a red satin evening gown and very shiny shoes, precarious shoes. Behind her a team of stylists has assembled the way magpies gather, proprietorially, around something discarded and gleaming. The woman waits in front of the mirror, which is shrouded in black satin. One of the stylists breaks from the flock to lead a small girl in party clothes and a man with frizzy hair and a forlorn gait into the room. The man is a forklift operator in a small town in the southern U.S. He loved her fine the way she was.

'So,' says Taisie. 'What about Joe?'

'He would have been interested in this,' I say.

'In what?' she says.

She's teasing me. She knows he never watched TV. But for some reason I can't bring myself to say the word *pregnancy*; it feels almost obscene in its adult ramifications. When I was a child there was always a sort of shimmery scrim between myself and adulthood, until one day – *shazam!* – I found myself tiptoeing like an alien amongst the enemy, wondering when they would see past the permanent, shoddy disguise.

'No,' I say, pointing to her belly, 'that. And also,' I add, looking down into my lap, 'I keep remembering things I forgot.'

'Like?' she says.

'Well. Like this one time we're hiking in the woods on Bowen Island and we don't see a soul, not even a deer, until we get to the salmon run and this incredible family appears from across the bridge. It was a mother and three daughters – the blondest, tiniest things I'd ever seen, so they made delicate little Joe look like this hairy gorilla Amazon, and I looked like I'd just rolled out of some tree trunk where I'd been surviving on roots and berries. That's how luminous they were, and how spare, as if everything about them was there for a specific, superior reason.'

'I know people like that,' says Taisie grimly.

'"Hello," said the woman, only she said it with no tentativeness whatsoever, like she was making an important list, and *Hello* was the last thing on it. Her girls stood next to her, a row of pretty chickadees, each a head shorter than the last, and also said *Hello.* They had rich, clipped accents, and when Joe asked, they said they were from South Africa, and the woman leaned back slightly, placing her hand like a cup under her belly. Which is when I noticed she was pregnant.'

'*Pregnant,* eh?' says Taisie, and pokes me.

'"Congratulations," I said. "When are you due?" And immediately I regretted it, since something inside me was certain that *due* could not be the right word. "Three months," I could hear her saying through the bustle of my thoughts. "I'm quite small, but I have small babies, easy births." And I was still thinking *due* was for library books and hydro bills, and wishing I could get these things to stop trotting across my mind. But then it occurred to me that South Africa was where all those penguins washed up, so I crouched down low to look into the face of one of the chickadees and asked her if she knew of any tarred, tuxedoed waddlers washing up on her shores. "Oh, yes," she said. "Mother and I took care of one. It was quite arduous washing all that oil from its feathers, quite a number of them died." "Yes, a shame," said the mother. "That was right after our neighbour was shot."'

'Jesus,' says Taisie.

'I know,' I say.

On the TV, the assistants have wheeled out the contestant's ninety-two-year-old grandmother. They introduce her and the audience erupts into raucous applause. A couple of people even hoot.

'You know,' says Taisie, 'I never used to get it, the applause for old people. I thought: So what? They're old! It's not really a talent or a special accomplishment, not *really*. And, I mean, it's a bit condescending too – isn't it? – clapping for the wrinklies?'

I nod and wait.

'But last year I went to see this bluegrass singer, and she said she was the youngest of fourteen children, and then she dedicated a song to her momma. She said, "This one goes out to my momma, who is ninety-one years old." And I thought: Fuck me, ninety-one years old, fourteen children, what the woman has *seen*, right? And I got it, I really got it, and I clapped extra hard, so my palms bounced right off each other . . . '

I give her knee a little squeeze.

'Just living,' she begins, then continues quietly, 'it can be an accomplishment, can't it?'

I toast her with an imaginary champagne flute.

The woman of the hour is about to see her new Self for the first time. The room is hushed as the black satin is whisked away from the mirror. The camera pans over the crowd and settles on the reflected image. For a moment the woman stands perfectly still. Then she doubles over as if someone has punched her in the stomach. Which, in a way, somebody has. I read an article about this writer in her seventies who said that in her head she was stuck at age thirty-eight, no matter what tale the mirror told. *Well, Self,* I say, *I'm not sure we're there yet, at our sticking point.* But it's possible it's close. It's possible it's very, very close.

'Tell me again why we like this show,' I say to Taisie. But Taisie is in Snoozeville, her eyelids almost completely lowered on the world, her chin bobbing against her chest as she inhales and exhales for two.

I rest my hands on her feet and finish the story. 'Then,' I tell sleeping Taisie, 'the woman turned back to Joe, and I realized they had been talking about the travails of childbirth, because the next thing she said was, "In Africa, the blacks in the fields will simply stop whatever they are doing and push out their babies then and there, in a squat, strap them to their backs and go on working. Just like that." The woman placed her hand on the head of the oldest girl and sighed. "It's lovely here, but quiet, so polite," she said. "Even the trees are polite."'

I close my eyes. 'Taisie,' I whisper. 'I wanted to talk to Joe about the strange beauty of those children, the ruthlessness of the mother, the way in my head the correct words kept feeling so wrong, but on the way back home we got distracted by some teenagers in big pants making out up on the observation deck, and then the hump of a whale breaching in the distance. We started arguing about what we wanted for dinner.'

Once: *How can anybody be their own best friend?*

The next day, Taisie goes into labour. The beginnings are much less dramatic than I anticipated. She glares and holds up an index finger prohibitively when I ask what I can do. There is nothing I can do. There are processes, once set in motion, that do not heed preset human choreography. I find this causes me some small relief. I phone Marco, who arrives in mere minutes, a vinyl overnight bag clutched in one hand.

'How far apart?' he says, still breathing heavily from his journey.

'Um,' I say, 'enough time for her to wipe down the countertops and take out the garbage.'

'Ten minutes,' Taisie says. 'My housewifely skills have improved.'

Marco takes her in his arms. 'Ready,' he says. 'I'll call the midwife.'

She nods, although I know her well enough to see the skittering incredulity behind her eyes.

'I'll take Anton for a walk,' I say. 'Do you need anything?'

'No,' says Marco, suddenly manly and in charge, 'a walk is a good idea.'

I think I would like to trip him by mistake, can imagine the length of him sprawled over the kitchen tile.

'The baby's on the way out, or in,' I tell Anton, momentarily confused.

'Uh-huh,' he says. 'Let's go to the zoo.'

He means the low-rent zoo in the park. Peacocks with their runway walks, thug-like buffaloes and – my favourites – mountain goats looking to head-butt each other when they're not looking to the horizon.

We tour the animals for half an hour, then stop to buy hot dogs from a friendly vendor. Anton confides that he would like to be a hot-dog seller when he grows up if the pilot thing doesn't work out.

'Joe would have liked you,' I tell him.

'Who's Joe?' he says.

'Oh,' I say. 'Nobody, really.'

He doesn't press for more. He has Nobodies in his life too.

When we get back to the house, the contractions are coming one on top of the other and the racket is of the nerve-jangling variety. Anton and I sit in the living room and play checkers, pretending not to notice the long, low moans, which are possibly the most purely animal noises we have heard all day.

The midwife, Lena, an expressionless Iranian with a light tread and an olive complexion, comes padding down the stairs and tells us not to worry, soon our friend will be able to push. But a few minutes later, a flashing, yelping ambulance is parked outside the house, Taisie is being helped down the stairs by a ghost-faced Marco and within seconds they are all out the door.

Anton watches them leave, then sweeps the checkers from the board with the back of his hand in a gesture that can only be learned. Next he upends the board and attempts the same with the table. He begins to scream, his fists so tightly clenched that when I pry them open there are bloody crescents where his fingernails have marked his palms. After about an hour, although he has not stopped screaming, his body loses sound. He topples slowly over onto the floor and lies there, his lips still stretched apart in anguish. I lie beside him until Marco calls from the hospital.

'The baby is fine,' I tell Anton. 'Taisie is fine. Please, let's go to sleep.'

A few days later, Taisie comes home from the hospital with a bundle tied to her boob and asks me to stay awhile. She says, 'As long as you like, but get a job to help with food and fun stuff for Anton.'

I tell her I need to think about it.

Lately, Anton has been asking me questions I can't find answers to. Two nights ago he pulled an old atlas down from the shelf and started pointing.

'Where did you used to live?' he said.

'British Columbia,' I said, 'over here.' I turned to the correct page, North America spreading down across the crease of the book like a spill.

'Were you dancing a lot there?' he asked, his finger circling the province rhythmically.

'Yes,' I said. 'My specialty is west-coast swing, from California. Down here,' I said.

'Is that where they had the flood with all the black people?' he asked. 'I liked how they got to float along on their houses.'

'No,' I said, 'that was in Louisiana.'

'Right,' he said, 'Hurricane Katie.'

'Katrina,' I said, 'they named her Katrina.'

'Why?'

'Because we name storms and babies according to their sex,' I lie. (This is preposterous, I know, but how to respond to such queries?)

'How do we know their sex?' he said shyly, his volume downturning on the word *sex*.

'We turn them upside down and examine them, or we use instruments to predict their nature,' I told him, acting professional.

'When will Taisie name the baby?' he said.

'I don't know, honey.'

'I like the name Martin,' he said. 'It's also a bird's name.'

One second I decide I must leave Taisie and Anton and the baby – which, at three weeks, remains nameless – and the next second I decide to stay with them forever. I do a lot of dishes and sometimes laundry, and I stare at the baby when Taisie cannot. This morning we lay him on a placemat on the kitchen table, then sit down as if to sup.

'You know,' says Taisie, 'that midwife was magic. She was like the best kind of boss, while Marco kept doing this useless whispering in my ear.' She touches the baby's nose, then lets him grab her hand.

'Have you decided on a name yet?' I know better than to pressure her, so I speak lightly, as if discussing a possible change in the wallpaper. 'Anton thinks Martin is a good name,' I say.

'Yeah,' she says, 'I don't know. Has he talked to you about his mum and dad?'

'No,' I say, 'not in so many words.'

'Sometimes I just think what the fuck, you know? I mean, they shot them in a church. I mean, if God sees everything, why'd they think they had to do it in His face?'

'They weren't thinking about God,' I say.

The baby begins to whimper. Taisie picks him up and latches him on to her breast.

'What have I gotten you into?' she says, and for a second I'm not sure if she means me or the baby, and then I realize she means all of us, herself and her hapless, handsome boys. 'They wanted to believe they *were* gods.' Tears gather in her eyes but do not fall. 'I need to transfer to a soft seat.' She winces and shifts. 'Hemorrhoid,' she adds, standing up.

We walk over to the couch in the living room, where she does a strangely graceful combination squat-lean in order to sit, then winces again.

'Where's your doughnut pillow?' I say.

She wipes her face energetically, like it's a window she's having difficulty seeing through, and points in the direction of the kitchen. 'Maybe Martin,' she says. 'Martin might work.'

When I come back with the pillow, the baby is barely suckling, his face mashed into his mother, his little paws relaxed.

'He's asleep,' Taisie says.

'Yes,' I say. I give her the pillow. 'I'm not sure you want me living here, Taise.' I look down because I can feel the truth writhing like a live thing in my throat. 'I'm very selfish,' I say.

'I know,' Taisie replies, 'but you sure can dance. Can you take him?' She pulls the baby away from her body and holds him out to me.

'Okay,' I say. 'I'll put him down.'

I walk up to Taisie's room and over to the bassinet. I place the baby on his blanket and he opens his eyes, looks up at me, or at the space between us. The baby is still not quite of this world; he stirs like a fugitive who has been hiding in a cave and can't yet absorb the strength and significance of the light. I think of what he has to look forward to, his limbs forcing their way through the atmosphere, finding ways to move to the music he hears.

'Hello, Baby,' I say.

There is something I had been meaning to tell Joe for a long time. I look into Baby's face as I tell it: 'The funniest thing ever happened the summer I was nine years old. My parents rented a cottage up in the Gatineaus in Quebec, and a bunch of us from the cluster of cabins would spend our days on the dock, cannonballing and ass-cracking our way into the evening. But our favourite scenario involved a man walking into nothingness. He'd begin where the dock met the shore, swinging a briefcase, or miming a tip of the hat – he was a businessman with a devil-may-care walk. One of us would take up the narration: *One day, a man was walking down the street.* The businessman would begin his stroll down the dock, whistling or waving obliviously. *When, suddenly, the street ended.* The businessman would step off the end of the dock, a look of complete and utter surprise on his face before he hit the lake. God, we'd roll around on that dock hiccupping and hyperventilating until we couldn't talk, until we couldn't breathe.'

I stop to wrap the baby up in a blanket like a giant burrito, like Taisie showed me. I place my hand on the baby's head, feel the soft down and warmth of him as I tell him how the story ends. His eyes are still open; when I begin to speak again it is easy to believe he is listening to me. 'When the businessman hauled himself up and onto the dock – hair plastered to forehead, lake water rolling down neck, streaming between innocent shoulder blades – we would watch him shake himself dry. Then the businessman rejoined the group, someone else staggered up and it started all over again … '

The baby's eyes are closing, then opening, closing then opening. I leave my hand on his forehead until I am sure he is asleep.

# Wanted Children

'DID YOU SEE THIS?' Paul cocked his head to the side then skewed it aggressively towards his laptop, which he had perched on a pile of old newspapers on the kitchen table.

'See what?' Beth refused to turn from her careful work at the counter. The naturopath had said six drops of the kava-kava root tincture and three of the impatiens, star of Bethlehem, cherry plum, rock rose and clematis. In spring water. She squeezed the top of the dropper delicately. Two drops, followed by a narrow quicksilver dribble. Could the dribble be considered a drip? How many drips in a drop? How many snowflakes in a snowbank? There was a joke in there somewhere. The precision of it all, the crucial measurements and ratios, the equilibrium and relative concentration and dilution – it was doing her in. But the naturopath had said it would help her regain a sense of her place in the world, settle her nervous system, her overactive mind and frequently, inappropriately aroused nether regions. She would feel better, centred, the healer had promised.

Beth smiled. The water clouded, then cleared. She lifted the glass to her mouth, opened her throat and let the mixture slide home. It tasted like moss, mould, cheap perfume sunk deep into cheaper upholstery. She gagged and grabbed the edge of the sink, then closed her eyes without thinking – as if shutting off one sense might dull another – and listened to Paul like he was bearing a message from a fleeting and inconsequential dream.

'Beth, I'm serious, this is serious.'

Beth opened her eyes and looked out the window. It was summertime in Bloor West Village, and the purple finches, with their wine-speckled plumage, were regular visitors to the feeder. *As if they've been dipped in raspberry juice*, she remembered reading in a guidebook. The birds flitted and pecked, then retreated from a domineering grackle.

Paul whistled through his teeth and Beth watched him sit back hard in his chair. 'Check this out,' he said. Something had scared him, and it was this that finally drew Beth to the screen.

It was an abstract, staged photo, something someone with too much studio time and grant money had cooked up. A black river – a river of tar or paint – with creatures rising sluggishly from its depths. Swamp monsters – perhaps it was a movie trailer? Beth shook her head. 'So?'

'It's Cuyabeno,' Paul replied. 'It's your river, Beth.'

The trip had been Paul's idea. They'd been trying for two years to conceive, then stopped, then succeeded, then miscarried. Then there were too many options dangled before them, too many well-meaning, putty-faced friends at the door. Paul began to clear out corners in the basement, Beth took long walks in Etienne Brulé Park. The park was a long strip of winding land on either side of the Humber River, one-time superhighway for the coureur de bois of the park's name. Brulé was only twenty-three when he became the first European to see Lake Ontario from the mouth of the Humber. What must he have been thinking as he stared out into that inland ocean, surrounded by his Huron comrades? Beth imagined a watery portage trail suddenly opening up into all those steely grey waves, a pristine September sky. The fall of 1615: Toronto was nothing more than a carrying place, a spot to heave burdens onto strong backs and into hardy canoes. Yonge

Street, longest street in the world, that broad boulevard of strip clubs, fast food, head shops and hairdressing salons, had nothing on the Humber in its heyday – explorers, missionaries and traders vying for bewildered souls, the softest of fur pelts, the prospect of getting there *first*. Oh, it was romantic and incorrect, she knew, but when Beth visited the park she often thought of Brulé, and would forego the two landscaped paths for the less manicured trail that ran right smack up against the river's edge.

The alternative was the commercial strip on Bloor where for weeks they'd attempted to distract themselves, buying crumbly, extravagantly priced cheeses from the new high-end deli, top-of-the-line B.C. and Australian wines from the LCBO and organic beef from the butcher. Quaint, functional and quietly fantastical, their neighbourhood had an air of the hobbit – hobbit with Eastern European roots, as some of the lingering Ukrainian bakeries and specialty shops could attest. Even the homeless folk tipped their hats with one hand while they held out the other for change. The buskers strummed mournful Ukrainian folk tunes on battered guitars, and on Sundays the loudspeaker at Saint Pius X played stately choral music, designed, it seemed, to chide and cajole the wayward. Filtered through a subpar sound system, the music crackled and snorted as it met the street. But God was already smiling on Bloor West Village; there was no pressing need for prayer.

And on every street corner and in every tidy parkette, Beth spotted the strollers. They were little buggies of anguish – their sturdy wheels and bright utilitarian fabric, their multitude of clipped-on accessories and cushioned interiors. She wanted to puncture their tires, spray-paint their protective sides, slash their UV-blocking visors. Paul knew this, he saw this, and he said, 'Let's go away. Somewhere where people don't think this way, the way we think. So obsessed with achieving the "supposed to."'

Beth had nodded, semi-entranced by Paul's ability to imagine quick fixes and act on them with a kind of jittery intensity, a follow-through she had never mustered. When he suggested Ecuador, the emerald light and mercurial moisture of the rainforest, she had shrugged, then wondered sheepishly, 'Isn't it a bit, I dunno, cliché?'

'It won't be cliché for long,' he said grimly. 'It will be gone.'

'That's what I mean,' she said. 'It's like we're peering in at a dying, caged animal, isn't it?'

'Maybe,' said Paul in a way that suggested he hated himself, 'there is a way of helping.'

He looked like he wanted to stick forks in his eyes, so Beth agreed. Paul had a friend who had been through the region with an NGO and gave them tips and details: what to bring, whether to tip or haggle, which immunizations to endure and delicacies to sample, that sort of thing. They were to spend two weeks in the Amazon basin, in Cuyabeno National Park.

The trip had been literally breathtaking, fourteen days and nights when Beth spent whole minutes trying to teach herself to breathe again. Was it the humidity or simply the intensity, the drama of it all? They called it the world's pharmacy, an Eden: sweet balm and scourge, the innocence and viscera of new beginnings. But it was also something more sinister and random, something cloying, squawking and stealthy. To say it was unlike anything Beth had ever experienced might have been inaccurate – there were woods in northern Ontario whose fog of blackflies and sneering impenetrability maybe came close. But where the native people of her northern province had been decimated or interned or suffocated by white man's guilt, these jungle lands were still inhabited by their original denizens – men and women with wide, implacable faces and smooth, rubbery skin who clambered up the banks of the river with regularity and ease, clutching plastic jugs of gasoline, babies strapped to their backs with long strips of cloth. Miguel, their tour guide, was such a man. Short and compact in body, barrel-chested, with a few uneven black sprigs of hair for a beard, he had a thin, rosy scar along his jawline and the haircut of a more urban, moneyed man. When he smiled, Beth noted his strong, small, pointy teeth.

This was in a café in Lago Agrio, waystation for travellers, frontier town for the desperate and entrepreneurial. She and Paul had been waiting a long time on a patio, clinking their cups of Nescafé against their saucers.

'Do you think that's him?' Paul pointed towards the street, where a mocha-skinned man was pulling a trolley towards their patio. They were to expect a guide who spoke five languages, a war veteran, friendly and 'uninhibited,' the eager teenager who booked their trip had reassured. But the man with the trolley was not the right man, and neither was the man cradling a basket of fresh mangoes. When Miguel appeared, it was from within the rendezvous restaurant; he was everything they might have expected and nothing they had anticipated. His arms made his T-shirt bulge with their baseball-sized biceps, and he was sporting cheap orange flip-flops, which he continued to wear for the duration of the journey, exposing his long, yellowy-tough toenails and making the rest of the tour group, in their beige, super-tread hiking shoes, feel subtly, wonderfully mocked.

On the bus to the oversized, motorized canoe that was to take them to their campsite, the dust from the window made Beth cough, and the rutted roads caused the bus to jump. The inside of her head was all jangly with priorities and survival, and she felt sunburned although she had not been sitting in the sun. She nodded to the two Germans who had joined the group, and then pushed past Paul, who was nodding off, a thin line of spittle reaching downwards from his bottom lip to the strap of his day pack, which he had, wary of pickpockets, left attached to his back.

'Do you mind?' She motioned to the vacant aisle seat next to Miguel.

'Not at all,' he said. 'You are welcome.'

She sat next to him, not speaking, trying to catch her breath.

'You are having some difficulty, some respiratory difficulty?' He turned towards her, face creased with concern and something else: amusement or mild lust?

'I'm fine,' she said, and took in a big lungful of air, right down into her diaphragm, as she'd learned in a few yoga classes and tricky situations.

'Good,' he said, and went back to his book.

Beth closed her eyes, but that made her dizzy, so she opened them. It was difficult now she was sitting on the aisle to find a place to look. Straight ahead meant a row of seatbacks, brown vinyl and grimy, the blond Germans and various black-haired people sitting in them. It meant absorbing the reality of the interior of the bus, a rollicking, wretched press of passengers, bulky bags, boxes and bound chickens. It meant considering which qualifications, exactly, were required to drive a bus in this – she nearly thought *godforsaken*, but settled on *strange* – country. And looking outside, well, that would involve craning over Miguel to the window so that her head was positioned directly above his crotch, her shoulder pressed against his.

Also, Beth was experiencing traveller's terror – the pervasive notion that each moment that passed represented a small treasure trove of noteworthy difference and that she would *never pass this way again*. She pivoted her body and her breast grazed Miguel's arm. Muttering an apology, she squinted out at the side of the road. Outside was both hazy with dust and excessively green. The foliage looked prehistoric – gigantic ferns bowing chaotically to the palms reaching high up into the cloudless sky. This was it: the jungle. Miguel shifted to turn the page of his book and she felt obliged to speak. 'What are you reading?'

He closed the book to show her the cover, a sepia-toned watercolour of a barn with a fair-haired woman standing in the foreground looking to the horizon. In the top corner of the book was a gold seal, one of Oprah's marks – *Book Club*, it exhorted. Miguel was watching her. She had no idea what to say. She was flabbergasted; the man at the tour agency had told them Miguel still had a bullet in his thigh from fighting in the border dispute with Peru. Finally she settled on, 'Any good?'

Miguel nodded eagerly. 'Very good, and it helps me to practise, to stay fluent, use new words.' He opened the book to the page he was on. 'What does this mean?' He pointed to a word and underlined it with his finger.

Beth looked at the word. She did not know what it meant. She took the book from Miguel and read the blurb on the back. A multi-generational saga set in the American Midwest with a complicated, malevolent patriarch at its core. 'Must be dialect,' she said, shaking her head. 'Sorry.'

'It's okay,' he said.

But she knew she had fallen in his estimation. She looked out the window again. There were black pipes running alongside the road that seemed to be made of the same plastic used to make heavy-duty sports-drink bottles. The pipes didn't look very serious, especially next to the profusion of vine and leaf that surrounded them. They passed a length of pipe covered in white spray paint. Beth caught the word *OXY* repeated in messy, angry capital letters. 'What is that?'

Miguel closed his book, placing a purple bookmark in its pages. 'Oil pipelines,' he said. 'My people, the people of the river, the Siona, they want the oil companies out. They're sabotaging our home. We have stopped them before,' he said. 'We are well-organized, and although it is not entirely in our nature, we protest peacefully.'

'Is it true you have a bullet in your thigh?' Beth blurted, somewhat fanatically.

Miguel nodded. 'My partner was not so lucky,' he said.

From across the aisle, Beth heard what sounded like a deliberate sniff from Paul. Perhaps it was warranted. But she was mesmerized by Miguel's offhand manner, his apparent obliviousness to his own glaring, gaudy contradictions.

Beth wondered where Miguel was now, six months later. She envisioned him paddling valiantly, hopelessly, through the unthinkable sludge his river had become. Or maybe not. Instead: in a hotel room in town, his head between the legs of one of the other 'uninhibited' citizens of El Oriente. The women of Lago Agrio had been as colourful and intent as the jungle birds; their tight green leggings, pink stilettos and bands of quivering exposed flesh spoke mostly of joy and heat.

Paul was speaking to her, saying something about the political situation in South America. 'It was Occidental, Beth. You know, the one they've been protesting for years. Here, then, is irony. Finally, the natives get the company to admit their free trade has been anything but. The people manage to oust them from the land, to reclaim what is theirs. And then, *this.* I wouldn't be surprised if it's the Man simply asserting his dominance. Oops, spilled some oil in your fresh, piranha-infested, life-giving waters. Sorry about that, but you shouldn't have asked us to leave so rudely. We were, after all, your guests. And were we not gracious? Did we not give your people training and jobs? Oh, we know. The rule of law. But what about the rule of the jungle?' Paul was clicking around the website as he spoke, searching madly for clues.

She still could not quite grasp what he had shown her. There were ramifications, she knew, houses made of cards, delicate ecosystems, butterflies on one side of the world flapping their diaphanous blue wings, while on the other side lucky humans sampled sushi from the newest hot spot – everything explained by a near-invisible knotted string you could follow back, if you chose, to a pot of money and a few greedy men with polished scalps and eyes like hunks of coal, dreaming of the ninth hole on a heavenly green and profit charts that explained their own lives to them in triplicate. Americans, she mused.

And then panic pushed like a spring shoot through the loam of her thoughts. She knew the earth did not belong to her but to her grandchildren, and perhaps not even to them. But what if there were no children, no grandchildren, and the generational link was lost? One day she would be old, bereft, perhaps still angry … The image of that equatorial river she had begun also to call her own, lying like a dark, drugged serpent, flashed into her mind. She turned to Paul. 'I'm going to the river.'

'I'll follow,' he said, with a knowing, almost servant-like condescension.

She shrugged, thought for a moment about what she might need, then shrugged again. She reached the park running, had to stop and crouch in the parking lot, hands braced on knees, to catch her breath. The day was overcast and humid; she could feel the threat of rain in her sinuses. The scattered copses of trees and fertile patches beneath the bridges had the look of hiding places for humans or their detritus. It was the sort of day bad men chose to bury body parts.

Paul had caught up with her. She turned for a moment to look into his familiar, fretful face. He was stuttering out facts like a telegraph machine: 'You know, it's Petroecuador now, but it hasn't always been this way. The Ecuadoreans managed to wrest back control, but only after a long and underhanded battle. It was the Americans first. Occidental. They were the ones who invaded what was essentially forbidden territory, protected and precious territory. And then they did sneaky things like sell part of their shares to Encana, a Canadian company, Beth, who then sold to the Chinese. If you think we are blameless in all of this, you are wrong. We Canadians drift in on the Americans' wake. Oil or diamonds – it doesn't matter, we'll take their sloppy seconds with our shadowy lesser dollar.'

She scrambled her way down the concrete wall that had been built to counter flooding, found a log designed for sitting and looked towards the old stone bridge, the site of the Old Mill, its ruins replaced by a spa and stacked-up condos. A fisherman was standing under the bridge, his hip waders making him appear large and mournful. He prepared his bait, cast into the deeper waters downstream and hooked a salmon while Beth watched. In the fall, the salmon would be running thick through these waters, leaping with a ferocious joy, using every ounce of their life force to clear the man-made steps that had been installed to control the flow of the river. Their connection to their home, to their little patch of earth and rock and water, was that compelling, that terrifying and true.

The water was higher than it had been for weeks; in June there had been fierce, unseasonal rains, then in late July the sun had come out and the river had receded, but the most recent downpour had made the trees thrive and weep again. The river was murky. Above them, to the west, a subway train went rumbling by. Out of the corner of her eye, Beth caught sight of a small black airborne shape, a scrap of red. And there it was: everything familiar, everything home, dogged by its Ecuadorean shadow, its strange tropical double. Here: a red-winged blackbird darting out from the shelter of a shrub. And there: a toucan decimating a small, hard fruit with its unlikely beak. Here: a pair of squirrels trapezing through the low branches of a maple. There: a monkey grooming his mate, bold and fastidious, perched on his very own Amazonian awning.

Paul tapped her shoulder. 'Let's not stay here, Beth.' He did not appreciate the river the way Beth did. Six months ago four boys had mugged him on a Saturday night as he strolled with two friends, reminiscing and taking turns toking like teenagers. The boys held a long serrated knife to Paul's throat; they fancied themselves gangsters. Later, close to dawn, the police found three of the four hiding in a gully. They were peppered with red-ant bites, their pockets clanking with change. 'Beth, I'm taking you home. You're in no condition to be traipsing around down here like some goddamned explorer of yore.' He grabbed her arm.

Beth shook free, but could not remain sitting. She got up and swatted at the seat of her pants, but nothing was clinging there. The damp had simply seeped in down to the skin, it would not be brushed away. She had to cut back up to the main path before she could make it down to the beaten sandy trail next to the water again. Paul zigzagged behind her, panting and riven by loyalty. On the far shore, a night heron was picking through pebbles and bits of trash. The bird stepped carefully over a pop can. Beth stopped to trail her hand in the water. At the edges, the river was lukewarm, but in the centre, in the depths, it would be cold. A man had drowned here, having jumped in after his dog. The dog survived. This was a fable of sorts.

That first night in the jungle, she and Paul had huddled close on their mattress, flicking the flashlight on and off like schoolchildren, peering out through the mosquito netting at the matte surface of the night and the six other gauzy, tented sleeping areas that surrounded them under their wooden shelter.

'They're like bridal beds, aren't they?' Beth said.

'Or ghost ships,' Paul replied, and Beth turned to him, surprised. They kissed then, softly shocked kisses that helped them both to sleep, despite the rustlings, the constant exchange of information and emotion under the canopy, along the riverbank, despite the scurrying geckos and dazed spiders Miguel had warned them might come tumbling from the rafters. Despite their recent history and despite themselves, they kissed like chaste children and slept like gentle dragons, side by side, through the night, until the clear commands of the camp cook woke them.

And then there was the issue of moving formally from sleep to waking, selecting the appropriate attire without parading around naked. Paul managed to pull on a pair of shorts and wiggle a T-shirt over his head before emerging to introduce himself to the pair of Germans, who had farted unselfconsciously – loud chains of farts – as the morning light crept in, and the group of cheery Spaniards sitting on the steps smoking cigarettes as if sucking in the dawn's nectar. Beth put on her quick-dry pants in a supine position but had to stand to do up the zipper. As she reached to fasten the button, she ran her hands over her abdomen, as had become habit.

Filaments of a dream returned to her.

She had been walking past a schoolyard, and she saw them, the children, in clusters and singles, trading insults, passing around secrets like coins. What did they *know*? What leavings and keepings were rattling at the bottoms of their bright, oversized knapsacks? It began to rain, and a teacher who looked far too young for the job began herding the children up the stairs and into the building. And it was then that Beth saw them – the children's dreams. They were floating above their heads, untethered, but somehow bound. *Paul!* she cried. *Look!* The dreams were hovering, they were dancing through the air, less like speech bubbles than interwoven threads of light. And the children seemed so cavalier with their dreams; they seemed not to notice they had them. They dawdled on the steps. They shoved and hugged each other roughly. *Look!* she shouted at Paul again, and he turned towards her, as did the children, whose eyes looked suddenly pale and intent, as if they had themselves been woken violently from sleep. And then the dream ended, or Beth's memory of it did, and she found herself in the Amazonian rainforest.

Before zipping up her pants, she caressed the pouch of flesh above her belly button. She looked up because she thought she could feel Miguel watching her across the expanse of swamp that separated the sleeping shelter and the dining area, peering out towards her, silhouetted against the mosquito netting like a shadow puppet. Perhaps they all appeared this way, funny outlines backlit by their particular cultures and accents, trampling and maundering their way through the jungle, laughing and drinking around the slab of a wooden table, starting comically at all the same sights – the tarantulas waving their chubby arms at the atmosphere, the sloths hanging like overstuffed handbags from the branches of ancient trees. Watching Miguel watch her, she was overcome by modesty; she had not yet thought to put on a shirt, and she could feel sweat beginning to accrue underneath her breasts. She reached for a bra and stroked her tummy one last time.

It had been concluded that there was nothing technically wrong with either of them. At first Paul had scoffed, said something about natural selection, overpopulation, all for the best, and she had felt an odd pull in her gut, as if one of her arteries had gone spelunking in the region of her uterus. They had walked for two hours in High Park after the third specialist gave his verdict. It was February, the temperature was sub-zero and they had to dodge Canada geese strutting and *tsk*ing like cops along the path. They did not speak; although the words were there, their footsteps over the snow and ice told a more complete, forlorn story. They wore parkas and Thinsulate accessories, but the wind blew straight through them. After they had circled the park four times, Paul said, 'Chicken breasts for dinner?' and Beth nodded, veering towards Bloor Street and home.

In retrospect, Beth was surprised and encouraged by their daring in taking the trip, or perhaps their faith that the daringness would pay off. Yes! It *was* intrepid to be so far from the creature comforts they were used to, and it should have brought them closer together, the risk they were taking, the shared adversary, which was the weather, or the atmosphere really – so thick, so talented at insinuating itself into your lungs, your very pores. No real civilization anywhere close by; eight hours by motorized canoe to the nearest hospital – and piranhas surrounding them! It was easy to act blasé about these things, but the fact remained that she and Paul, both Britons from way back, were not constitutionally designed for the rainforest. They did not exactly fit in.

On their third day out, Miguel rigged up fishing rods using long sticks they had selected from the edge of the trail, a length of strong twine, a rudimentary hook and a bucket of bait – pieces of raw meat that shone like rubies in the humidity. The moisture in the air made a sound like impatient insects and the reflection of the trees in the water made it seem they were gliding through an absurd upside-down land where anything could happen. They hung their lines over the side of the boat and waited, then exclaimed at the cleverness of the creatures when they felt a tug, or several tugs, and pulled up their lines to see the decimated bits of beef. They were about to return to camp when Beth felt another tug at her line and began exclaiming excitedly, 'A bite, a bite, Miguel! Miguel, a bite!'

'Pull it up,' he urged, standing in the canoe, hands on hips like a squat human teapot.

So she hoisted up the line, and there it was – small and prehistoric, scales seemingly pasted on over bone. The piranha thrashed weakly on the line, then stopped and appeared to be musing, with some malevolence, on its own fate. Miguel caught the fish up in his hand, then plucked a large leaf from a nearby overhang. He extended the leaf to the piranha and watched it chatter tiny, nonchalant puncture holes through the plant matter. Miguel held the fish up to his face and bared his own teeth for the cameras. As if he and the piranha were kin. Then he called Beth up to stand beside him, and Paul took shot after shot of her holding the piranha aloft, smiling next to Miguel.

When she had taken her place on the bench next to him again, Paul put his arm around her. 'I'm so proud of you,' he whispered. She understood his breath against her cheek as a kind of communion and felt herself smiling again. They both sensed Miguel looking in their direction, taking no pains to disguise his glare.

'Oh, Paul, he's a bit of a sad figure, really, isn't he?' Beth said.

'Yes, but he likes you, and maybe you like that he likes you, no?'

'Maybe,' Beth replied. She kissed Paul on the mouth. 'Maybe.' And it was true, there was an anger in Miguel whose shape she recognized.

Then the driver of the boat, a stooped man in his seventies with saggy knees and a round drunkard's nose, stood up quickly, as did Miguel. They peered at the sky for a second, then exclaimed, 'Ponchos!' to each other and to the group.

The two men sprang into action, pitching balled-up rain gear to each passenger. The sky opened like a giant trap door and water fell from it. Beth, Paul and their fellow tourists scrambled to pull the ponchos on over their heads, laughing at their own ineptitude, at the silliness. It was Mother Nature herself directing this slapstick, and it made them all giddy, although the canoe was quickly filling with water and the boat's gunnels had sunk to mere millimetres from the surface of the river.

Beth and Paul huddled together, watching the water rise around them. When Miguel threw them two sawed-off bottoms of bleach bottles, they gamely began to bail, although nothing seemed that serious, not really. They scooped and poured like toddlers, side by side, laughing. Beth knew that they had truly loved each other in that moment. It was as if they had just met, or had never exactly met.

But then on the second Wednesday of the trip, the group had travelled in tiny, tippy, handmade canoes to the opposite shore, 300 metres downstream. On the way they spotted pink river wraiths – freshwater dolphins cresting in the calm waters.

'We will visit one of my friends,' Miguel announced cryptically.

They disembarked on a small beach where sandbugs began immediately to chomp at their exposed flesh. Through it all, Miguel remained serene in his orange flip-flops, smiling as they flailed and slapped at their skin, scrambling in their packs for repellent. When they looked up, sweating, he was already waving a walking stick up ahead, soldiering farther into the thick woods and unknown.

'Isn't it exciting,' Beth said to Paul. 'I wonder where his friend lives. I wonder what he does in here.'

'I imagine he lives his life, Beth. Just with different dining room furniture.' Paul did not react well to bug bites; his legs were covered in loonie-sized pink welts. 'Besides,' he said, pointing up ahead, 'I'm not sure Miguel knows where he's going. Maybe he's not as canny with a compass as your coureur de bois, eh?'

Beth searched for Miguel and found him zigzagging over a small patch of land, stopping to make peculiar bird calls, his hands cupped up near his lips. 'He's signalling,' she told Paul. 'We don't always have to resort to cellphones.'

And sure enough, within minutes, a three-tiered whistle call came sailing back from an easterly direction. Miguel began leaping and running over the log- and mulch-strewn ground, bounding over obstacles and jumping to high-five low-hanging palm leaves.

'He expects us to follow when he's carrying on like that?' Paul said.

But they did follow him; they had no choice. There were times when they lost sight of Miguel altogether and the two of them paused, turned to each other, searching for signs of their own selves, the crumbs that might signal a trail of existence. If not for the other members of their band, who came stumbling through the ground cover with their digital cameras outstretched, they might have believed themselves to be truly abandoned and alone.

'C'mon,' Miguel finally called to them. 'We are almost there.'

And he was right; all of a sudden they were there. A small settlement presented itself in a long narrow clearing amidst a profusion of what must have been cornstalks.

'Meet my friend,' said Miguel, waving his hand towards a woman tending fire in a large pit circumscribed by stones. The woman straightened for an instant to pull her long black hair back from her face and over one shoulder. She wore grimy white shorts and a baggy red tank top over a pink camisole. No bra, Beth noticed. How wonderful not to have to worry.

Miguel sat them down on a log and told him that his friend would now demonstrate a traditional recipe. Miguel's friend did not look up again from the fire. She bent to retrieve what looked like a turnip from a large pot near her feet and began to shred it into a wooden bowl. A kitten sprung from behind the log with an angry oversized rooster in hot pursuit. Then a mongrel dog roused itself from behind a post and began to chase the rooster. The assembled group watched the kitten, rooster and dog as they circled the woman's cooking shelter. Then they sat and observed the woman shred her root vegetable. After about fifteen minutes, a young girl – maybe fourteen? – with an infant straddling one hip came striding, barefoot, from between the cornstalks. She smiled at Beth, who smiled back. When the girl began walking away, towards the river, Beth rose to follow.

'Beth,' said Paul. 'No.'

Beth patted Paul on the shoulder. 'I'm all right,' she said. 'I'd just like to know her name.'

Beth followed the girl into another small clearing, empty of structures. 'Hello,' she called out. 'I'm Beth.' She patted both hands against her chest and stepped closer to the girl, who was still smiling, her head cocked to one side coquettishly.

'Juana,' said the girl. 'Me llamo Juana.'

'Encantada,' said Beth, and for a moment the two simply stood staring. It was a moment that opened up like a hard coconut cleft in two to reveal its white tender meat, the flesh and milk of its insides.

Then Beth pointed to the baby, whose round brown eyes had pivoted towards her. 'And what is the baby's name?' she said.

'No.' The young girl shook her head.

She had misunderstood, or not heard correctly. Beth tried again. 'El nombre del niño?'

'No,' the girl said again.

Perhaps it was a girl? 'El nombre de la niña?'

Again, the girl shook her head and shifted the baby to her other hip impatiently. She was bored with this. Beth was not showing her anything new, was she? Still, the baby must have a name, she looked to be at least three months old. 'Nombre,' she said again. She pointed to herself and said, 'Beth.' Then she pointed to the girl and said, 'Juana.' Finally, she pointed to the baby and shrugged emphatically.

The girl stomped her foot. 'She no have name,' she said. 'No name.'

'What do you mean?' Beth cried. 'She is so beautiful and new. She must have a name!'

Juana smirked. 'No name,' she said.

Beth leaned up against a tree, steadying herself. If the baby had no name, then perhaps it was not ... claimed. Perhaps it had not yet been properly tied to this place, these people. Maybe there was a chance. In a flash, she saw it – the plump, umber-coloured child, tucked under a yellow fleece blanket, being ferried along Bloor Street like a royal in her sturdy stroller. If she got homesick, Beth would show her the Humber. They would gather bouquets of pale purple phlox and Queen Anne's lace and she would tell her the story of Étienne Brûlé, who learned to live among the Hurons. She would show her the CN Tower, that useless, soaring, space-age thing. Oh, there were those little pots of organic baby food in the No Frills grocery store, weren't there?

Juana moved closer to her, reached out to touch Beth's cheek and hair, the silver camera that hung like a medal around her neck. Beth brightened. 'Would you like me to take your picture?'

'Yes, yes,' Juana said happily, bobbing up and down.

'Okay,' said Beth. 'You should stand over there. Maybe I should hold the baby.' She held out her arms to take the child, but Juana backed away, cradling the baby's head under her stern chin.

'No,' Juana said.

And then the group had spilled into the clearing, muttering and perspiring, craning their necks to see a flock of parrots winging by.

Next to the Humber, Beth could hear thunder rolling in over the lake.

'Paul,' she said, 'do you think we should go back, find a way to help them rebuild?'

Paul sighed heavily. Soon the sky would open, and it was possible the humidity would break.

'I mean, if we are responsible, maybe we should just take responsibility ... ' Beth knew she was whining a little, but couldn't help herself.

Paul threw up his arms, which almost made Beth laugh. '*Jesus*, Beth, do you even know what happened to Étienne Brûlé?'

Beth nodded. Brûlé had eventually been disowned by his countryman, Champlain, it was true. And then the Hurons decided he'd betrayed them to the Iroquois, or at least this was the speculation. And those were harsher times, weren't they? 'They killed him,' she said quietly.

'Yes,' said Paul, pleased with her accuracy, but not nearly finished with his own story. 'The Hurons killed him.' He paused to take a breath, then turned towards her and whispered sadly, excitedly, 'Then they ate him.'

And that was when Beth pushed him. If he had fallen differently, with more agility and pliability, the water might not have borne him, the way it did, to the centre of the flow. But within seconds, Paul was struggling in the depths of the river, carried farther and farther away from Beth by a wicked undertow.

For a few seconds, he seemed not to care; there was surrender in the position of his body. But then Beth watched as he clambered strangely towards the shallow water on the opposite shore, and she watched as the current caught him by the ankles and pulled him back into its grasp. It confused her to think about what she wanted – how rarely people's plans and yearnings find their proper, perfect form. Beth stepped into the river. She felt it push gently on her thighs, then with more force on her torso, until her feet lost purchase, pedalled uselessly, freely, above the rocks and minnows of the riverbed. She lost sight of Paul, then found him again, as she would continue finding him for many years to come. The current would carry them both back to shore and one day they might laugh about this. But for the moment she focused on the rushing water between them, its opaque mystery, the smell of rust, fish gut and human effluent. She noted its very force, a liquid force that pulsed around the globe, hastening into places humans could not reach.

The evening after Beth met the nameless baby, Miguel invited her on a jungle walk. Paul had gone to bed early, blaming the bug bites and cheap wine for his fatigue.

'It is possible we will see some night animals, the nocturnals,' Miguel said as they traipsed carefully along the path. 'Do you have any like this in Toronto?'

Beth laughed. 'Maybe raccoons,' she said. 'They're the cleverest creatures you've ever met, and they've adapted to us, so now we adapt to them.'

'Adaptation,' Miguel said. 'Is that how you call it?'

The light was beginning to fade, making shapes waver, turning living tableaux into unreliable dreamscapes. Miguel placed his hand at the small of her back and invited her to take a closer look at an orchid the size of a thimble that was growing in the crook of a tree.

'Can you see?' he said. 'Here.' He slid a penlight from his pocket and shone it tightly on the flower. 'It's precious, isn't it?'

'Yes,' Beth said. And then, in a rush, 'There was a child, back there, in the forest. She was maybe three months old, so sweet, and she didn't have a name. I was wondering, if there might be a way, if she is not wanted or if she is a burden of some kind, I know I – we – could provide a good home. We live in a village of sorts – clean and comfortable, with very good educational opportunities and lots of diverse friends and toys for her to play with, second-hand clothes, because we don't like to be wasteful, and love. We have love for her. We can't have kids of our own, or at least that's what we've found.'

'I don't think so,' Miguel replied.

'But I don't understand!' Beth began to sob, then stopped when she noticed Miguel chortling to himself, bent at the waist with the laughter that was coursing through him. He stopped for long enough to hold out a fibrous piece of bark he had pulled from the trunk of a tree. The bark was a coppery colour, flecked with a darker, richer brown, and the piece he had stripped sat in the palm of his hand like a special seashell.

'Try it,' Miguel said. 'Rub it here.' He ran his index finger across his gums. 'Chew on it,' he said. 'It was what we used when we went to the dentist, to do the dental work. A way of freezing, of feeling no pain.' He passed her the bark and she put it in her mouth like a lozenge. It was true what he said; within seconds her tongue felt clumsy and numb. She looked at him, shocked, and found she could not speak.

'Shh,' he said, although she had not uttered a word. He sidled up close to her, from behind, and put his arms around her in a restrictive embrace.

I should resist, she thought, but fear was making her tingly and compliant. She wondered if there was a place where she truly belonged.

Then Miguel's fingers were down the front of her pants, his lips tender at her neck, his fingers rubbing and hooked up inside of her. 'Here you go, Toronto,' he said into her ear. 'A souvenir.' And Beth came, gasping soundlessly into the hand he had clasped firmly across her mouth. 'Now,' Miguel said. 'Now do you understand?'

When she returned to the camp, Paul was sitting cross-legged on his sleeping mat. Beth could tell by the studied rhythm of his breathing that he had been crying. She lay one hand lightly on his shoulder and he let her. Why did people's wounds never match up? Was life only always going to be terrible, terrible timing?

'That baby was … ' Paul whispered.

'I know,' Beth replied. 'I know.'

# Geraldine and Jerome

GERALDINE WENT FOR AN ULTRASOUND of her left breast and tried to make friends with the technician.

'I like your hair,' she said. She didn't really. It was trying too hard, had the look of one style superimposed on another, something from the eighties, asymmetrical and pop-star-esque, plopped on top of a pixie cut, the feathery innocent bangs. Plus the woman seemed not really to notice her, and she was wearing a wide brown belt over a large white shirt that made her look part handyman, part artist. But Geraldine supposed it was what people did; they snuggled up to their kidnappers, curried favour with their captors, tried to forge connections with those who held their fate in their hands. Although lately her will to live had been ragged at best, she still wanted the woman with the two wrong haircuts to like her.

'Thank you,' said the technician brusquely. 'Could you please scoot up a little? And just lie still.'

Geraldine scooted, then lay still while the technician squirted some gel onto her wand.

'It will be cold,' the technician said. 'Sorry.'

Geraldine's flesh went goosebumpy in anticipation.

The technician pressed some buttons, seemed poised to begin, then sighed. 'I'm sorry,' she said again. 'You'll have to go back to the waiting room for a while. There's something wrong with this machine. We'll have to wait for the other one to be free.'

'Back to the waiting room?' said Geraldine. She was only wearing a blue paper napkin on top.

'I would change back into your clothes.' The technician sighed again. She had replaced the wand and was clicking around on the screen, pivoting on her tall stool.

'Okay,' said Geraldine. 'Will you call me?'

'*Someone* will call you,' the technician said testily. Then she smiled at Geraldine and Geraldine felt the smile like sunshine.

'Sorry,' said the technician for the third time. 'It's not supposed to work this way.'

'It's okay,' said Geraldine. 'I like your belt.'

'Thanks,' said the technician, in a way Geraldine understood to mean dismissal.

There were magazines in the waiting room that had women dressed in outfits people had voted on – and sometimes one woman came out on top because she paired her minidress with high-heeled boots instead of strappy sandals and sometimes it was a bracelet or a hairdo that tipped the balance. The readers decided; it was a democracy. She liked these magazines.

But when she stepped into the waiting room there was a boy there. A teenager. He was sitting in one of the chairs with his knees thrust out into the middle of the space. He was tall but his slouching made him even larger than he needed to be, considering the venue. His ball cap was pulled low over his eyes and at first Geraldine thought he might be asleep, but then she realized he was just hiding – in the way that hoodlums hide. And Geraldine got angry – how *dare* he? She decided she would sit next to him. He wanted all that space to himself – well, he could not have it! She would have some too; she wanted to slouch and thrust too. She took her seat purposefully.

'Excuse me,' she said, searching not for absolution but attention.

The boy looked at her.

Fourteen or fifteen, Geraldine guessed. Why was he here?

'Oh,' said the boy. 'Right. You waiting?'

'Yes,' said Geraldine.

The boy glanced at her again, then quickly scanned the empty chairs that surrounded them. He canted forward slightly then tapped at the underside of the brim of his cap. 'I'm Jerome,' he said.

'Oh,' said Geraldine. 'I'm Geraldine.'

Jerome nodded.

Geraldine had not expected this. She began reaching for a magazine, then stopped herself. 'I guess we're both Gerrys then, aren't we? I mean, me with a G and you with a J, but still.' Geraldine had been Gerri (with a tiny heart over the i) until she turned sixteen, and then the more sophisticated – she imagined – Ger, until she met her husband, Simon, who insisted on Geraldine. It's less jaunty, he said. It has a gorgeous seriousness to it.

Jerome shook his head. 'I don't like it when girls have boy names. It's confusing.'

'Well, not really,' said Geraldine. 'It's just different.'

'It's *messed up*,' said Jerome. The way he said this seemed to imply some mess-up of Shakespearean proportions. A reversal that could precipitate unchecked chaos.

'Are you ... are you waiting?' said Geraldine. Of course he was waiting. But for what? For whom?

'Yeah, waiting to rob me some ultrasound machines,' the boy said.

Geraldine made a sound like a laugh. 'Don't steal the one in that room,' she said, pointing. 'It's not working.'

Jerome smiled. 'Are you okay, lady?'

'No,' said Geraldine. Geraldine used to be the type of person who apologized to hydro poles and thigh-high furniture. No more. Bereavement had made her reckless and easily incensed. 'I don't understand why you have to wear your pants like that. Your belt around your thighs, waddling around like a penguin. And why don't you let people see your eyes? It's a bit suspicious, you know. You're not doing yourself any favours, especially considering you're ... ' She stopped.

Jerome stood up out of his seat, moonwalked in a neat circle around the magazine table and came to a stop directly in front of Geraldine. He reached his hand into his pocket and drew out – nothing. Then he held his thumb and forefinger up in a pinch and drew them across his mouth in a slow mime. 'Zip it, lock it, put it in your pocket,' he said softly.

Jerome took his seat and resumed his former slouching position, ball cap now slightly askew on his head.

Geraldine was shocked but managed something like a *tut, tut* under her breath. Jerome countered with a remarkably similar sound, a subtle teeth sucking that communicated with a sharpness and succinctness lacking in Geraldine's utterance.

Geraldine, schooled, reached for a magazine. And after a moment, Jerome did the same. Out of the corner of her eye, Geraldine saw the cover; it was a design mag, glossy and heavy and square, with a fat vase full of poppies on the cover.

Geraldine's magazine was *Chatelaine*, not one of the tabloids plastered with tirelessly perfect people. She leafed through absently. Some recipes designed for the busy family – heart-healthy burritos and miso soup with veggies – and an article about a woman lost at sea that captivated her with its headline and arty illustrations. The woman had not exactly been lost – no, not lost – but kidnapped. She chose to go sailing, on a sailing expedition, and she ended up at the mercy of the captain/instructor, who, it seemed to Geraldine, was also a sociopath and a tyrant. The trip was extended by months. The captain did not respond to radio signals. The woman's husband thought she was dead. He grieved, he mourned, he absorbed the loss, and then she came back! She came sailing back into his life like some modern-day Lady Odysseus and he had to figure that out. They had to figure that out as a couple. It was the reverse of real life, really, where someone was snatched away from you but you imagined that he was not really dead, only vacationing, only lost at sea, held for ransom … You wished and yearned and dreamed that he was still alive and then … he was still dead.

The couple did not last. How do you learn to live with a ghost? How do you live as a ghost? Geraldine shook her head at the magazine – the gall, to publish such a strange, head-spinning story and then leave it in the waiting room at the breast-cancer clinic. Did they not understand that people like her – widowed at fifty-two, lumpy boobs – wanted outfit contests and gossip, not contemporary tuna casseroles and explorers risen from the dead? She closed the magazine. Jerome appeared to be sleeping. His chest was rising with some regularity and his hands hung relaxed off the ends of the chair's arms. Perhaps Geraldine should also sleep. Sleep took her suddenly these days; often the mere thought of it sedated her, bringing weight to her limbs and eyelids.

When Jerome woke up, the woman, Geraldine, was still sleeping, her messy bun lopsided on the top of her head. He wondered if she was sick like his mother. He wondered if she had children, and where those children were now. He imagined dinnertime at Geraldine's house. He saw speckled granite countertops – he had learned about these from his magazine, they were the rage. He saw eggshell-coloured walls and eggs lined up in the fridge like little round white soldiers. He saw a long wooden table and a place for everyone. The food on the plates was colourful and subdivided, complete.

At his house, Jerome was the cook. It had not always been this way; the arrangement had evolved. There were a few things he was really good at – sausages and mashed potatoes a babysitter had taught him (she called it bangers and mash – rude in his opinion), a jerk chicken his auntie cooked, a beef stir-fry he just made up and refined with some help from the internet. And he made sure the fridge was full of the types of sauces that could make plain pasta taste fancy, the freezer stocked with pizzas and pot pies. He never wrote it down but he had a schedule in his head too: what dinners for which day, a checklist for what was running low. He knew the aisles of the supermarket, the placement of products, like he knew the stairwells of his apartment complex – which were sketchy, which might mean the right kind of business.

His girlfriend Carla was a terrible cook. She was like a kid in the kitchen. The one time he went to her house for lunch she slapped together a peanut-butter sandwich for him – it was like a flat little cake made of white bread and brown frosting. Not nutritious at all. But he didn't say anything. She was an only child. Two parents but mostly TV.

Jerome stared at Geraldine. She looked like an animal asleep – a dog dreaming, legs twitching, eyeballs all crazy with chase under the lids.

Geraldine woke up with a start and a sob that was followed by another sob and another, until she was shaking in her seat, her arms wrapped around herself for protection and warmth and something else she did not want to name, or could not. Intimacy, maybe. Love. A poor approximation of the touch of someone she had known and not known for twenty-three years.

And next to her, Jerome's face, alarmed.

'Do you have cancer? Do you have breast cancer?' he called to her as if the sobbing might have deafened or retarded her somewhat.

'No,' said Geraldine. 'Well, I don't know. My husband's dead.'

'Fuck,' said Jerome. 'That sucks. When?'

Geraldine breathed more deeply, calmed by his concern. 'Six months ago. I'm sorry, Jerome. I didn't mean to upset you.'

''S'okay,' Jerome said. 'I wasn't really upset. How did he die?'

'A car accident,' she replied. 'A drunk driver.'

'I never knew anybody died in a crash,' Jerome said. His friend Tyrell was stabbed in middle school by his other friend Joseph, and his friend Rogelio once drove his mother's car into a cement planter because he smoked too much pot, but no one hurt or killed by cars. 'Did you see the body?'

Geraldine loved this question, its clueless indelicacy and important curiosity.

'Yes,' she said. 'But only after they had cleaned him up.'

Jerome nodded.

'I wanted to see him bloody and broken. The social worker said no, to live with that vision would be … terrible.' *But it would be real*, Geraldine had said. *Real is not always the best thing*, her therapist had said later. But Geraldine wasn't so sure.

'Maybe,' said Jerome. 'But you'd *know*.'

'Exactly,' said Geraldine. She thought at that moment that she would gladly buy crack from this boy, whatever it took for him to feel accepted and useful. 'What 'bout you? What you in for?' Geraldine made her voice a bit twangy and cowboyish.

'Oh,' said Jerome. 'My moms. She had to have a breast removed. A mastectomy.' He said this last word carefully, reverently, cognizant of its seriousness, the power and respect that accuracy commands. Jerome had never encountered the word *euphemism*; nevertheless, he was not a boy who believed in the cloaking of facts. 'Tell me,' he sometimes said to the boys in his crew. And what he meant was: The Truth.

'I'm sorry,' Geraldine said. 'How awful.' Something about Jerome moved her, even as his attitude and general comportment continued to irk her.

There was a feeling Geraldine got sometimes, talking to people who, like her, had endured a terrible loss. It was not a kind feeling. She felt almost disdainful of those who believed that what they had endured – a mother whose MS had wasted her slowly over the years; a brother who hung himself in the garage, using the box that contained his children's old board games to stand on; a dear friend whose heart attacked while she was teaching a Grade 2 class; a child, dear God, a child – was somehow equivalent to her own pain, her own cavernous emptiness. *Really*, she would say, *how terrible*. But these were mere words. She did not feel them. Instead, what she felt was indignation. She had been wronged, terribly misunderstood, and knew it was up to her to set matters straight. This very burden of proof, this responsibility, also angered her. She could not say exactly what it was she had done or who she had supposedly harmed, although on some level it seemed she *knew*.

She had a friend when she was in high school – potty-mouthed and beautiful – who used to say her mother made her so angry she could feel it in her cunt. Geraldine disliked the word, of course, how could she not (half *cat*, half *blunt*, all back-of-the-throat bile), but she understood what her friend meant. Perhaps she did not have the empathetic reserves required; they had all been exhausted in missing Simon. Or perhaps she had always been selfish and it was only now, when forced to confront her own vulnerability, that this selfishness was coming boldly to the fore. She could not feel sympathy for any of these people in her cunt. In her core.

But she felt it now. She felt it for Jerome. But no, not sympathy but kinship – like they were rowing along together in the same little rickety boat.

'Yeah,' Jerome said. 'It's awful. What about you?' His eyes flicked down to her chest, then up to her face. He cleared his throat.

'Yeah,' said Geraldine. 'These.' She cupped her breasts with two hands briefly, hoisted them up to her chin and released them. 'I get a lot of lumps – fibroids – and they have to check them out. Just to be sure. To be safe.'

'Right. Fibroids. To be safe.' Jerome spoke quietly, robotically.

He looked suddenly stricken, Geraldine thought. With grief? Confusion? 'Better to be safe than sorry!' she sang out.

'Sorry for *what*?' Jerome said. Anger had seized him by the nape and was shaking him so that his brain butted up against his skull. Carla said his temper would be his downfall one day. *Tragic flaw* were the words she used.

'I don't know,' said Geraldine. 'I mean … I'm sorry.'

'Better safe than sorry,' Jerome parroted. He kicked his foot out in front of him violently, but there was nothing there to kick, no physical connection, and the movement unbalanced him, sent him reeling into Geraldine, who pushed him gently back into his seat.

He closed his eyes. *I have to have one lopped off,* his mother had said wryly, holding his hand. At first Jerome had not understood the word. It sounded like *chop*, but also like *floppy*, and the French word for rabbit, *lapin* (he had always remembered that one, and *vache* for cow). He saw a cartoon bunny, but knew there were breasts involved, and for a horrible moment he pictured his mother with two floppy ears protruding from her chest. He saw a cleaver glinting on the counter.

'Oh, God,' said Geraldine. 'Can we just start over?' She felt terrible.

Jerome shook his head, then turned to face her. In fact, he got right up in her face.

Geraldine recoiled as much as her seat allowed, then corrected herself.

Jerome shook his head again, and sucked his teeth reprovingly. 'You got kids?'

'A daughter,' Geraldine replied. 'But she's gone.'

'Dead too?' He looked like he might cry.

Geraldine understood. He was primed to see tragedy everywhere. And tragedy *was* everywhere, if you peered through the right lens. 'No,' she said. 'Away at school. McGill University – in Montreal.'

'Oh,' he said.

Geraldine might have said Mars. Still, she persisted. 'She came home for the funeral, of course. But I didn't want her to interrupt her studies, the momentum of what she's doing. It's important to have a purpose, I think, at a time like this ... She's studying chemical engineering, still unusual for a woman, really.'

'How old?' Jerome said.

'Oh, she'll be twenty next month – I can't believe it. Twenty. It's just such a large, round number, isn't it?'

Jerome nodded. He had imagined younger children, despite the streaks of white in Geraldine's hair. He tried to picture Geraldine's daughter, but instead thought about Carla, and how she'd let him do it to her for the second time. How it felt in there. How much he wanted it and the deep expansive sadness he felt when he got it. She was a Brazilian girl, long hot-pink fingernails and soft melting brown eyes. She did something with her eyelashes so they stuck straight out like zombie fingers reaching up from a grave. The effect was disturbing and gorgeous. She was smart too, and not just on the street. Had an 80 average she hid like a prison record. Jerome was a little bit scared of her and probably in love with her. He wanted to keep doing it with her so he could find out.

'What about you, Jerome? What do you want to do?'

Jerome was startled by the question. Maybe she'd seen the thoughts playing across his face? He imagined saying it: *I wanna do Carla.* He laughed.

'No, I'm serious. A fine, sensitive man like you, you must have ambitions.' Geraldine was smiling encouragingly, like a guidance counsellor.

'I need to make money. Take care of everybody.' Jerome sniffed and looked away. He had a little brother, a littler sister. No dad. But he had connections. And people who were loyal to him.

Geraldine watched him pull something from his pocket. A handkerchief? No, it was his cellphone, one of the new ones with a screen and a keyboard and a headpiece, and probably a refrigerator in there too somewhere. Jerome was staring at the screen, his brow furrowed.

'Is everything okay?' Geraldine didn't mean this. She meant: Put that thing away while you are having a conversation.

'Yeah, yeah.' Jerome waved at her as if she were his secretary.

Just then a woman entered the waiting room from the direction of the examination rooms. She was wearing a lab coat and carrying a clipboard. She looked at Geraldine, then at Jerome, then at the rest of the seats, untenanted, in the waiting room. Then she looked down at her clipboard with the same frown Jerome was giving his cell. Geraldine was getting used to feeling lonely, but this was a new strain of the same disease, the exclusion she felt while the two strangers deciphered messages and weighed options.

'Are you Alice Yanofsky?' the woman finally said.

'No,' said Geraldine. 'I'm Geraldine.' For some reason she felt it unnecessary to give her surname. 'I'm waiting because my machine, my ultrasound machine, it was broken.'

'Oh,' said the woman. 'I don't know anything about that.' She frowned again.

'That's Jerome,' said Geraldine. She pointed with her thumb towards Jerome, who was still busy with his phone, although the introduction of a new human to their surrounds seemed to have piqued his interest somewhat. He held up a casual pointer finger and nodded at the lab-coat woman. *One minute.* Geraldine raised her eyebrows.

'I'll check back in a few minutes,' the woman said. Then, somewhat quizzically: 'Thanks.'

Jerome pressed many buttons on his phone, then slid it back into his pocket. 'What did she want?' He gestured towards the exam rooms.

'Oh,' said Geraldine, 'nothing.' She pulled a stick from her bun and let her hair tumble down to her shoulders. Then she twined the hair around her hand and fixed it back into a neat knot.

Jerome watched her, amazed.

'Nothing to do with us,' Geraldine added.

'Nah,' said Jerome. 'Still, we been waitin' a long time.' He knew something about waiting. When he and his mother arrived at the hospital the day of the mastectomy he could follow her only so far. A nurse had led Jerome's mother away, and she returned wearing a hospital gown and a shower cap, wheeling an IV beside her, the long tube finding a home in a pale green vein in her arm. She looked old, Jerome thought. And young too. He didn't like to think about what that might mean. She sat next to him just like Geraldine and they read magazines. Then a man wearing purple scrubs – why would they let a man wear those? – came and said

Jerome's mother's name. He smiled at Jerome and said, *You can come this way – there's a special room for friends and relatives.* Jerome did not like the sound of this. He had been to funerals, and this procedure – these quiet rooms, this general hush and formality – had the same unsettling feel. But he nodded and followed the man, then was too busy reading all the signs along the hallway to notice when his mother left him. He had not said *Goodbye*, or *Good luck*, or *I love you* or even *Kanga-poo*, which was their thing they sometimes said to each other.

He nodded at Geraldine in case she had asked him a question.

'Yeah,' said Geraldine. Waiting was *the worst*; she wanted to help. 'Let me tell you a story.' She paused.

Jerome made a sound she took for assent.

'It's an old story about making choices in life. It's one of Aesop's fables. Do you know Aesop?'

'Yeah,' said Jerome. He didn't. The guy sounded Jewish. And the story sounded lame. He didn't trust anybody who told him he had *choices*, that he should *make smart choices*. People didn't *choose*; they reacted and survived. Or sometimes not. 'Tell the story,' he said.

Geraldine was nodding quickly. Jerome had pleased her.

'Okay, great. So this is the story of A Man, His Boy and His Donkey. Once upon a time, there was a man who decided to go to the market with his boy and his donkey. On the way the boy got tired, and the father decided to let his son ride on the donkey's back. A group of men passed the man and told him the boy would only get lazier if he let him ride, that the father should be riding because he was older. So the father pulled the boy from the donkey and rode it himself …'

Jerome half-listened to Geraldine as the group of travellers met another group of haters who said the father was cruel for letting the son walk, and another who said they should both ride, and still another who said the poor donkey was being overworked and abused.

It was lulling, the way Geraldine spoke, and Jerome could imagine having her voice in his life on a regular basis, a favourite track on his iPod. He was trying not to, but he liked Geraldine. He felt sorry for her, but he liked her too. He could tell she wanted something good for him even if she was old and white and mostly clueless. As a rule, Jerome didn't appreciate people expecting things from him. It made his throat close up a little. But he had noticed something surprising about Geraldine: she needed him.

Finally the father and his son tie the donkey to a long pole and carry the animal to give him a break. Jerome found this inexplicably sad.

In the hospital that day, Jerome had taken his seat in the corner of the Visitors' Waiting Room next to a small, low table covered in pamphlets about healthy eating. The pamphlets made Jerome hungry but he couldn't leave, could he? What if they needed to contact him? What if his mother needed him? And he had read a sign on the way in that said No Food or Beverage Allowed in Visitors' Waiting Room. Jerome was not a strict rule follower by nature, but this directive seemed somehow related to the outcome of his mother's surgery. That there was a way of keeping the sick, starving and sad alive through the solidarity of the living, hungry lot who surrounded them seemed reasonable to Jerome. It was a complicated superstition but as soon as he had created it he believed it absolutely. No food then. And no moving from his chair. It was two hours. He could do that.

Except it was not two hours. The surgery was scheduled to finish at 3:15 pm. At 3:17, Jerome thought there was a delay, which is why no one had come to talk to him. He had seen the messenger who scurried back and forth between the waiting room and some secret space at the end of the corridor. He was a short brown man with slicked-back hair. Jerome broke his own rule, got up from his chair and asked the man where his mother was. *Write her name down here,* said the messenger in a hushed voice. *I'll go see what's happening. Thank you,* said Jerome with the same hush. He printed the name carefully, in caps, on a small slip of pink paper. The messenger took the paper solemnly and was off down the corridor. He returned after four minutes. *Still in surgery,* he said to Jerome. *That's all the information I have.* Jerome slumped back to his chair. He felt incredibly hungry and also like he might throw up at any second. He put his head between his knees and stayed like that, trembling, until the messenger nudged him at 3:49 to say his mother was out of surgery; she was being transferred to recovery. What Jerome knew about life was perhaps contained in that space between 3:15 and 3:49 pm. It was a barren island he had inhabited during those thirty-four minutes. Nothing but the cutting wind of his own thoughts for company. He understood that the island was much worse than the pain of poverty or prison. He never wanted to go back there.

'Jerome,' Geraldine said. 'Are you listening to me? The donkey drowned because of the father's stupid decisions.'

'Right,' said Jerome. 'So what?'

'Well,' said Geraldine. 'The story is about a man trying to please all the people all the time.'

'No, it's not,' Jerome said. 'That man is an idiot.'

'Well, yes, that's the moral.' Geraldine could feel herself getting annoyed.

'That ain't the moral,' Jerome said.

'Then what is?' Geraldine shifted impatiently in her seat, refused to look at him.

'Don't tie your donkey to no stick – else you are the dumb-ass.' He smiled, happy with the cleverness he'd fashioned there.

Geraldine decided to play this straight; she would explain. 'But you really *can't* please all the people all the time. And it's important not always to care what other people think.' She had been through this with her daughter, all the peer-pressure business, new drugs on the scene, porn everywhere.

Jerome snorted. 'You need to care about what other people think. That's the *only* damn thing you need to care about.'

'But if you try to please them all the time you'll just end up looking silly.' Geraldine had spent a lot of money and time on her therapist, and she mostly believed in her. She reiterated her point: 'You can't please all the people all the time.'

'You can try.' Jerome grinned at her.

What Jerome said delighted Geraldine absolutely – its insouciance and lack of logic. Every now and then, she thought, you bumped into somebody who showed you a different way of living, a fierce commitment to a life that you could never claim as your own. What would the future hold for them both? There was no way of knowing.

(Geraldine will continue to come in for her yearly scans, to be safe. And although her fibroids will keep thriving they will remain benign. Six years – to the day – after the morning she met Jerome she will wake up and realize she has forgiven her husband for dying; it will not be a happy realization, only a tired one. Sometimes, when she comes to the breast-cancer clinic, she will think of Jerome and wonder. But often not; there are a lot of magazines.

Jerome's mother will remain cancer-free for eight years. Then the cancer will come back, in her cervix this time, and it will kill her. Jerome will have narrowly escaped a stint in a juvenile detention centre and a drive-by shooting. At the time of his mother's death, he will have been studying tool-and-die-making at Seneca College for a couple of months and will consider dropping out. But Carla will convince him to persevere. Jerome will be reminded of Geraldine at only one time in his life. When they are burying his mother, he will think: She was wrong. It does no good to see the dead as they are at the moment of death, or as they appear in their coffins. It does nobody any good at all.)

But maybe, just maybe, Geraldine thought, there was something she could take away from this. A piece of Jerome to put in her pocket. She wanted to find a way to tell him this, but they were locked into something now; she had to carry on. 'But you'll never succeed in pleasing *everybody,*' she said.

'Nah, maybe not.' Jerome made his hand into a neat pistol and shot twice, up towards the heavens. *Bam, bam.*

Maybe aiming at God, maybe saluting Him.

'But I got mad hope,' Jerome said. '*Mad* hope.'

# Dominoes

I DIDN'T REALLY MEAN TO drop out of school. When I started at the university I thought learning how to name and explain things might bring me purpose, lucidity. I attended lectures and turned in my papers on time. I stood dead in the centre of the swirl and storm of theory. I applied myself. But then I started going to the student-operated pub between, and sometimes during, classes. The pub was difficult to find; it was located in a catacomb next to the cafeteria, and if a person wasn't careful she could end up in the boiler room or the yearbook office. Still, it was worth it once I arrived. I spent whole days sitting in one of the vinyl chairs, their shiny purple backs stapled like patchwork beetles. I went into the pub with every intention of leaving, my time parcelled out efficiently, a half-pint of beer resting modestly on the rickety wooden table in front of me. But when the time came for me to get up and walk the short distance up the stairs, out the door and across the quadrangle, I stayed sitting, less paralyzed than somehow anchored to my surroundings. And then it always seemed too late. Too late to do things properly. Too late to do anything but wait for the next song to come on the radio. Sometimes a voice less disapproving than bewildered would intrude on my whiling away of the hours. *What are you doing here,* it would ask, then wait patiently. *I'm biding my time,* I'd reply softly, humbly, *I'm biding my time.*

It doesn't feel as if I've dropped out, really. I still have library privileges, and the seventy-five-dollar cheques from Mum (for *sundries*, she actually wrote in one of her cards) keep coming every month, or more often if she can manage it. Now I'm taking this evening course, a writing workshop, so that one day, if I have what it takes, I will be a real writer. My instructor has the best posture I have ever seen. Every day I watch her riding her bike away from the recreation centre, and am convinced that there is nothing but willpower and gravity anchoring her bum to the broad, black reupholstered seat. She scares me a bit, like helium balloons. Our last assignment was to choose a clear, quirky, luminous incident from our pasts and to build a story from there.

I got a letter from Mum the other day, and in it she enclosed this clipping from the newspaper about your buddy Richie. The article wasn't very long. There wasn't much to tell – a bit about the murder, the arrests, how it shocked the community. And then the punchline, like something from a TV movie: Richie, two months short of a chance at parole, six years into his sentence, had hanged himself in his cell. So sad, Mum wrote. And she asked me the questions she could not ask you: Remember his mother, Mrs. Henley? Did you ever discuss with Jeremy what happened with Richie? Such a tragedy, wasn't it? I wanted to call Mum to talk to her about it, but I didn't because she doesn't know I dropped out. I wanted to call you to talk about it, but we don't really talk.

So I started thinking maybe this was a story.

It happened in High Park, at nighttime, and there were three of them with baseball bats. When you think about it, you might think of a crack, wood on bone, something clear and conclusive. But I know it was a thud, soft and stupid. Spiro was kicking him and yelling something about one less faggot, and looking at Richie like he was chicken shit, so Richie took the bat and brought it down on the guy's chest, and then he couldn't stop himself; he just kept swinging until he stopped the *ouf* noise. It was then he noticed the lines of blood streaming out of the ears like two solemn ant processions. But Joey still went at it, even after Richie and Spiro had backed off. When Joey finally stopped, it was like the guy on the ground wasn't even a person anymore. He was just this mess of rags and blood and arms and legs all quiet like sleeping animals, so they ran back to the car and they drove away. On the back seat was a two-four of empties Richie meant to return for the deposit money the night before, and on the dashboard an old air freshener Lori had bought him. Spring Rain. Fucking hell, said Spiro. That thing smells like shit.

Richie's life had always run alongside ours, like a wild horse next to a train. We were steady, on schedule, simply because he was not.

The thing is, Richie was your story, Jeremy, and to put myself there ... Well, I'm just a beginner. I'm afraid I would be tempted into machismo and melodrama, a scene in the bathroom, gazes exchanged in a cracked mirror over urinals. The cowboy stances, the dainty tip-tapping to shake the drops free, the post-pee shudder. How you would have had something, a yearning or a yen, for what Richie had, his assurance, an innate sexual power that emanated from his crotch and collar, which was denim, worn soft and grimy. Frayed: tiny extra hairs rubbing against his neck. And maybe in the story, if I were you, I would recall the time when you were eleven and expanding into your boy-self, an innocent to Richie's thirteen. You rode your bikes down to the river, through back streets, over curbs, along Bloor Street, that border of traffic, thighs pumping strong then slack, coasting on your banana seat, overweening child/man. Down then, into Etienne Brulé Park, the river valley named after a French scallywag and coureur de bois.

'Beaver pelts, that's what this country is built on,' Dad once said, so that for years I envisioned the sleek skins buried under the foundations of factories and apartment complexes, mixed in with bones and concrete, lost nickels and root systems. You hid your face behind your elbow every time Dad said *beaver* and Mum stuck her front teeth over her bottom lip, but quickly, without sound, as if acting out a charade only for herself.

Then you rode through the ravines to where the brush is thick on the bank and there is an eerie privacy for a place so close to the well-tended public path. Beaten-down reeds and crayfish, a stink like breeding. Jos. Louis wrappers and torn magazines, the brown murk of river rushing shallow over rocks and man-made waterfalls. You would sit there on stumps and skip stones, smoke cigarettes. (All this is conjecture.) A weeping willow would trail its bowed leaves to the ground.

Still, I understand that sometimes people have to go off slyly, on their own or with someone else. It's what we need: little amulets of time and space. It's what Dad did in his workshop with the two-by-fours and piles of screws and sawdust, the tape player pumping out Tom Paxton tunes.

What I imagine is myself, bigger, barging in on your little scene in the park and saying something cop-like: 'Where's your father, young man?' But then I remember Dad was having his gall bladder out at the time, and that gets me thinking about how he gave them to you, his gallstones, to keep. They floated, imperfect mustard-coloured eggs, in a large Mason jar you had on your dresser. It sat next to an old piece of hockey net and a silver cardboard box with a condom nestled in it – out of its package but unused – like an alien finger left to dry in the earth's unfamiliar atmosphere. I know this because often, when you were out, I would roam your room like an African cat, padding and predatorial. Sometimes I watched you in the mornings, still sleeping, lips loose, cheeks puffing out with stale nighttime breath.

I think maybe this is what she meant, my instructor, by 'quirky,' by 'luminous,' but I also know it is only one of many places my story (your story?) could go, and only the very edge of the truth (okay, the love) we shared.

When I first moved here I imagined the mountains might inspire me, or act as a kind of landscape tonic, wake me up a bit like a good aftershave should. It made me understand why you had to get away and find a spot of your own, even if it is just an hour outside of Toronto, and instead of mountains you got smokestacks. It's overwhelming, though, the brand of beauty here. All that water and land and sky give me a heady feeling, which is not the same as a smart feeling. The people wear nice clothes, though, surf-like and active, and they all have travel mugs and snappy gear with fastenings and paddings, although I'm not sure they ever travel very far. I started running because everyone else does, and I think it was a good idea. It forces me to measure out my life in the distance between telephone poles, which is okay. Setting small goals like that. When I went to buy new shoes, the salesperson, a man with shaved legs and busy tendons in his calves, made me test them on the street outside. I had to run up and down the sidewalk with the glowing sides and stripes calling attention to my stride.

I miss the subway and the lake. I miss High Park with its autumn colours, mulch and long, long memory. I miss you like I've been missing you my entire life.

So Richie is gone. The guy he killed was gay. And we didn't know any gay people then.

The thing with teenagers is they transfer all the affection they might have had for their family as children to relative strangers as soon as they hit puberty, and the trail the love leaves wags behind them like a vestigial tail. It's what makes them move so awkwardly. Lori was thin with chunky thighs and the kind of jeans you had to lie like an acrobat on the bed to zip up. She sometimes crimped or teased her shoulder-length brown hair into mini fountains at the front, and her eyeliner matched the blue of her eyes exactly. Once I helped her pick up the insides of her purse when it fell open and spilled in the parking lot: a red glossy compact, two hard tampons, wrapped tight and pointed like bullets, wallet-sized photos of her and Richie where she has him in a headlock and they are both laughing. On her key ring: a rabbit's foot dyed orange, plus a little plastic tag that read *Sarasota* in swirly writing over a picture of the setting sun. For some reason her voice always sounded slightly asphyxiated, unsure, although she herself never seemed so. In her last year of high school she got braces, which added to her mystique, made her more closed-mouthed, so that when she did speak her words seemed loaded, cryptic. We all loved her.

I wish I could say I was born a writer. In Grade 7 I wrote a story for Mr. Lara about a post-nuclear-war world where wraiths with black oblong pancakes for eyes trailed mournfully along the earth's decimated surface. He gave me a B minus. 'He's not even English,' my best friend Julie hissed. 'He's from *Trinidad.*' But I still felt sorry when someone wrote *Dirty Packi* on his blackboard.

'I'm sorry,' I said, when I arrived early one morning and found him leaning up against one of the desks contemplating the message.

'It's okay.' He erased the 'c' in *Packi*, then wiped off the entire thing. 'I'm not even a Paki. You will encounter this often in the world, Maddie. Carelessness and hate in combination. Strange that what bothers me most is the inaccuracy of it all.'

'I'm sorry,' I said again.

'It's not your job to be sorry. Just know exactly who you are. Name your fortunes and misfortunes and live your life.'

There was the day I overheard Mum talking to Aunt May on the phone, deeming you dyslexic. The glee I felt printing it in blue felt pen across your pink Hilroy notebooks. *Dick-Sex-Lick. Dick-Sex-Lick.* Until the only space left was a small unsullied triangle in the corner only big enough for one word, and which to choose from amongst the three? A bad word was a bad word was a bad word.

I asked you about it later, the dyslexia. High school was new territory for me and it was a mystery what went on behind those doors they labelled *Remedial.*

'What do you do when they take you in there?' I said. We were sitting in the rec room, fighting over a ragged afghan.

'Oh, you know, drink baboon blood, give each other tattoos, that kind of thing.' You grabbed the afghan and secured it around your legs like a granny.

'No, really,' I said. 'I mean, are they nice to you?' I felt suddenly shy but determined.

You glared at me and made a move to leave but the afghan restricted you. 'They're okay,' you said. 'But it's too hard, so fuck 'em.' I thought I could see tears in your eyes.

'Yeah,' I said. 'Fuck 'em.'

When we got a bit older we didn't talk to Richie much at school. He hung out near the senior doors, but he didn't go inside much. There was a covered pathway leading up to the door where kids slouched to smoke, lining the narrow passage like mould. Richie had a coveted spot on the step leading up to the door, close to the warmth of the foyer in winter. He wore sleeveless T-shirts in the warmer months so that you could see the cigarette burns – tiny, puckered blooms in the skin – on the tops of his wiry arms. Stepfather was the story. Lori was often by his side. Someone said she refused to see him after what happened. Still, I used to imagine her sometimes, waiting outside of the prison, in the spring rain, her hair shorter, maybe streaked.

You were always accident-prone, loose like an animal with your body. I spent a whole summer trying to break my wrist, bending it back, testing it against the plywood headboard of my bed for pain. Why? Someone long-suffering in a book. Beth from *Little Women* with her sickbed lethargy and loveliness. I longed for it.

You once came shuffling into my room, smiling, blood streaming from your mouth. You had bitten clear through your tongue when you fell off a swing. 'I almost made it over the top,' you mumbled like a drunk. That was the same summer you got the pink pear-shaped scar on your chest. You and Richie had been burning bugs with your magnifying glass when you caught fire. He had to put you out with a hug.

There was one day in high school – it must have been a few months before the murder – when I came home to Richie's car parked in the driveway. When I walked around the side of the house I could hear your voices and smell the meat cooking. It was only April, too early, really, to be eating outside. But when I walked up beside the porch, there you were.

'C'mon, Maddie, pull up a chair.' Richie was smiling, brandishing a pair of tongs.

I sat down on the step. 'Hi.'

'How do you like it?' He flipped open the barbecue lid and peered inside.

You were wearing an apron, one of Mum's plasticized ones with a picture of Oxo cubes on the front. 'She likes hers practically still alive,' you said.

'Rare, eh? Some rare meat for a rare girl.'

Was this an insult? I didn't care. I took the steak.

Richie closed the lid, sat next to me and tapped out a smoke. 'How do you think you'll die?'

'From death,' you said, even though there was a possibility the question was directed at me.

'No, really.'

'Dunno. Cancer. Falling piano. You?' You lit his smoke for him.

'Not sure, but I sure hope I lose my marbles first.'

We all laughed at that because it sounded like something our mums might say.

The day Dad died, Richie's mum came to the door with a bundle of chrysanthemums and a supermarket strudel. Richie had been in jail for two years at that point; Mrs. Henley had the cheerless stamina of a prisoner's mother. This was when we were still allowed to coast around inside our shock, buffeted by its outsides, glad to be sad. Dad was gone, but we were the most *there* we had ever been, weren't we? Loving each other purely, distractedly, all aglow, like a family of defeated angels. I was in a state. Still, I noticed when you cleared a space on the mantel for the sympathy card she brought.

There was a phone call deep in the night of the murder. It rang one, two, three, almost four times. Then it stopped. Later, Dad said that was around the time you went off the rails. There are times I want to believe you picked it up, then spoke, low and comforting, into the receiver, but mostly I hope whoever it was gave up and left you to your own depths and devices.

It is possible I made up the late-night phone call. Writing is supposed to be the ultimate act of empathy, but it's not. It's forgery; the ultimate act of a mooch.

One summer we rented a cottage in Bracebridge, and you invited Richie up for the weekend. I was eleven and beginning to chub out in the places that would eventually become curves. I wasn't sure how to dress, or what stance I should adopt while discussing things. There were certain phrases I felt certain I should commit to memory. *Smooth move, ex-lax. Yeah, you and what army?* Even, *Why don't you go fuck yourself?* I noted all of these diligently, then was silent and dry-mouthed when it came time for the comeback. I was mortified with my entire self. I lay on the floating dock and waited for my skin to be brown but not blemished, my hair to be blond but not brassy, my brain to be bold, never bossy. You and Richie practised ass crackers off the side, and once, when you thought I was asleep, aqua-shat next to the reeds near the shore. It's a floater, I heard you say. Don't let it follow you, man, from Richie.

Sunday morning we all three went out, breaststroking sloppily to the raft.

'What's with the pudge, Maddie?' you said when I stopped to recline and bob around on my back.

'Yeah. Pudgeville, Arizona,' said Richie, and splashed me.

'Nothing,' I said, when I should have said nothing.

'Nothing,' you said.

'Nothing,' Richie said.

'Nothing,' you said again.

'Nothing like a little pork on your fork,' said Richie.

'Put pork on your fork,' you sang.

'In Ontario!' Richie continued. 'Put pork on your fork!'

We reached the raft and hauled ourselves up onto the dry warm boards. I lay down on my stomach and was silent, watching you both. You took two heavy-footed strides, then straddled the air before the splash. Richie paused, shook his head to free the clumps of wet hair at the back of his neck, then smoothed the clumps back down behind his ears. That's when I noticed. He was still wearing his watch. I took a second to rehearse, then realized there was no time. I wanted more than anything to be helpful.

'Hey,' I hollered, as he was preparing to jump. 'Hey, you're still wearing your watch!'

Richie ran his eyes up and down my body as if he were frisking me, then averted them dismissively. I understood then that I would never catch up; I could never measure up to you, to what you and he had. It was a realization that started in my gut, then spread over my body like a rash. I could feel every inch of my skin flushing, beginning to itch.

Richie lifted his wrist in the air before speaking. 'The watch is waterproof.' There was scorn, and something else in his demeanour. Pity? He made a splash that put yours to shame and you swam off together to a distant rock. At no time since have I felt the intense humiliation of those moments as I observed the watch glinting in the sunlight at the apex of Richie's every arcing stroke. After all this, what you felt for me, what you might feel for me now, is still only an amalgam, a layering of what I think I know, what I seem to remember, what I observed. What still knocks me out is that this huge incident – *murder*, for God's sake – seems to have gotten lost in the hazy scrabble of those years. Was it hidden from us? Partly, but we didn't ask. Richie was one of the killers, which was unfathomable. The dead guy was gay, and like I said, we didn't know any gay people then.

(One of the important rules when you're writing a story is to carefully choose your moment. You should have one -- and one only -- pivotal, astonishing instance from which the story hangs and balances. This moment should reverberate and resonate throughout the story; it should shine. Also, more than one death is not a good idea. It's more weight than the story can bear.

But the problem with deaths is that they line up like dominoes in the heart. Nudge at one, they all come clattering down.)

It's not exactly a full or bristling moment I would choose to write about. (A family of *defeated angels*? A bit OTT, my instructor will say. And she's right, she really is. But how do you transfer years of yearning onto the page; how do you shape your *family* into action, into story?) Okay, so the moment I choose is something more static, a slowing down after all the action. And it's not exactly from childhood either, but for some reason it reminds me of the corner of my Grade 3 pillow slip, where the sateen was worn from the hours I spent rubbing it against my cheek and between my fingers.

It was a night three days after Dad died, when old snapshots still lay like bits of discarded gift wrap on the living room floor, and we were clean from the inside with grief. I found you sitting like an Indian chief on the landing, stuck between upstairs and down, and when I asked you what you were doing you said, 'I can't decide.' So I sat with you until Mum woke up and found us.

'We can't decide,' I told her. You were wedged into the corner, and I was kneeling by the banister, so Mum took the bottom step and settled in with her cotton nightie pushed to one side over her knees.

'Go get the sleeping pills, Jeremy,' she said after a while. More than a few minutes of nothing together was more than any of us could bear.

You came back with the bottle wedged showily between your thumb and pointer finger and held it aloft, staring at Mum. 'We could take them all,' you said, and shook the bottle appraisingly.

I shifted my bum to the side and sat with one leg stretched out like a ballet dancer. I watched you and Mum watching each other.

'I would never do that,' Mum said. 'Never.' On the outside of you and Mum was me. I waited.

'Okay,' you said, 'but one extra.' You shook the pills out like candy, and we swallowed without water. The next day, after the funeral, you were gone.

# Bye Bye Flangle Nuts

'NOW, CLOSE YOUR EYES,' Rosa said. 'But close them as if they're open, or you're surprised, if you know what I mean. It's maximum important not to bunch the lids up.'

Jeremy leaned his head back and thought that even when his eyes were closed he had to pretend he was awake. And he didn't need to pretend, because he was. Always. Awake.

'That's good, but you're doing something totally fucked with your eyebrows now.' Rosa smoothed one of his brows with her index finger, leaned close, possibly to kiss him or identify an imperfection, then pulled away. He heard her rifling through her instruments, pictured the glorified tackle box teeming with tiny pots and slender brushes, her irked efficiency as she worked free an eye pencil or cheese-shaped sponge.

'Awake with your eyes closed,' Rosa said. 'We're going to make you gorgeous.'

He nodded.

'Stay still. Remind me to call Maddie about Mum later, will you?'

He nodded again.

'Stay still,' Rosa said.

Jeremy stayed still and thought about his sister, Maddie. He had been asleep when she called mid-afternoon – six months ago now – sleeping off the twelve beers and fearlessness of the night before. The phone rang at least eight times that he could count before Rosa picked it up. How fantastic it was to know that the racket was over with, what irreplaceable relief. He turned his head into the pillow, flipped himself over with effort and felt sleep squatting on the bridge of his nose.

'Jer,' Rosa called from the doorway. 'Jeremy, it's Maddie.'

'She can call back.' Dim-witted of Rosa not to know this.

'I don't think so.'

He hoisted himself onto one elbow and kicked some covers free. 'Bring it here,' he said. 'Just toss it over.'

But Rosa had walked it over, holding the receiver in her hand like a piece of fine china, choosing her path to the bed with uncharacteristic, mincing care. So he knew then, as he had known the night before, the premonition enveloping him like scent. His father dead. *I made it happen. But I took it back, I took it back.*

'What should I do?' he asked Maddie.

'Come home,' she said. 'Come home.'

'Open,' Rosa said, 'and look up.' She unscrewed the lid of a mini UFO-type disc, muttered to herself, then screwed it back on. 'Where's … ' She patted her pockets, went back to the tackle box and fished out a finger-shaped tube. 'Up,' she said.

It took discipline to stay like that, gaze fixed on the light fixture, fighting the distractions of country-style wallpaper, coffee maker and obsolete clipped coupons. It took concentration and a monk-like resolve. When you blinked, there was always the danger you would lose it all. Rosa smeared a thick, chilly liquid underneath his eyes, rubbed it into the soft, giving tissue there.

'Okay, close again.' She fingered his eyes shut. 'We just need to get you looking even. Too bad you didn't shave.' Her tone was strict but merciful.

Rosa had called the bus station. Only later had he realized – with a thrill shot through with regret – that he could have chartered a plane, a high-speed train, sweet Jesus, even a taxi. A rinky-dink two-seater, a paraglider, a yellow checker, a high-class French commuter mover. From Hamilton to Toronto? Was it possible to charter a plane? *Whatever.* When you are drunk or someone is dead, these options open up to you. To hell with the cost, you cry, I have somewhere to be! He pulled his suitcase from the back of the closet and began to toss socks inside. Seven pairs. Would he stay longer? 'Rosa,' he yelled. 'Where are all my socks?'

She had appeared beside him like a shape-shifting, dishevelled saint, pointing with good grace to the hamper. 'They're dirty,' she said, 'but we can find them.' Thirteen pairs in total. It seemed right. He lifted the lid of the suitcase and scanned the careful balls, curled into themselves like snails. Tube socks, dress socks, work socks. White, grey, brown, navy. Did he not own any black socks? Tears pricked at his eyes.

'You'll need something black,' said Rosa. 'For the funeral. A shirt and pants.'

*The funeral*, he thought. It soothed him. It was something to do, wasn't it? A goal. At the bus station, Rosa kissed him on the mouth and forehead, embraced him for too long. 'I'll see you in a couple of days,' she said.

He nodded. *Why not?* 'I'll see you in a couple of days,' he said.

The bus made a sound like a horse as it pulled into the station. Not a whinny, something more throaty, deep and full. A pissed-off horse noise. Oh, the steps up to the bus were tall! How ridiculous to have to lift your knees with such purpose simply to board. He found a seat at the back, near the bathroom, slid his case in the overhead compartment, folded his duffle bag in two like a sad sausage and forced it under the seat in front of him. He was on his way home for a funeral.

'No,' he had said to Maddie, meaning, *Just you try to say that again.*

'Yes,' she said. And, 'I don't know.' And, 'Maybe brain aneurysm.' She spoke these things as if she were not joking.

He knew of a man who had died of a brain aneurysm, alone, on a fishing boat. A friend of Rosa's father. According to Maddie, their own father's demise had been much more demure, pastoral even. He had been feeding the birds in the backyard, bundled and magnanimous, when it happened. Yet, Jeremy couldn't help it: in his version, it started with fish refusing to bite, a cloudless afternoon, six bottles, twist-off caps, a cooler in the bow, a tangled line and cursing. A lightning bolt came from the sky, only the sky was the inside of this guy's head. A curse and a carp and a bolt, sound struggling to match up with light. But he knew for his father it would have been different. What he meant was there had been a mistake.

'Okay, you'll just feel a pressure along your brows, and some tiny sort of flicky pains. I'm just, like, tweaking and defining.' Rosa uncapped two midget pencils, *shup*, *shup*, held them together, and then up to the light to check out their shades. 'Your eyebrows are quite fair and sparse, really, for a man.'

He liked her talking to him like this, like he was a science project or a show dog. He liked being told what to do. And he could tell she was pleased too, happy to have made it this far in the transformation business. 'I'll be a cosmetics agent,' she had confided when she first got up the guts to register.

'You mean, you'll sell twelve-dollar lip gloss and creams dressed up as dreams to lonely ladies-in-waiting.'

'Maybe. So what? Besides, people like having their faces touched. And what's with the rhyme, MC Expert-Head?' She nudged him with her knee, stroked his cheek unprofessionally.

He had not spent the night in the same bed with her for weeks, frightened as he was by his own unwitting trances and outbursts. He would start out beside her, limbs stiff like a soldier, eyes closed in a toy-box parody of sleep. But then the curtain would part and the show would begin: his father reaching quaintly for a handful of seed, weighing the grains in his hand appraisingly, then extending his palm wide, all hope. The birds would have begun to assemble like slivers of iron gather and pause before rushing towards a magnet. One might even have attempted descent, hovered uncertainly over his father's head, his shoulder. And then he would have felt it – what? An in-burst. A pain centred over his left eyebrow, zinging and pure. Was there, as they say, a fast-forward reel of triumphs and tragedies beginning with birth? Or one moment that floated, helium-filled, into his field of vision, occupied it fully, unapologetically, until he succumbed to the darkness? Or maybe none of this. Instead, a set of tracks in the snow – three-pronged, tiny and intent – and then nothing. Did he know that Jeremy loved him and hated him? That his son *knew* him, had predicted this very outcome? Did he cry out for succour or solitude? Or both?

The questions tailed Jeremy to the couch, lurked like poltergeists in the television. He was exhausted and wanted to sleep. But sleep itself frightened him. What would he see without the benefit of conscious borders and bylaws? It was important to stay in control. Nevertheless, he tried them – potions and mantras, hot baths, massage and tranquilizing drugs that sent him hurtling down a steep surface, clambering for purchase. He let Rosa straddle him, with her thin middle and lovely side-winding breasts, and he rummaged around there, emerging a man momentarily, thankfully lost to himself. He would surrender for a few ragged hours and wake with a start, raging against his own body, so easily, utterly duped, so vulnerable to its own reckless rhythms.

He had not told anyone, not even Rosa. How to say it? *Rosa, you know how my dad died and everything? And you know that show Carol watches with the smarmy, bad-pleated-pants dude who talks to the recently croaked? Well, I'm like that too.* But that wasn't exactly true – it wasn't that he had predicted his father's death. More that the possibility had overwhelmed him – and he had let it. Rosa had a pack of tarot cards she and her friend Carol stroked and fanned, laid out in crucifix patterns on the table like kids in cahoots. 'Oooh,' he once heard Carol crooning, 'the High Priestess. That's totally about opening to what could be and acknowledging the Shadow. And Death – not really death, y'know, more like taking care of unfinished business and no point avoiding the inexecration of the future.'

'I can't believe you're into that crap,' he told Rosa later as they stood spitting toothpaste down the drain. 'There is a thing called science, you know, and if you're not into educational TV shows, there's this concept called common sense.' He took her toothbrush and ran it under the water, then flicked the bristles appraisingly. Hygiene was not always Rosa's main thing. She sat to pee, then fluttered her eyelashes winningly. 'It's just a different way of looking at the world, at your life, getting different angles and perspectives and, like, finding your bliss.'

Your *bliss*? It made his brain hot and dry to hear this.

Out the window of the bus an angry line of cars idled, the drivers shellacked and safe, singing along to someone else's heartache. The bus inched along, and Jeremy thought of the anxiety he should be feeling, drew the shape of it in his head: something many-cornered and impossible to slot into place. An octagon: plasticky yellow edges. Or a pentagon: large white building for warriors and decision-makers. Or maybe not corners, but lack of corners. Something oversized and dense – like one of Rosa's sponges. Sponges. They lived like squatters at the bottom of the sea. Barely lived. Squatting and feeding; soft, unlikely things. We harvest them, he thought. How odd.

Some honking had begun; there was a holdup. An eighteen-wheeler was cornering badly, redressing errors with minute adjustments of its wheels. Outside the bus, doors slammed, cellphones were proffered to waiting ears and unripe advice was hurled at the trucker, who kept on with his conscientious cornering, trapped in his mission. Inside the bus the passengers had succumbed to a solemn intoxication. Across from Jeremy a woman was dabbing her finger to her tongue in her quest to turn the slippery page of a magazine. The truck finally freed itself, the whole lot of it bulking into the intersection, then rumbling off to its destination. But no one outside seemed happy with this; they shook their heads and wearily flipped each other the bird. A tall man wearing a khaki hunting vest over his three-piece suit shook his fist like a thwarted revolutionary in the direction of the retreating truck, then folded himself angrily and efficiently into his eggplant-coloured SUV.

On a nearby building, artists had been at work. An eagle soared in a pink and blue sky, a thick peach-skinned boy with jowls and vacant baby eyes leapt from his airborne skateboard. Mushrooms sprouted in technicolour beneath him. Green bubble letters outlined in purple floated in the wall's foreground. *Bye Bye Flangle Nuts*, the puffy message read. Jeremy lifted his hand to wave.

'Don't move, squirm bucket. You think this job is easy?' Rosa smoothed Jeremy's hair behind his right ear. This was not part of the process, he knew. This was how humans sometimes made it through. 'You've got good cheekbones, though, glamorous for a guy.' How much flak would he get from the guys at the steel mill – a whole eighteen-wheeler full, stacked to the gills – if they could see. How little, how meanly, he cared.

The night he *knew*, he'd had a final pint by himself after his buddy Al left. *A Miller as per uszh.* It went down easy, helped him wind his scarf around his neck, zip his coat to the top, roll the rim of his toque down over his ears. He stamped his feet with certainty inside and outside the bar. It was a winter thing. It was possible it helped, or at least provided a comforting physical script. 'Fucking February,' he said to a snowbank as if naming, furiously, a poem. It was cold. The sidewalks, painstakingly cleared, had slicked over with a hard hybrid of ice and snow. But where his sober self might have integrated this, shortened his stride, his drunken self, an oblivious monarch, noted it only in passing. The air around him warmed infinitesimally and large flakes began to fall, with nasty purpose, from the top of the night. He felt fine. Not warm, but fuelled and rhythmic, his mind narrowed to a gleaming metal tube. One foot, then the other, hands fisted in pockets. My father will die, he thought. It was not a pleasing thought but it did little to interrupt. In fact, it floated right up into the forest of snow. And then he was sad, as if sad for a far-off country's strife and pettiness, its people's lack of true solace.

'Stop making that face – all bunchy and shit. Like a bulldog swallowing a wasp.' Rosa was Italian but never flaunted it, instead plucking expressions jauntily from the air as they went flying past her. She knuckled Jeremy's chin gently. He tried to relax while she used her thumbs to knead magic into his cheeks. 'Translucent,' she was saying. 'This new product. Everything is so much less 2-D now, y'know. They use reflections and molecules and the true inner glow of your skin. Of your self, I guess.'

Don't you dare say *soul*, Jeremy thought. Don't make it about soul. What he understood now, what he had perhaps always understood, was that life was about instinct.

His friend's mother, Mrs. Henley, had met him at the bus station, tapped him on the back, sniffed six times in rapid succession. 'Your mother and sister,' she said. He allowed himself to lean into her, but only slightly. Jeremy had been close to her son, Richie, when they were teenagers, but had not spoken to Richie for years. It was how he liked it.

'Yes,' said Jeremy. He knew she was thinking of her own stark, scooped-out existence. 'Yes,' he said again.

'He loved you.'

This was less comfort than statement of fact. There were fathers who loved – no matter how falteringly – and those who could not. Richie's stepfather could not. All through high school, there were marks on their bodies, mother and son, that corroborated this truth. When he was seventeen, Richie had beat the crap out of a guy, killed him with a baseball bat and his own willing fists and feet. He was in jail. (Still, after so many years, it sounded tabloid cowboy, untenable.) Richie's father took off with the shooter girl from the local bar and only came back once, to retrieve his key-chain collection.

Mrs. Henley was a good driver, which surprised Jeremy. Whatever quaver he observed in her personality was missing from her firm turns and casually assertive shifting of lanes. He sat back in his seat and did not speak.

Maddie was at the door before he had a chance to knock, her hug man-like, even her chest, with its new woman's breasts, unforgiving.

'I've been phoning,' she said, and held up her finger like ET. 'People need to know.'

'Okay,' he said. 'Where's Mum?'

His mum was in the back room. He sat next to her on the couch and she patted his knee. When Maddie came in and saw them just sitting there she looked perplexed, then purposeful. She took her place on Mum's other side and the three of them stayed like that, as if posing for a portrait at Sears, the background liable to slip up and scroll away without warning.

Later, people made them eat, and they found they were hungry, and later still, that they were sleepy. But so lonely! So fundamentally unable to see their way clear to the morning. Jeremy's bedroom had been remade: a sewing room full of spools and swatches, his KISS poster rolled tightly, red rubber bands circling either end. Maddie knocked on his door. 'We shouldn't leave Mum alone,' she said.

And Jeremy knew what she meant: she might die too.

They walked together to their parents' bedroom, pushed open the door without knocking and stood breathless, watching their mother. The three of them slept together, that night and the next four, gathering like tribe members, tugging the covers politely, judiciously, to the edges, and making sure, at all times, that they were touching.

*This* was instinct: it was puppies or baby snakes even, skin to skin, next to a rock, in a cave, the corner of a barn, hidden and cosseted against the rawness of the world. How long could they have stayed like that – dreamless, drugged by closeness?

But one morning they woke up and counted each other's white hairs, and their mother was angry. 'You're too young,' she said to Maddie. She pulled tweezers from the bedside drawer and began to pluck roughly at her daughter's temples, holding the silver pincers up to the light with each success. Maddie's eyes reddened with every yank, but she did not cry.

'Get out, both of you,' Mum said. 'Sleep in your own beds.'

'I'm finished with the base now. It's like being a painter, only you start in the negative. You have to create a clean canvas before you can start.' Rosa had stopped touching him, but he did not open his eyes. He preferred the puzzle of not-seeing, envisioning her bustle as she tidied one set of tools, dragged out another. So resolute now. But it hadn't always been this way. There had been times, deep in the winter months, January mostly, when she'd been all raw eyes and odd rashes, lumpen under the covers on the couch. 'I just can't,' she'd say, like every word was its own heavy sentence. 'Why can't you,' he said. She had taken his face in her hands. 'It's not that I want to sleep like this, like a stone, or like I'm stoned, or even that I want to die. It's that I don't *not* want to either. It's like a laziness that's been ramped up and made muddy by all the things that can't be fixed in the world.' He nodded, held her warm hand for a limp moment and went out drinking.

Jeremy loved the funeral, and not because it was like a party or a solemn ritual, although it tried to be both of these. Everyone kept saying how important it was to celebrate his father, to remember him when he was alive, as if they could recall him any other way. The service was in a church – United – which was not so much Jesus, really, as school lunchroom, that same institutional feeling, safe and staid, with adult secrets and stale smells around the periphery. There was a minister but it was a woman. No, not a party or a service, but a distraction, almost a holiday, with a whole circus of people and an itinerary. Rosa was there with Carol, but they hung back like bridesmaids, ceded the spotlight. And friends he had not seen in years came forward one at a time, shook his hand and sought out his eyes with their own, nodding in a kind of awe or acknowledgement. He could not remember the speeches – every single one like a momentarily hypnotizing, forgettable song. His father's coffin, closed and sleek, shone like the mahogany inside a yacht, and Jeremy was only really jolted awake when one of the speech givers – Mike Elton, a retired cop – rapped on it on the way back to his pew. It made Jeremy so proud, that knock. It was a closed-mouthed, puffy-chested sign of respect, and he felt it deep in his breast, could still call up the tone and timbre, the one, pause, two, three, pause rhythm of it. Afterwards, back at the house, he parked himself in a corner and tried for inscrutability. Rosa had left – a practical at the Sally Caponi Institute that would determine her mark for the semester. He was glad to see her off. Someone had to have appointments to keep. He had booked two weeks off work and still had six empty squares on the calendar to wander through. He was not afraid of time and space. It was his version of Rosa's muddy not-caring that terrified him.

It was then that Mrs. Henley had sought him out, found her place by his side.

'A lot of people,' she said.

'How's Richie?' he replied.

She took his hand. 'You know, he told me once about the mushrooms. How you knew them all by Latin name, would point them out like some professor when you two went riding in the ravine. There was one, he said, called the ear mushroom. He always liked that one.'

Jeremy smiled at her. *Auricularia auricula. Or, not so operatically: tree ear. In less language-conscious, perhaps more clannish times: Jew's ear. Smooth, fleshy to the touch. As unlikely as ears themselves, whorls of skin and soft cartilage stuck arbitrarily on the sides of heads.*

*The mushrooms had a shellacked newborn look, more purely ear-like than their namesakes.*

He had done a speech in Grade 4 about mushrooms, mycology. How many hours had he spent examining – memorizing! – the striations, shapes, smells and unexpected qualities of chanterelle, agaricus, cremini? How he had fallen into it! As never before and never since, roaming backyards and dim places in parks, plucking his specimens easily from the soft rotten places they sprouted. With the aid of his mother, who helped him see words whole, line up sentences so they meant something, he gathered enough material – genealogy, geography, curative properties and cuisine – to speak for a good forty-five minutes, and was forced to cut it down to twelve. It almost made him cry – the lore and science that fell away as he trimmed and tucked, practiced speed-speaking to squeeze in an extra sentence or three. But when he was finished, a shroomy essence remained. He rehearsed it for his mum and dad, knowing it was inadequate, but reasoning that the passion he felt for his subject would come through in his celebratory enunciation, his unintimidating, helpful physical stance.

When he finished, he looked at his parents not for approval or admiration but with a confidence he had never felt before, a knowledge of having made himself bigger without having to posture or puff up physically. It was power he felt, and it warmed him. His mother had been staring fixedly at him the entire time he spoke, and now she tried out a word he had used, *mycelium*, but without sound. Then, with the same relative soundlessness, she brought her hands together in a heartfelt, if meek, fluttering of applause.

'You're a champion mushroom expert,' she said.

'Mycology,' he half-whispered. 'Mycologist.'

'And what a speaker!'

'Mushrooms,' said his father. 'I never would have guessed it.' He pronounced this not to Jeremy but as if to another, avuncular self looking on. Then he closed his eyes reflectively. When he opened them, they were glassy with unshed tears. 'I'm proud of you, son,' he said.

So it was no wonder, really, when Jeremy was advanced to the school speech finals, chosen as one of ten to hold forth for an auditorium full of ladies and germs, ha-ha, fellow students, distinguished teachers, ha-ha, and honoured judges. It was just the universe, which Jeremy was sure now lived comfortably inside him, making its grand design known. It was fate. No, not fate: biology. He had a strategy for the day. He would focus not on the people themselves, or even the back wall of the room, covered as it was with yellow felt banners proclaiming victory, but instead on the spores he imagined emanating from each audience member, their chairs rich in compost, disdainful of chlorophyll. He would speak to their mushroom selves. This worked. The opening – *What living creature, neither plant nor animal, grows without roots, seed or leaves, always wears a cap and has never been afraid of the dark?* – slid out easily. He didn't even have to count out the pauses, they just breathed themselves into being. And the first third worked too; he was nervous but combatted this with a charming overemphasis of the facts. *Thirty-eight thousand varieties! Of course not all of them edible!* It was halfway through the second third that he faltered. He was talking about shiitakes (having avoided the obvious pitfall in pronunciation here), and had loosened up considerably. He was even using hand movements to mime the harvest, or to imitate, in a facile manner, the various ways in which spawn could spread and shift and float in the forest. And the spore people were enthralled; they were listening as one.

Then he noticed his father. He had locked on to his son with a resolve Jeremy had not seen on any other occasion, no matter the ceremony or circumstance attached to it. It was not – no, *never*! – that his father *wanted* him to fail. In fact, Jeremy saw in that instant that his father thought this impossible, could in fact envision the multitude of mulchy paths his son would tread, eyes trained to seek out the inflated parasols – with their delicate spokes and crenellations –

that represented his very livelihood, his life. At nighttime, Jeremy's step would be less sure, but no less focused. He'd carry a torch to stab, épée-like, through the dark and illuminate the crooks of living things – knobby trees, right-angled deer, the raven's wing. And there, in the places these creatures had fled or rooted, would be the prize. A whole clan of *amanita muscaria*, their red caps gleaming, or *albatrellus ovinus*, practically weeping, definitely perspiring, in anticipation of his arrival. Back in his office – an oak desk, wheelie chair and two filing cabinets in the corner of his lab – the phone would be vibrating insistently in its cradle. He was an expert; people were always wanting to talk to him.

All of this passed between Jeremy and his father in less time than it takes to identify a morel.

Jeremy blinked and continued talking, but he could not stop looking at his father, who was now channelling a crystalline stream of loving envy. *My father knows I'm good and he wishes he were me.* This thought slid under the words Jeremy was speaking like a mechanic glides himself, smoothly, wheeled and jumpsuited, under a car. It would be melodramatic to say the thought broke Jeremy's heart, but it severed something irrevocably in him; it crippled him. He finished his speech, but without conviction. A girl who had researched the origins of the wristwatch came first, the runner-up a boy with a talk-show shrug and a T-shirt emblazoned with *Here Comes Trouble* in purple sparkle paint. Jeremy went home to his bedroom, flushed his harvest, a few at a time, down the toilet and stacked his books on the landing at the bottom of the stairs. In the morning he returned them to the public library on the way to school. They slid easily through the drop slot, but landed in broken stages on the other side. He did not become a mycologist.

'You should visit Richie,' said Mrs. Henley, without commitment. 'I brought some strudel.' She pulled it from her bag. The dome of the plastic lid was dented. 'I'll put it away.'

Jeremy bit his lip and inclined forward in assent. Who could chart the course of a life? Not Mrs. Henley, with her strudel and steadfast sorrow. Not even Rosa, with all her miraculous, face-saving tools.

His father was gone and so was Richie, and now Mrs. Henley, off to open cupboards and find space for provisions. *I should go home. Home to Rosa.*

'All right, champ, this requires some poise on your part. What that means is if you move I'm fucked. Got it?' He nodded. 'No moving!'

'Okay,' he said. 'Okay.'

'I'm using the liquid eyeliner for a cleaner line. We wanna open things up a bit, almost make you look a bit shocked at the state of things ... '

She wasn't talking to him, but he made a sound like he bought what she was selling. She pulled the skin of his left upper lid out towards his temple with the pad of her middle finger. 'Raise your eyebrows up.'

He complied, and felt a wet, delicate coolness trailing across his skin like a miniature slug. Her hand was so steady!

'Okay, open. Let's do the other one.'

She was pleased with him, he could tell by the plumminess in her voice. He was unaccustomed to this – pleasing people – and if anyone had thought to ask, he might say it was why he loved Rosa. She dabbed an old-fashioned shaving brush into a pearlized palette in her palm. 'Head back, and suck in your cheeks, but just a bit. Like you took a shot of tequila and it hasn't hit you yet.' He smiled. 'Don't smile,' she said. 'Close.' The brush came skimming over his face, across the chin, up the cheekbones, left, right, quickly down the ramp of the nose. He would have rolled over, exposed the soft part of himself where all the vital organs lived, if Rosa asked.

'Head up again.' Rosa tapped his forehead. 'So I was thinking maybe I could do a reading for you, eh? Try to get to the bottom of all of this no-shut-eye business.'

Jeremy took a breath, held it in his lungs, then exhaled. Fucking tarot cards. He knew why he couldn't sleep. It was the same reason the mushroom speech had failed. What keeps a person from greatness and a good night's sleep? His own porous self, batting possibilities back and forth, delving too deep into other people's private motives and cloistered pasts.

'We're almost done here, honey.' Rosa was swiping muted tones of shadow across his eyelids. The coloured chunks were set into a tray like a paint set; shiny shards glinted up from their surfaces. 'What we want is an everyday look that can be tweaked for evening, made glamorous with a few strokes here and there.'

How could he tell her – so optimistic and persistent with her tools – that he couldn't sleep because he kept *feeling* it: his father's node of jealousy and sharp, explosive end. He kept feeling it and he did not want to dream it. And how could he tell her that he was *relieved*, and this was why – like a helpless animal, all-seeing and dumb – he had divined his own father's death. He could not, not now, with her fingers on his face, the dispassion and drive in her every calculated move. It was making him sleepy.

On the bus ride home to Hamilton he had closed his eyes, and it was possible he slept, although what he recalled now was less like dream than reality in meltdown. Was it memory? He could not say. The day before Richie killed a man, he and Jeremy met in the park near the river and pulled out a six-pack they had crammed into the opening of a hollow log two days earlier. Before he left the house, Jeremy's father had called him down to his workshop in the basement. 'Son,' he said. Jeremy snorted. The two men shared a stocky certainty of the body, and as his father bent forward over his workhorse, Jeremy could see, for a second, his own forearm straining into the future. 'You know I've always wanted the best for you, but I don't know how … ' His father paused, a sob gathering in his throat. 'You and this boy Richie. We seem to have lost. I don't know.' Jeremy nodded, wanting badly to spit, to hork a big ol' loogie direct into the old man's cauldron of trailing dreams.

'Stay in tonight. Maybe we could.' Jeremy shook his head. 'Can't,' he said. 'I have to go out.'

Jeremy sat on the log while Richie opened two beers with his belt buckle. 'Fuck,' Jeremy said. 'My dad.' The fingers of Richie's right hand retracted like a sea anemone; Jeremy could see a muscle in his friend's tricep where there had been only blank skin. It was a warning: *There can be no comparison.* They drank and listened to the water webbing its way around rocks. Then Richie wound one arm around Jeremy, and with the other pulled a dainty plastic pouch from his jean-jacket pocket. Five flattened dried mushrooms jostled like family in the pouch. Richie upended the bag and shook the mushrooms free. 'Magic,' he said. They spent the afternoon and evening in the dirt around that log, crouched and curled close to the earth, to each other. There were whole legend-spewing, weapon-forging civilizations in the cracks between stones, a spa for Yorkville ladies in fox furs had launched inside a pop bottle, the way the sky bent and rippled meant good fortune, the smell of car exhaust was a constellation, and their very cat faces sprouted silvery-fine whiskers for extra-sensing and formal occasions. They talked about how to live when nobody understood. They fell asleep next to the log.

When he woke up, he was nearly home. Outside the bus, the landscape repeated itself. Still the flesh-toned, jowly skateboarder jumped. Still, the sky was ripened peach, the letters inflated, autonomous and wise. *Bye Bye Flangle Nuts.* Where did they all go – the living and the dead – when their eyes were closed?

Jeremy felt the soft tickle of a brush across his cheekbones, over his nose. On the inside of his lids he began to discern short squat somethings amongst the trees of multicoloured lights. Mushrooms. He let them make themselves known, noted them and released them to their own private fevers.

The mushrooms were slowing their pace; there were golden strands linking them. The farther they travelled from each other, the thinner and more resilient, the more gleaming and near-invisible the strands became. God, they were beautiful.

'*Amore?*'

Jeremy opened his eyes.

'Oh, wow,' Rosa said. 'I thought you were a goner. Finito, bandito.' She was shaken and hiding it.

'Nope,' he said, in a tone meant to show he had tricked not her but himself. 'I've just been sleeping.'

# Dingbat

DAD DIED IN FEBRUARY of my seventeenth year, in the backyard, while feeding the birds. Mum found him flat on his back, looking for all the world as if he were napping on the soft pile of snow he had just cleared from the space beside the feeder. When I got home from school, the ambulance had not yet arrived. Mum would not let me in the front door.

'Go back to school,' she said, her face white as bone.

When I kneeled beside my father, I was cheered by the fact that his eyes were closed. Dead people stared blankly into some unfathomable beyond. I laid my hand against his face. The skin was not warm, but it had a tender elasticity to it. I pulled his toque down over his forehead. There was a tiny curlicue of wax sitting like a hardened spot of Dijon mustard inside his ear. He was not dead.

'Dad?' I said, and leaned down close, so that he could hear.

A paramedic shoved me to the side.

Mum and I sat on the steps of the back porch and watched the uniformed men work. And it was work. They pushed and prodded at him, blew into his lungs, shocked his heart. We could see our breaths in the air, but sweat soaked their baby-blue shirts into navy. They did all that they could do. Still, they could have done more.

We got to touch Dad one more time before they took him away. Then we sat back down on the steps. A blue jay landed on the stoop outside the shed, hopped over to the garden and pecked hopefully at the snow. From the street, the slow roar and clank of the snowplow. And, at the corner of my lip, if I stretched with my tongue, the taste of blood from the same cold sore I had had since Christmas.

'Go call your brother,' said Mum.

I nodded, started towards the door, then stopped. 'What should I tell him?'

We stared at each other, dumbfounded.

'Tell him to come home.'

That winter and through the spring and summer, Mum made soups from a gourmet cookbook someone had given her for her wedding anniversary three years earlier. She did not seem sad to me. She did not seem happy either. She did not seem to be anything at all. For six months we ate gourmet soups at every meal and received bills that still showed my father's name through the little plastic window at the front. The sympathy cards, which had arrived in an extravagant volley in the first two months, came less often by months five and six. I opened the envelopes cavalierly, with my index finger, and peered in without pulling the cards from their envelopes. In the midst of these came several official letters addressed to me.

I refused all three of the universities' offers. I told Mum it was because I was going to be a writer or a painter, or, quite possibly, a sculptor.

'You never liked art,' she said.

'I know,' I said, 'but it's never too late to try something new.'

'Yes it is,' she said, 'oh, yes it is. You should be a scientist.'

'Mmm,' I said.

Really, I wanted to be an artist because I believed artists lived alone in apartments with silky Indian-print scarves draped over everything, had a series of fascinating lovers and were never lonely because they had their passion to sustain them. It was not entirely clear to me how they reached this particular state of grace, but I understood that it was probably important for me to track my experience in some way. I started keeping a notebook to pin down my thoughts. *Grief makes you stupid*, I jotted furiously; nothing seemed more perfectly true to me. *I have been made wise and raw by death*, I wrote in caps across an entire page, seized by a burning focus that began in my sinuses. *Death is timeless. When someone dies, we are made tense by the idea of tenses.* I penned aphorism after contradictory aphorism. In the margins, I drew sunbursts, triptychs of tiny balloons with sudden leaks, and labelled them *brain aneurysm*, then hid my notebook at the back of my closet in a ratty pillowcase with pink shamrocks stitched around the edge. I lay on my bed and thought about my mother, how I could never leave her, and how it was absolutely imperative that I leave her. And I thought about sex – how great art is so often culled from lusty encounters.

'I think I'm going to start having sex,' I told my mother, who was stirring a carrot-curry soup on the stove.

'Maybe we should get a dog,' she said, without looking up.

'I think I'm going to start having sex,' I said again, adopting her pseudo-questioning manner. I scratched my cheek casually and watched her add what looked like paprika to the pot. I cleared my throat.

'Just don't get pregnant, dingbat,' came the response, and I realized that, more than shock, I had expected my pronouncement to evoke something like pride from her.

I had sex for the first time in a tent with a friend of a friend named Ben, his beered-up buddy asleep beside us. We were camping next to sand dunes, the kind that emerged from the water like mesas, plateaus for the sun-hungry in the middle of Lake Erie. Sex for the first time felt like it was happening in the basement of a toadstool because of the musty smell and the grey-green light seeping through the tent flap. My mouth tasted of flat Molson Canadian from a king can and I remember noticing, although not with any sense of indignation, or even irony, the tiny towel that Ben had placed fussily under my hips. I remember that I wished, then unwished, that the condom would break, that I would get pregnant and full. Because that would be fair – if whatever tripping, caustic god that lived up there amongst the faraway stars could give me another life to replace my father, a smaller version, cherubic and demanding. Was I thrilled? Not exactly, although there was something prickly about the whole thing, something gently dangerous. Afterwards Ben took me by the hand and walked me along the beach as if I were a toddler, which made it difficult for me to feel in any way initiated.

I remember the stones underfoot more than the stars above, which seemed to me ugly and unnatural, as if someone had tossed ice-melting salt against an asphalt sky. Ben's hand in mine was dry and callused, his grip strong. He worked most weekends dry-walling, and I tried to feel grateful that he had sacrificed two shifts for me.

Ben had his Neil Young tape for the way home so we didn't have to talk. We could roll down the windows of his pickup and count cows. We could sing.

When I got home, Mum stretched the phone cord across the kitchen and waved the mouthpiece at me.

'Your brother's on the line,' she said.

'Tell him I'm in Paris.'

'Don't be a dingbat. Take the phone.'

And I did, although I loathed Jeremy intermittently and without conviction. Loathed him for having found a life of his own, even if he did work in a steel mill with a girlfriend named Rosa whose puffy, sneering lips and thin plastic belts around her thin waist made for a curious appeal.

'How's Mum?' Jeremy said.

'Good,' I said. 'I mean ... fine.'

'You should make sure she gets out.'

'Of the house?' I said.

'Just *out*, Maddie. Just take care of her, okay? I gotta go.'

He hung up.

As a child I had often wished for sisters. In Grade 4 I had a friend Denise who had three of them. They called each other *Sewer*, like the French word for the relation. Denise was precocious.

'A bit too precocious for her own good,' said Mum, semi-admiringly.

In October of that year, Denise discovered a new word. She'd leap from her desk at least three times a day and position her hands firmly on the handles of her hips. 'That's redundant!' was the rallying cry.

We took to using it as a taunt in the schoolyard. It had the same satisfactory rising and falling action as *retard*, and the middle was nicely reminiscent of *dunce*. It was even useful as a skipping chant, the three syllables matching the *clip-clap-clip* of the rope hitting the pavement. *Re . . . Re . . . Re-dun-dant.* It was how I felt talking to Jeremy. It was how I felt about my life.

In late July Mum and I drove an hour and a half to the Canine Castle to buy a dog. I had been driving for only a year, and it showed. Mum held tight to the holy-shit handle the entire way, but didn't comment when I flicked on the windshield wipers instead of the turn signal, then swerved awkwardly to change lanes. The woman who sold us our puppy was petite except for her bulgy forearms and jutting chin. She checked the dog's mouth and behind, tapped its nose, then gave us a pink photocopied list of required shots and how-tos.

'If you have any trouble,' she said, and snorted delicately, 'call this number.'

We were shocked into submission. The puppy was so small. He lay in my arms and murmured. On the way home, I sat in the passenger seat with the dog while Mum drove efficiently, her hands at ten and two o'clock on the steering wheel.

We spent a lot of time sitting on the couch, watching the dog. When the dog was asleep, Mum would read the newspaper and I would read poems by contemporary Canadian poets. Sometimes it was difficult for me to contain my enthusiasm.

'Listen to this, Mum.'

'Okay.'

'It's Anne Michaels.' I cleared my throat. '"The dead leave us starving with mouths full of love."' I put the book down. I looked at her for confirmation. She stared back, unblinking. She seemed to expect more from me. Always, she seemed to expect more from me. I flipped the book open again. 'Which we then lavish on the dog,' I recited.

'It doesn't say that,' Mum said.

'No, it doesn't say that.'

'I didn't think so.' But she was smiling.

When we weren't on the couch, we were walking the dog in the brash light of late summer. The park was beautiful and quiet, an oasis of trickling creeks and carefully treed banks, with a woodchip path that shifted and crackled like granola under our feet. The dog strained at his leash. He loved the park, with its tufts of spiky, smelly grass, its long-necked Canada geese and its catalogue of sticks that had been scattered willy-nilly by the wind across the soft ground. We watched him lift his leg to pee, again and again, against signposts and benches, tree stumps and whole tree trunks, rocks, bushes and piles of crumpled pop cans and newspapers. Once we were far enough from the road and its roaring cars with their ominous metallic undersides and hungry tires, we took him off his leash.

'I think you should go to university,' Mum said, one particularly humid afternoon. 'It's not too late to go in the new year, is it?'

'No, but … ' I pitched a stick, and we both watched the dog scamper and grab, then leap and scramble.

Mum pulled her T-shirt from her stomach and shook it rapidly to create some air flow. She turned towards me.

'I'm not sure it's the right path for me.' I tried to look thoughtful, but I could not think. I could not even think of how to appear thoughtful.

The dog was panting and cavorting in circles around us. Mum bent down and rubbed his trusting, rumpled head. I watched her.

She looked up at me. 'I suppose you think,' she said quietly. 'I suppose you think that I'm going to become one of those women who chases hooligans with my cane, because that's what the old and bereft do, am I right? And that creature will be yapping at my heels.' She pointed to the dog and raised her voice. 'And I'll call it names like Pookie and pick up its shit with a small plastic baggie. And I'll call you at inopportune times with bits of inconsequential news and smatterings of guilt, am I right? Well, am I right?' She began shaking her T-shirt again.

I was too brittle with my own self to answer. I held her hand, took the leash from it and turned to go home.

Dad always liked to tell the story of Mum sleep-singing in a high clear voice one hot night.

'Well, I was just lying there on one of those infernal nights in August when something woke me. A voice. At first, I was certain it was one of you kids in trouble, or just fooling around – a tummy ache, or a battle over the blankets, some such thing. So I sat up and looked around, saw the two of you lying in sweet bundles on the floor, noticed the moon out the window looking like it was about to swoop down at me, and that's when I realized. It was an adult voice I was hearing. And it was singing.'

At this point he would pause to allow the scene – the predatory moon, the mysterious voice, the guiltless children asleep on the floor – to sink in. Often he would dab at the corner of his mouth with a serviette before continuing.

'In any case, once I'd shaken off my dreams and my incredulity, I realized it was your mother doing the singing.' Then Dad would glare at me and Jeremy as if we alone were responsible for bringing Mum into his life. And he would not go on until we asked.

'*What?* What was it she was singing, Dad?'

We couldn't help it. We would plead with him – as kids because we couldn't bear not to hear it, and as teenagers because we knew what was expected of us, and because, although we rolled our eyes, we still couldn't bear not to hear it. There was always a moment before the singing began that was less of a pause than a space; it was a smooth, timeless space that the story had carved out, and we were living in it. Then would come the careful falsetto:

> *Christmas is coming, the goose is getting fat,*
> *Please put a penny in the old man's hat.*
> *If you haven't got a penny, a ha'penny will do.*
> *If you haven't got a ha'penny, then God … bless … you!*

My mother, who was the crux and star of the story, never spoke or sang during the telling, although her smile throughout had something of the smug about it. And sometimes, towards the end, she would let out a brief, girlish laugh. Because she knew, as we all did, that it was not like her to be the showman, to solo so brazenly, even if it was under cover of the night.

On Thursday afternoons, Jeremy's friend Richie's mum came to visit. Mum made tea and served chocolate digestives. Mrs. Henley was sad and capable. She always did our dishes and insisted on running the vacuum across the rug in the front hall. 'It's the least … ' she would say. 'He was such a good man,' she told my mother. Then one day we forgot she was coming; we took the dog out to the country for a run and sniff. When we came home there was a note scotch-taped to the front door. Mum read it quickly, folded it, then put it in her pocket. 'That woman is depressing,' she said. 'Kind, but depressing.'

One morning in September, I came downstairs to find Mum sitting in the corner of the couch in her housecoat, the dog draped across her lap like a discarded stole, her face wet with tears.

'Your father came to the door,' she said absently when she noticed me. 'The knocking woke me up. He forgot his keys. He was laughing and carrying on on the porch, slapping his forehead like one of the Three Stooges.'

'Oh,' I said. 'Did you let him in?'

'Of course not. I couldn't.'

'Oh,' I said. 'Should I feed the dog?'

Every Hallowe'en for as long as I could remember, Dad had dressed up as a warlock named Newman the Nefarious. His costume varied from year to year. Sometimes it consisted of stripey black lines he had smeared across his face using Mum's eyeliner, and an old stained blanket he draped across his hips and shoulders toga-like. Other times it involved head gear: a baseball cap with a rubber spider sewn on the front, a straw sun hat with bits of blackened newspaper and other trash affixed to its brim. They were not brilliant costumes, but as Newman he infused them with a blundering menace that thrilled the children who turned up at the door. Their parents were often not so pleased, probably because Newman's breath smelled strongly of Glenfiddich and cinnamon gum, but most of them returned at least twice, tethered to their offspring, who loved him. With Jeremy and me he was equally alluring and threatening. 'You are not my family,' he'd say with a guttural growl when we approached him. 'I am Newman the Nefarious. I have no family. I have only my pots and my potions, my mice and mittens. Do not mess with Newman the Nefarious.' And he would hunch over himself and mutter darkly before waving us away.

The Hallowe'en after Dad died, Mum and I gamely decorated the porch in orange and black streamers and stretched bits of cotton across the railings for cobwebs. But we had to close the door after three visits. Who can endure a child's questions when it comes to loss? *Where's Newman?* the superheroes, princesses, werewolves and gypsies asked, then rattled their plastic bags hopefully. *Where's Newman?*

After we had turned out the porch light, we sat across from each other at the kitchen table eating dainty chocolate bars from the good salad bowl. Mum smoothed out the creases with her thumbnail, so that the wrappers appeared to have been sucked dry and starched. Once a wrapper slipped from her grip and fell to the ground. I intercepted it quickly and handed it back to her. 'Chocolate is death to dogs,' I whispered. We stacked the empties in the middle of the table. When the pile was too high to balance, Mum turned to me.

'Do you feel sick yet?'

'No.'

'Me neither.' She passed me another mini Mars bar.

Emptiness is making us invincible, I thought, but had the good sense not to say it out loud.

Before the camping trip, Ben and I had spent a lot of time in his truck in parking lots or cul-de-sacs, making out and talking in a light, jokey way.

'Did I ever tell you about when half my face was frozen?' I loved to compare war stories from childhood with friends; we would often boast of strange injuries or illnesses we had overcome. My best story involved Bell's palsy; how, at the age of four, my face had tricked everyone, including myself, into believing it was infirm and elderly. And half-paralyzed! This was the hook that always got them. And Ben was no exception.

'No way.'

'Swear to God, Ben.'

'Show me.'

'What?'

'Show me how you looked.'

'I can't.'

'Don't be a wuss.'

'Like this.' I pulled one side of my face down with my open hand and smiled. But it wasn't the same, and I knew it. The whole of my face was smiling, despite the pressure of my hand, despite whatever lopsidedness was going on inside me. But I can still remember, with a sharp-edged clarity, the night my face froze. Dad had told a knock-knock joke, and I was hiccup-laughing. My corn was piled to one side on my plate, and my plastic tumbler was full to the brim with apple juice. I was reaching for it when my father's broad pink face changed. 'Stop making those funny faces,' he said, and grabbed my arm roughly. But I would not, could not, stop making the funny faces. Not then, and not for six weeks afterwards.

What I remember most about my father during my spell with paralysis was the way I would catch him looking at me sometimes, as if I had been stung by a dangerous insect whose name everyone had forgotten, and he was trying desperately to pin down its particulars, to recall the antidote. He would hug me at odd times, then turn away. My mother, if she was at all puzzled by my predicament, never let on. She busied herself sewing me a pirate patch for my lazy eye, and, when she was finished, snapped the elastic resolutely around my head. 'There you go, dingbat,' she said. 'Now go outside.'

For Christmas, we bought the dog soft elfin boots to protect him from the salt on the streets. But he refused to wear them, tearing them from his paws with his new pointy teeth.

The night before I left for university, I dreamt Jeremy and I were at the Ex on Labour Day. Jeremy's friend Richie had invited himself along at the last minute. We watched the parade from behind the Princes' Gates, sitting on electric-purple folding chairs, fanning ourselves with glossy leaflets. Solemn and tattered, the line of workers filed through the gates of the Exhibition. Richie cheered madly when the Miss Toronto float chugged by, then he sat back down, exhausted. My father was there, less ghost than sprite. He weaved his way in and out of the marchers, his hands in the air, waving. Pied piper to the union folk. As a grand finale, my brother and I were required to fly a stunt plane in the air show. There are rules, even in dreams.

Jeremy was explaining to me the best way to keep your sunglasses from falling off your face while the plane is performing a 360, when my mother appeared, casually, on the sidelines. She was not a ghost or a sprite, but she was everywhere. She pointed a finger towards the midway, where a vendor was selling breaded pork on a stick and a carny was peddling three chances to win a stuffed pink poodle. Everywhere, slick skinny men in snug jeans and leather headbands hawked bright, perfect, useless things. Mum had a megaphone in one hand, and two spirals of fluorescent cotton candy in the other. She brought the megaphone up to her lips.

'All I can say.' She paused, as if that were indeed all that she could say. Jeremy and I were standing now, listening. Mum coughed and gestured towards one of the kiosks, then spoke again. 'Is if you two die in that plane, you'll be working at one of those places for the rest of your lives.'

When I hugged Mum at the airport, she whispered something in my ear, and, for years, I have whispered it to myself when I find myself in a tight spot, or in no spot at all.

Then she began to wave, and called to me as if from a great distance, although I was still standing right there beside her. 'Goodbye, dingbat!'

When I didn't move, she pursed her mouth into a tiny, pink O, tight like a dog's bum.

'Bye.' I picked up my bag, began making my way over to the sliding glass doors, then turned to look back at her.

*A ha'penny will do.*

The doors slid open. I looked back at her again. I wanted desperately for her to forbid me to go.

But she didn't. She just stood there beside the idling station wagon in her red and beige paisley blouse that did not quite match her burgundy pants, and I noticed her shoulders for the first time. How small they were, how suddenly stooped and how completely, shockingly, her own.

# Frogs

NAADIYA ABBOUD WAS A dark brown girl, a Somali Muslim, slight of build, with a smattering of tiny pink blemishes across her chin, wide brown eyes, heavily lashed. She wore the same rose-coloured hijab most days, and green high-top Converse tucked under her dark denim jeans. As a student, she was vivacious and bright, although completely unreliable. It seemed to Vasile Dinescu that her lack of assiduousness when it came to her studies was of little concern to her, which is why it surprised him when she came to him at the end of class to ask for extra help.

'Sir,' she said, leaning over the slab of the lab bench, 'do you think I can talk to you after school today?'

He looked up from the attendance sheets he was updating and nodded. She had barely passed the first test of the year – nothing more than a lack of sustained attention to the diagrams and definitions in the text. But tears were welling tragically in her eyes, and the skin on her face had gone blotchy where the fabric of her hijab met her forehead. There were pressures at home, Vasile surmised. He would try to help her. He would make no overt promises but would also make it known he had no intention of contacting her parents, of, in teenage parlance, snitching.

'I'll be in the science office.'

She nodded, stepped away, then back again, touching the barrette that held her hijab in place with one careful hand and reaching into her pocket for her cellphone with the other. 'Where's that?' she said, preparing to make a call.

'Room 206, next to the stairwell.' Ah, no, she was entering the information into her device, making it a date. 'Do you need some extra help?'

She nodded again, then turned away – more resolutely this time – calling to one of her friends in the hallway. Then she was gone, padding softly in her sneakers.

Vasile shook his head to clear it. There was something about that girl. The way she had spoken, with an intensity and clarity of purpose. Was she flirting with him? He thought not; in any case, the prospect terrified him. He was not of the ilk that admired nubility beyond its representation of youth – of an era necessarily and thankfully no longer available to him. It was somewhat of a relief not to look for that, not to *want* that anymore. When he first arrived in Canada from Romania, he had, in order to refine his English, which was already passable, taken a class in poetry. The poem that had stayed with him like a pop song was by Theodore Roethke, 'Elegy for Jane' (*And how, once startled into talk, the light syllables leaped for her, / And she balanced in the delight of her thought* ...). It was awkward and creepy to be a male teacher of young women, the poem suggested. (*Over this damp grave I speak the words of my love: / I, with no rights in this matter, / Neither father nor lover*). It exiled you into a position of necessarily non-physical, non-overtly affectionate mentorship, but demanded of you an investment, an intimacy – okay, yes, a *concern* that in other quarters might go by the name of love. You could weep over your student's grave, but you'd better make damn sure no one saw you.

Besides, he loved his wife. A colleague had recently sent him a YouTube clip of a crude comedian who explained his interest in women vs. girls. Women, he had exhorted, were not women until they had squeezed a couple of children out of their vaginas and had these children trample on their dreams. As a former doctor in a pronatalist socialist republic, Vasile could appreciate the directness of this assertion. Ceauşescu had specialized in this dream trampling with his ban on abortion and designation of women who managed ten or more children (*ten!*) as Heroine Mothers. So this new humour was necessarily less scathing than the gallows humour that circulated in Romania at the time (*Beginning in the year 1967, rape will be considered productive labour and will not be punished.*), but no less accurate. He was mortal, and he liked to be reminded of it; the more we as a species untether ourselves from our limitations, the more difficult to ascertain the world becomes. Okay, he liked the way technology made his life easier, but also shied away from the moral quandaries it seemed to engender almost every minute of every day. But science and morality – they had always been strange bedfellows. Where was he going with this? Closer to the crux: why did Naadiya want to see him? He doubted she would even show up. A teenager's brain was not designed to keep scholarly commitments after dismissal. To swim against the flow of students yearning for freedom required a monumental effort – a rebellion against that strongest of forces, instinct.

The lunch bell rang.

'I don't like to stand too close,' said the young teacher whose name Vasile had forgotten. She was tall, with a confident Roman nose that seemed to lead her person. Christine, he thought. What was the surname? Something vaguely and inoffensively European. French perhaps? Her posture was newly self-assured and somewhat forced – he could sense she had spent time coming to grips with her height. She wore a bright blue cardigan that tied like a fortune cookie at the waist, stylish wide-legged blue jeans and a coral-hued lipstick on her mouth. Vasile was certainly not, as his students might say, a fashionista, but he felt the ensemble suggested far too much colour contrast between the woman's lips and torso – there was something touristy and sunset-esque about it. What was it she taught – history or social science? He couldn't quite recall. For a moment, he wondered at what she had said. *Too close?* Was he offending her somehow – exuding a certain non-collegial maleness?

'They say the rays,' she continued, and pointed at the microwave, '*not* good for you! At least a metre away is what they say.'

Ah yes, Vasile nodded. 'They' had made such proclamations before, and it was an attractive prospect, to be able to gauge and control your environment, seal yourself deliberately and definitively off from danger. He nodded again at her as the microwave beeped. She stepped forward to retrieve her meal. The fragrant steam wafted towards him. 'Indian?' he said.

'Yes,' she replied, nodding quickly. 'I made it last night – spicy dahl. I find the spice gives me energy in the middle of the day.' She was in her mid-twenties, keen like a squirrel, a *veveriţă*, bristling with industry and vim. She had already presented two school-wide initiatives at staff meetings, and it was only the beginning of October.

'How are your classes?' he asked, stepping forward to program the heating of his own meal.

'Oh,' she spoke, and her eyes said, *So glad you asked.* 'Some are more challenging than others.' *But I will not be beaten or dulled by the institution, by the constantly changing, consistently confounding curriculum, by bureaucracy, by seeping professional apathy. I'm here for the kids! For their minds and livelihoods, for their very futures, which I hold like delicate doodads in my terribly capable hands …*

Vasile felt himself mildly accused. He smiled at her, the *veveriţă* with her twitching, anxious nose. 'Can I give you some advice?'

'Sure,' she said. *Of course, old man. I am young and kind, and I know it is politic and generous to engage your type.*

'There will be days … ' Vasile paused. The spicy dahl steam rose between them. 'There will be days when you are so bone-tired that you will look out at them sitting there, waiting for you to give them something, something true and shining that holds their attention or will prove useful at some later date. Or maybe they just want badly for you to tell them who they are – a chatterbox, a troublemaker, a genius – so that they may continue to live up to the role they feel has been foisted upon them. And you will reach far down inside yourself and find … nothing. There will be nothing left. On these days you must write two words on the blackboard.' He paused again. She leaned forward expectantly. 'Work Period,' he said.

Christine stepped away from him, disappointed. Vasile could tell she thought he was not being exactly 'appropriate' as per the staff handbook. She wanted to get to that dahl, but he had not yet finished. He stepped closer to the door, so that she would be forced to excuse herself in order to push past his bulk and into the staff room. 'Then,' he said, 'at the end of the class, after you have dismissed the students, I would recommend the following: run your palms along the blackboard, erase the words with your palms, then pat them, like so.' He patted his belly and his thighs. 'Directly on your person. That way, when you bump into the principal in the hallway, she will see the extent of your dedication marked on your good clothes and you will feel yourself excused – or at least unworthy of comment.'

Christine looked at him, into his eyes. She was unsure of whether to laugh. He lifted a corner of his mouth, giving permission. Her laugh was dry and short. Vasile's meal beeped. 'Lunchtime,' he said.

'Yes,' Christine replied. 'Have a good one.'

Vasile's first class after lunch was another Grade 10 science. A small class, but boisterous, they tumbled into the classroom, cursing and laughing, took their places at the lab benches, but did not stop talking, even after he had cleared his throat twice, loudly. It was his least favourite part of the job, having to quiet them, to focus their attention on his person. He had been in the employ of the Toronto District School Board for eighteen years now, and still, the corralling of these young people felt strange and affected.

'Class, your attention up here at the front, please. Quiet, please.'

The nattering and jostling subsided. They were not unruly, really, just young, coursing with hormones and full of french fries from the cafeteria. And once he began to speak, they listened, or at least appeared to, their faces tipped up towards the blackboard, then back down to their notebooks, as they scrawled down the lesson.

He suspected it was his ghost of an accent that kept them rapt. It was reassuring, the not-quite-rightness of his English; they were not native either, or at least their families were not. What they were was Diverse. Which, as one might imagine, could mean many things. Mostly, people used it to mean Black, although sometimes it also meant Poor, or Neglected, or 100% Likely to Do or Deal Drugs in the Next Five Years. It was language used to cloak and gentle the truth. Never mind. He understood the power of naming, the great mess of meaning that trailed after a word like cans clanking along behind the bride and groom's car. And, it was true, there was a kindness in this gentling that at times it found its proper mark.

But in his classroom, Diverse meant Vietnamese, Jamaican, Guyanese, Somali, Albanian, Portuguese, Iranian, Indian, Afghani. It meant Christian, Muslim, Hindu, varying levels of devotion. It meant On Welfare and Working Hard and Striving for the Comfortable Middle Ground. And it meant Canadian. Which was another word with its own cans clanking. And trumping all this Diversity was Youth – its arrogance, energy and lovely obliviousness. He witnessed it all the time, eavesdropping, observing:

'Ugh, I never want to turn twenty.'

'Why not?'

'That's when you have to start watching the news.'

And:

'Man, that girl is so haunted.'

'What do you mean?'

'I, like, totally booked her talking to Bryan, standing totally close and all up in his face, while Sha-shauna was, like, right behind her. Afterwards Sha-shauna was looking for her and she just dipped.'

Their dramas were all-consuming and extreme; they were ridiculous and charming and seemed to find their roots in daytime talk shows. He could understand why they did not want him to interrupt. But interrupt he did.

'Please be prepared for the frog dissection next class. You will need to make sure you have reviewed the chapter in your textbook regarding amphibian physiology – chapter 12. You must also go over the handout regarding proper procedure for dissection. Remember also that you will be evaluated on the precision of your technique.' He paused to allow some chatter to subside. 'It is no small thing to use another living creature in this way. You should arrive with an attitude of reverence, of respect.'

The students gazed at him, saucer-eyed. He had deviated from the script, had dared to speak not as a teacher but as a spirit guide of sorts. It entranced them for a moment.

Vasile was alone in the science office when Naadiya knocked. The two colleagues with whom he shared the space had sprinted out the door seconds after the bell rang. He understood it, the pressing desire to put distance between the overwhelming stimuli of the school and the shaky sanctity of the self. But minutes after dismissal, there was a new quiet in the school – a deflated sense of contentedness, as if the building had digested something, then belched up its essence. It was not like this of course on the main floor, near the drama and music wing, or in the basement gym, where rehearsals and practices went on, causing a ruckus with bleating trumpets and bouncing balls and proclamations of love and victory. Here on the second floor was a different story. A calmer, emptier story.

Naadiya knocked again. When Vasile opened the door, she was searching for something in her backpack, one hand submerged in the large main pocket.

'Hi, sir,' she said.

'Hello,' he replied.

She uncapped a chapstick – the backpack loot! – and ran the tip along her mouth several times. Then she threw the chapstick back in the bag, zipped up the pocket and slung the bag over one shoulder.

'Hello, Naadiya,' Vasile said again. 'Come in, won't you? Have a seat.' What must they think of him, with his strange gentleman's diction? It was nervousness that prompted it; he did not *think* in these words, they just made themselves when he opened his mouth.

'Sure,' she said, stepping into the room. It was a wheelie chair he had gestured towards and she took her place in it gingerly, using her feet to move back and forth, back and forth in the small space between his desk and the recycling bin. So they were both nervous. He understood then that she had something to ask of him, a favour of some kind. Advice? This seemed unlikely.

'Do you need some extra help, Naadiya? I know your last test results were perhaps not as satisfying as you would have liked.'

Naadiya looked down at her backpack, which was now at her feet, then up at the bulletin board behind Vasile.

'No,' she said. 'I mean, yes! I totally sucked at that test. I didn't study. Is that your family?' She pointed at the snapshot he had tacked above his timetable and a coupon for the pizza place across the street. Vasile swivelled his own chair around to check, although the same photo had occupied the position for the past three years. He could close his eyes and conjure the lines around his wife's eyes – how they extended out towards the entire world when she smiled. His son and daughter's easy lean – Maria between him and Caterina, Marcel on tiptoes, with one arm draped around Vasile's shoulder as if they were army comrades on leave. There was an unthinking kind of leaning that was as good as love, as joyful and unthinking. He missed that lean – the leaning love of young children.

'Yes,' he replied. 'My daughter, Maria, and my son, Marcel.'

'Huh,' Naadiya said. 'You guys liked the letter M, eh?'

'I suppose we did,' Vasile said. 'I suppose we did. They are grown up now. Maria is living in Montreal and Marcel has gone back to Romania.'

'Oh,' she said. Then, 'Romania. Is that where vampires are from?'

Vasile contemplated a number of responses to this query, then settled on one. 'Yes,' he said.

But she was not really interested. She had stopped wheeling the chair and was staring out the tiny window.

'Naadiya,' Vasile said. 'What can I help you with?'

She stopped wheeling and looked up at him ever so briefly, then up at the photo again and back at him. Her eyes had filled with tears in the space between the photo and his face. What was wrong with her?

'Perhaps … ' he began. 'Perhaps you'd like to speak with the school counsellor?'

'No.' She shook her head. 'No, no, no, no, no.' Almost absently.

It reminded Vasile of his daughter as a toddler, how she'd waddled around with that word perpetually on her tongue, already cataloguing forbidden objects and pathways. He looked at Naadiya, who was looking out the window again. The silence between them grew. Vasile didn't mind; he was good at silence. And it was what they said was correct: not to judge or advise, merely to listen, to – in therapy-speak – *be there.*

Naadiya sighed, but barely. She was not breathing properly. There was not much left in her lungs to exhale. Then she pulled her shoulders back and turned towards him. The tears were gone.

'I'm pregnant,' she said.

Vasile stared at her. She was not blinking, and it seemed he could do nothing *but* blink.

Blink.

What was she saying?

Blink, blink.

The words had been spoken as a challenge of sorts. Could she possibly think that he was somehow … Blink. Responsible? He should say something. Do something.

Blink.

He cleared his throat.

Naadiya just kept *looking* at him. He knew he had gone bulgy-eyed, incredulous, and that it was unbecoming, *inappropriate*.

Vasile fell back on his medical training, pulling out a notebook from the desk drawer. Although he had no intention of taking notes, he opened the cover, picked up a pen.

'How far?' he said.

She leaned back in the wheelie chair, exhaled more deeply this time. He had said the right thing.

'I'm not sure. I think, like, almost three months.' She lay one hand on her belly, an instinctive gesture Vasile had witnessed thousands of times. But she was so slim, not yet curvy with child. He envisioned the tadpole-like fetus, its size and viability. Then he looked into her face, so open and frightened and *young*.

'What will you do?' he said. Not: Have you told your parents? Obviously not. Not: Who is the father? A boy. The father was a boy, skittering and beautiful and mistaken. Like Naadiya. Or perhaps not. Was the father himself already a father, someone who knew better? Don't go there, is what Vasile thought, surprising himself with the lingo.

'I can't,' Naadiya said. She began to cry in earnest. 'I can't let it out.'

Babies and secrets. If you held them, they could be the most difficult things in the world to release – Vasile recognized this better than most. And to hold the two in combination. Well.

'Naadiya,' he said. 'Don't cry. I will help you. But are you sure you wouldn't rather talk to someone else? A woman?'

'No,' she said. She sniffed, then wiped her nose with the back of her wrist. 'I know you were a doctor. I know you understand these things.'

He nodded. 'You have options, Naadiya.'

'I have one option,' she said.

'I will find out for you.' Vasile reached out to pat her on the shoulder, but she was already standing up, hoisting the bag onto her back.

'Thanks,' she said. 'I'll come see you tomorrow, same time.'

'I'll be in my classroom,' Vasile said.

Naadiya nodded.

Vasile understood she had no need to enter this new appointment into her electronic device.

The next day Caterina needed the car, so he rode the subway and bus to work, camouflaged behind a newspaper and his own rumpled, oblivious look. He let staff and students believe he was clueless; this misapprehension on their part provided him a shield and a power.

A few stops away from the school, two students he recognized boarded and took seats just ahead of him. It was a white boy, a white girl, the girl's hair dyed a russet colour with black streaks, the boy tall and athletic-looking, save for the shaggy hair and jaunty red scarf. The girl was wearing a pair of turquoise spectacles with a 1950s cat's-eye shape. As soon as they sat, the boy leaned over towards Spectacles so that his lips – which were full and red to match his scarf – very nearly touched her ear. Then, in a sultry stage whisper, he spoke. Vasile, intrigued, also leaned towards Spectacles, and tilted his head in to hear.

'Well,' the boy said. 'You'll never guess what happened this past summer.' He smirked and breathed into Spectacles' ear.

Spectacles, unfazed, pushed her glasses up and did not pull away. 'What?' she said, then sighed.

The boy maintained his position and paused for a moment before speaking again. 'I *deflowered* someone,' he said. Vasile was surprised at the use of the term before he was shocked at its meaning; how difficult it was tell who was being ironic, and when!

The choice of vocabulary seemed also to have piqued the girl's attention. Her sigh turned into something more breathily anxious and eager. 'Get *out*,' she said. 'Who?'

The boy slouched back into himself, having created, for the moment, a stunningly desirable effect in his seatmate. He shrugged. 'I dunno. Some ugly girl. Afterwards she was all, like, wanting to be my girlfriend and everything.' He looked out the window, then tapped it angrily.

Spectacles craned towards him so she could see what he saw, feel as he felt. But nonchalance escaped her. 'So *did* you? *Were* you?' she said, looking intently into his youthful, sharp-angled face.

The boy turned back towards her. 'No way. I was, like, welcome to camp.' He looked down at his hands.

Was he ashamed, Vasile wondered, or simply bored? This was not Naadiya's boy; summer camp was a third- or fourth-generation thing, not designed with the observant Muslim in mind.

The girl gave his shoulder a fleeting pat. 'Totally. It's not like you assaulted her or anything,' she said.

The boy appeared rueful, then gleeful, then a combination of the two. 'No, I mean, she totally dragged me into the bushes,' he said.

Spectacles nodded understandingly, back in control. She, like the boy, was a callow youth, it was true, but Vasile did not believe she would outgrow this egotism; it pleased her too much.

'And then, you know … ' The boy looked down at his hands again, out the window, then back at the girl. 'The brain stops working after a while,' he said.

Spectacles nodded again, and kept nodding until the boy turned back to the window. Outside, the sky seemed to have swollen; it gave off a harsh grey glow that bled into the overpass up ahead. It could have been pollution or the beginnings of precipitation. It could be the end of the world, Vasile thought.

At school, he busied himself readying the frogs for first period. There was very little time for the students to complete the dissection; his choreography of the whole affair would have to be efficient and graceful. He lined the creatures up on his lab bench. The students would be responsible for picking them up and carrying them to their respective work areas. He would sort the instruments next, check to make sure there was nothing missing or defective.

But first, he walked to the back of the room to visit the rabbits. The students were responsible for cleaning the cage, making sure the animals had food and water, and they were conscientious in this regard, devoid of brashness or boastfulness. All was well in the hutch, the rabbits sleeping in innocent heaps in piles of sawdust. He surveyed the rest of the classroom. Vasile knew a place was not its people; still, a room could wait, breathlessly, for its occupants, a prison's hold on its inmates could be both loving and cruel, a field could feel itself being tilled or stampeded. He opened a window. The room needed air. The frogs needed air.

Once the students had placed their specimens on their desks, Vasile began to instruct, leading them through the procedure as quickly and clinically as possible. There would be few opportunities for 'teachable moments' on this day, there was simply no time. This learning would be purely experiential. It was less difficult to calm the class today; they were eager to get started. Vasile began.

'Step one. Make a lateral incision on both lymph nodes of your frog. Lymph nodes are found under the jaw on either side.' He demonstrated on his own frog at the front, two tiny perfect slits. The students, who had been brandishing their tools confidently, suddenly became shy and serious.

'Like this, Mr. D?' a boy sitting near the back – Richard – called out. Vasile walked down the aisle towards him, observed his work, and that of the others, who had been released, it seemed, by Richard's question.

Next they were required to cut through the abdominal muscles and bones, disconnecting the bones that linked to the shoulders, freeing the sternum.

'Free the sternum,' he said. It was absurd-sounding, but they did not notice, so intent were they on their work. Vasile continued.

'If your frog is a female, you'll have to remove the black eggs that sit in her abdomen.'

'Is this like caviar, Mr. D?' Richard piped up again. 'Can you, like, sell this for major cash?' He held several of the eggs aloft on one gloved finger for the rest of the class to see.

'No, Richard,' Vasile answered. 'No, you're thinking fish eggs. Feel free to sample these eggs if you desire. Although I am sure you will soon understand why they are not considered a delicacy.'

Richard brought the eggs to his mouth and waggled his tongue. 'Nah,' he said. 'I'm still full from breakfast.' The class laughed.

And then they found their rhythm: the liver, the small green orb of the gall bladder, the coilings of the small intestine, the stomach, the pancreas. Vasile paused in his instructions to allow some of the more fastidious students to catch up.

After Maria left for university, there had been a spate of letters demanding justification of his role – however small – in his country's history and in the smaller, more vital history of their family. The letters were long, handwritten – the script reaching ambitiously, rebelliously to the edges of the page – outlining her stance: pro-choice. The text was bursting with a young woman's righteousness and conviction. Maria's fervour tended towards the revolutionary; when she came home at Christmas, her head was shaved and she wore pointy boots with buckles – restrictive footwear designed to attract the eye and bind the user. It was masochism for show, in Vasile's opinion. So overstated, like her opinions, which she wore proudly on her sleeve: pro-choice. Over turkey and tofu, she elaborated: 'You have to weigh up the suffering. It's about the suffering. For example, I'm not a vegetarian because I believe we should never eat meat – it's that the means of killing for food are so inhumane, so vicious. I would eat an oyster! Oysters do not suffer when they die. They don't have brains or nerves. You have to weigh up the suffering. You have to consider all the parties involved.'

He answered her letters, a note of pleading in his tone, a forced eloquence he thought might refine his sense of guilt. The news reports from the Romanian revolution were writ large in her consciousness, inscribed on her childhood, he knew. His status, which had not always protected his family, had allowed him to purchase documents that facilitated their escape before people took to the streets. She was only ten when they arrived in Toronto, but old enough to note that the differences between she and her new friends went beyond funny accents and pop-star preferences. When he was not fielding her epistolary missives from Montreal, they spoke on the phone. He recalled a particularly heated exchange:

'Did you ever *think*, Father?'

'Of course I thought, I just couldn't let my thoughts stray too far from the reality of the situation.'

'Right. But did you not ever think about the larger picture? Of the web of consequences you created by perpetrating Ceauşescu's schemes?'

'No, we did not think in those terms, Maria.'

'In those *terms*,' she had shot back. 'They are not *terms*, they are the truth, they are what happened! My God, it was like something out of a horror movie, or the Bible – women boiling roots or shoving them up themselves, babies left to rot on the riverbank – and those orphanages! You were there, you were *complicit*. You *knew*. You knew about everything and you forced women to have babies they didn't want and couldn't care for.'

'Not always,' he had replied. It was a lukewarm response he knew would incense her further. 'You'd be interested to hear about the frogs, I believe.'

'Why do you speak like that, like a professor in a TV show? I'm your daughter, for Chrissakes!'

He suspected she might hang up, but he pressed on. 'Ceauşescu had the frogs imported in droves in aid of his pronatalist policies. You see, back then, they didn't have the technology we have today. So, instead of women peeing on those little plastic wands, they had to inject a female subject's urine into the frog to determine if she was knocked up.'

Maria was, of course, alarmed by this. 'But how ... ?'

'Ah yes,' said Vasile. 'How did they know? What *symptoms* did the frog display? Well, the pregnancy hormones in the human pee would make the frog produce eggs within twenty-four hours. And the beauty was that the frog remained alive and could be used again.'

'So they didn't kill them,' Maria said, relieved.

'Well, no,' Vasile replied. 'They merely enslaved them and worked them to death.'

'Why?' Maria sounded tired, unimpressed.

'Because the big C wanted everyone to have more children. So he enforced it with menstrual police and doctors who were conscripted to ensure ladies made babies. Sex was procreational, not recreational.'

'That's awful,' Maria muttered. 'You were a doctor, Dad. It was your duty to *heal*. And instead, you helped take away their freedom, their choice.'

'The frogs or the people?' Vasile said. His tone was facetious. He should have stayed silent, but his daughter's dismay goaded him somehow, made him ache for battle. It was because he knew she was right; he had been cowardly.

Caterina was the courageous one. They told the children she had been called away to care for an ailing aunt. It was like a fairy tale: abandoned children, parents with selfish ulterior motives, old women – witches – with potions and spells designed to solve problems, grant wishes. And absent mothers.

How lucky he was to have her!

When they first started dating he had almost lost her to a poet. But the poet was poor. *And he has these fatty little fingers,*

Maria had confided to Vasile, laughing. *I could not bear for him to touch me with those fingers.* She drew her own fingers across his cheek. *We will be happy, Vasile.* Because she was beautiful and stalwart, he believed her.

'The heart is pretty central,' he told his students. 'It is located behind the forelegs. The thin tissue around it is the pericardium.'

Maria had inherited her mother's sense of responsibility and irreverence. He had watched her playing with Marcel when they were children, building elaborate kingdoms out of toilet-paper rolls, twigs and scraps of fabric. Like all children, she was a fan of the riddle: *Cineşade pe perete şi-are numai o ureche?* she asked her brother, again and again. Who's on the wall and has only one ear? It was Ceauşescu, of course, a portrait in every classroom of the shoemaker who made good, one ear hidden by the angle of the shot, a grey slab of hair.

'Is my frog sick, sir? It has these yellow wormy things … ' It was Laura, a young woman of limited intellect, often distracted and easily, dramatically offended.

Vasile shook his head. 'No, those are the fat bodies. They allow your frog to store fat and survive its winter hibernation.'

'Oh,' Laura said. '*Gross*.' And: 'I didn't know frogs hibernated.'

Vasile nodded; he would return to hibernation. For now, the spleen, the kidneys, the lungs – all were awaiting discovery! The lungs especially were a surprise.

'But sir, they're so small!'

'Because they breathe through their skin, idiot!'

'No way!'

'That's so cool.'

'It is and it isn't. Cool,' Vasile said. 'It makes them very sensitive. Like a canary in a coal mine.' The students looked at him blankly. 'I mean, they're the first to feel environmental upsets. They're the first to suffer.'

Several students looked up at him, nodded. His time was running out, they would have to begin cleanup soon.

'For example, scientists are pretty sure the chrytid fungus was responsible for wiping out the golden toad of Costa Rica and the majority of harlequin frogs in the tropical forests. As the fungus is a skin disease, and frogs breathe through their skin … Well, you can see the difficulty, can't you? Weirdly, it also disoriented the poor creatures, forced them out of their comfort zones. Nocturnal species began taking noontime strolls, river frogs were found high in the treetops far from home. It turned their world upside down,' Vasile said.

The students began to gather their books, anticipating the bell. Just as well; he wasn't quite sure how to continue.

Vasile spent the last period of the day, his prep, tidying up the remains of the frogs. The formaldehyde made them rubbery, toy-like. It was absurd, but he felt a sense of the funerary, an air of pomp. His own mother had had an expensive and elaborate funeral in Romania, the tributes and rituals of a dignitary's wife. She too had been pumped full of embalming fluid so that her skin, when touched, possessed none of the comforting pouchy looseness he remembered. The tautness of her was repellent, quite literally. He felt his fingers bounce off her when he tried to stroke her hand. He said, *Goodbye, Mama,* as was expected of him, and then cried counterfeit tears, so much forged grief. He cried not at the loss but at the strangeness of her preservation, the unnatural tilt of her head under the badly coiffed wig.

The frog parts had to be disposed of. He was living in a culture of compartmentalization – there were bins, colour-coded, for his waste, for everybody's waste. But what to do with used pickled frog? There was a special company charged with picking up these bits and pieces, finding a place for them. He did not want to know how they did it; it was their job, they should be grateful, no, for such a job? It was a job that could exist only in a world of privilege, of opportunity. He sealed the parts up in a large plastic paint-can-like container and stacked the remains on a shelf in the office. The waste pickup was not until the following Wednesday, but the parts would not smell. He sat down at the lab bench to wait for Naadiya.

She did not knock this time, simply opened the classroom door and waltzed in. Vasile was momentarily, strangely offended by her gall, her sense of entitlement. Then she smiled at him, shyly. Ah, it was merely bravado then. He forgave her. She perched herself on one of the tall stools at the front of the room. He got up and walked towards her, greeted her.

'Hello, Naadiya.'

'Hi! Hello, Mr. Dinescu.' She waved a little wave, quickly, like a duck waving.

He stopped a metre away from the stool, unsure of where to go. He put his hands in his pockets. 'Are you ... How are you feeling?'

She sat up straighter on the stool. 'Good. I feel good.'

And she looked good. He could see it now, a new luminosity. But it was not useful to romanticize. 'No morning sickness?'

'No.' She shook her head. 'Nope.' She rocked back on the stool, balancing.

'No!' Vasile shouted. 'No! You mustn't do that, you could fall, you could ... '

Naadiya brought the stool back to earth.

'I googled some clinics for you,' he said. He had been amazed at the cluster, the constellation of stars that had popped up on the map. Here in Toronto, there were buildings, nondescript and functional, wherein it was possible for a woman to terminate a pregnancy. Nobody talked about it, but it happened calmly, quickly, perhaps heart-rendingly. Maybe it was better nobody talked about it. Perhaps it was the real measure of a civilized society. A form of internal, truly domestic peacekeeping. A necessary exit strategy. The clinics were everywhere, dotted along the subway line like the white pebbles left by Hansel. They would glow, he supposed, in the moonlight.

'Yeah,' Naadiya said. 'I found them too.' She looked like she was losing interest! In him? In her predicament? Vasile took a step away from her. He was frightened at how much he wanted her to need him.

'What's malignant hyperthermia? They asked me if my family has a history of it.' Naadiya started to lift the stool from the ground again, bracing herself with her arms against the lab bench, then stopped.

'Oh,' he said. 'It's a reaction to anesthesia.'

'Okay,' Naadiya said, shrugging. She dismounted and began making her way to the back of the room, towards the rabbit hutch. Once there, she crouched down, wove her fingers through the wire, and brought her face close to the cage.

'Naadiya?' Vasile said. He walked towards her. He was shocked – again – and somewhat hurt.

'It's next Monday.' She spoke to the rabbits, happily, buoyed by the fact of it. 'I need someone to drive me to the appointment.'

'I will drive you,' Vasile said, but already his brain was scurrying for alibis. Why would he be driving a young Muslim girl – his student! – into the downtown core, after school hours?

Naadiya seemed oblivious to this quandary. She cooed and hummed to the rabbits. 'Bye, bye.' She blew the rabbits a kiss. 'Thank you, sir,' she said. 'I just have to go now. I have to pick up my sister.'

'Yes,' said Vasile. 'Yes. See you Monday.' He returned to his desk as she made her way to the door.

The next day at lunch Vasile met the *veveriță* next to the microwave again.

'Hello,' he said. 'Spice today?'

'Oh no,' she said. 'Fish – brain food. But not too many carbs. They weigh you down.'

'Yes,' said Vasile. 'You don't want to be weighed down.'

Christine looked miffed. Perhaps she heard the serving of secret sarcasm he had hidden in his reply. He couldn't help it. He found her relentless cheerleading quality disturbing. He detected in it the root of some small fascism. Not that there was much value in a wholesale dismissal of the possibility of change – why live at all if hope was an impossibility?

'I mean, sometimes it's good to feel weighed down, grounded, y'know? But sometimes too light is bad, because then you just float away on your own little cloud. We need interconnectedness and an equitable environment in which to learn and grow.'

Vasile sighed deeply. The *veveriță* seemed momentarily aware of the speed and desperation in her chattering. She stopped.

'Have you signed up for any extracurriculars yet?' She removed her food from the microwave, stirred it with a folding spoon she had pulled from her bag. The bag looked to be a cross between some sort of camping gear and a briefcase.

Vasile watched her snap the spoon back into its compact shape. Sometimes he didn't think he was made for this new world; often he wondered if he was made for the world at all. Extracurriculars! How would the *veveriță* have responded to Naadiya's predicament? There was no doubt a rubric one could apply to this situation, protocols, a whole troop of professionals to summon and implicate … He imagined an announcement on the PA: *Monday's after-school activity will be a lesson in freedom and responsibility, biology and ethics. Do not miss the shuttle – we are leaving at 3:30 sharp!* He hated himself for thinking this way. The *veveriță* was staring at him.

'Are you okay, Mr. D – I mean Vasile, are you okay?'

Oh, she was young, and still not used to calling adults by their first names, an uncomfortable informality. It was endearing. Perhaps she was not a squirrel but a young bird, a nervous fledgling.

'I'm okay, Christine, just tired.'

'Oh well,' she said. 'This is a pretty tiring job.' The coiled energy of her stance seemed to suggest the opposite. 'You hang in there.'

'Thanks,' Vasile said.

'Here, let me get your food.' She reached up, opened the door of the microwave and passed the plate down to him. It was lamb and potatoes that Caterina had cooked the night before.

Once again – it was recurring, like a tic or a cough – Vasile realized how much he loved his wife. 'Thanks,' he said. A wave of general goodwill overtook him. 'Have a great afternoon!'

On Monday after school, Vasile and Naadiya drove together to the appointment, hurtling silently, like escaped lovers, eastward along the Gardiner Expressway. Just past Sunnyside Beach she began to weep, great soul-shaking sobs that seemed too large, somehow too … *mature* for her delicate frame. Was it the sight of the waves, the great sky, the glinting of the sun, an alchemy of light that prompted the outburst? Or was it Vasile's fatherly profile, intent on the traffic, stationed beside her? How could he ever know? How could anyone ever know anything about anyone? Vasile felt himself sliding into an unboundaried despair. *Fiica mea dragă, my darling daughter. You ask me what I remember of that awful, ill-lit time and perhaps you will be shocked at my answer. But more than anything, I remember the frogs. I dream them in their many incarnations and contortions. I weep for them the way I cannot for the women, for the babies born half-formed or badly loved. The frogs were exhausted, the women pissed more blood than urine, but we did not stop. Not one of us stopped for long enough to look at the frogs or to look at each other. A man in uniform was breathing down my neck and I was so very afraid.*

'Do you want me to turn around?' He spoke into the windshield, quietly.

Naadiya shook her head in the periphery. No. *No, no, no, no, no.*

Caterina had been sentenced to six years for the abortion she had procured. It would have been less had she given up the name of the woman who sold her the tubing, the saline solution. She worked like a peasant in the fields as punishment and toed the party line with an admirably authentic meekness. *There is a hole in my heart,* she told him. *I must hold my children again.* They wept together, heads bowed and touching over an unstable metal table, a guard, buttoned snugly into his uniform, peering at them with lustful curiosity and spite. Caterina's sentence was shortened to eighteen months and she returned to them, her body and spirit taut with what she had endured.

Vasile checked for Naadiya in her home form the following morning but she was absent. He searched for her in the hallways superstitiously, as if anticipating an apparition. But she did not appear. His gut clenched in fear. At every bell he hurried to the staff washroom, voided his bowels, then returned to class, empty and shaken.

In the last period of the day Vasile had only to administer a test to his Grade 12 students, a task that required him to look stern and stalk back and forth between rows periodically. He had just begun this invigilating when there was a knock at the door. The knock was authoritative and clear; it frightened him. Irony: to survive Ceauşescu only to be apprehended by the bureaucrats of the Toronto District School Board. His students waited for him to answer the knock. He strode over to the door, his trembling hands hidden in his pockets. It was Naadiya, looking tired but hardy. He stepped out into the hall and closed the door behind him. He heard the deliberate coughing, subtle rustlings as he left. Some students would cheat; it was human nature.

'Thank you,' said Naadiya, her arms wrapped around herself.

'You're welcome,' he said. 'You should be in class.'

She stared at him.

'I mean, you are all right?'

'Yes,' she said. She reached up to touch her hijab. Then she unclipped the barrette holding it in place.

Vasile had a moment of panic – the scarf would fall! They had already shared too much; he did not want to see her hair. But the scarf did not fall. Naadiya tucked it into place efficiently; the barrette had been insurance only. She held it out to him.

'Here,' she said. 'I couldn't think of anything else.'

'Oh,' Vasile said. 'Yes. Thank you.' He took the barrette and slipped it into his pocket. 'My students are writing a test,' he said.

'Yeah,' she said. 'I have Ms. Foster. She's totally gonna freak when she books – I mean notices – how long I took. So, bye.'

'Bye,' said Vasile, and closed the door.

There was a murmur and a subtle rearrangement – of desks and dispositions – when he re-entered the classroom, but it was not long before his presence restored the students' focus. They rotated their wrists like athletes, scratched at their scalps unselfconsciously, looked up – not at him, but at some elusive pattern: scientific etymology, formulae, classifications and recipes designed to help us understand the earth and its organisms. At the back of the classroom, the rabbits rooted around in their cage, nosed the air and each other. Vasile Dinescu was not an observant man, yet there was a residue of religion in him. He took a deep breath and allowed the air to fill his lungs, his abdomen, his limbs and his head. He began to float, his body hoisted aloft by loss and yearning. He began to pray. '*Doamne iartă-ne*,' he said. God forgive us! '*Broaştele!*' The frogs! He sent the prayer up into the ether, into the atmosphere, the atoms of water that created the clouds … He exhaled. Then he turned back to his students, some of whom were beginning to crane restlessly away from their concentration. He checked his watch and confirmed with the noisy wall clock. 'Time's up,' he said.

# No One Else Really Wants to Listen

HI ALL YOU MOMS-IN-WAITING,
I felt the baby move a little, I think, but I'm sort of worried because I'm having some spotting. Not a lot, and it's not bright red, alarm, alarm! But I feel a bit concerned. I'm wondering if anyone has any advice, or suggestions. I have an appointment with my ob-gyn on Wednesday, but I can't sleep right now. It's just on my mind, y'know?
– *New Country Girl*

WRT the bleeding – it could come from sex. I don't know about you chickadees, but since I crossed over into the second trimester I've been crazy-horny. It's like everything is super-ripe, y'know? No offence or anything inquiring about your love life – it's just normal to have a bit of blood from the friction. Sorry again if this is TMI.
– *Craving City*

No such thing as TMI in this forum, my friend. All info is good info. Yeah, ripe is one word for it. NC, the blood is likely coming from your cervix which is probably quite swollen and tender at this point. It might also be the result of straining on the toilet. Are you constipated at all?
– *Straight Shooter*

Nope, the elimination pipes are clear, and the bleeding continues – not heavy or anything, but it's there. I'm thinking I'll call Tele-Health and see what they say.
*– NC*

Good idea, NC. IMHO, it's totally better to be safe than sorry.
*– Craving*

New Country: I wouldn't worry too much – when I got pregnant not only my sense of smell but also my sense of tragedy became more acute. By this I do not mean, as some women exclaim, that I became more sensitive to the plight of others or that I was compelled to turn headlines involving the maiming of children face down on the kitchen table. Quite the opposite. During my first trimester, I devoured stories wherein the unlucky fledgling protagonists were killed – instantly – in a head-on collision; I spent afternoons imagining the last moments of infants left to freeze in some alcoholic father's backyard wasteland. You must understand, none of this was malicious or gratuitous. Perhaps it was a test of my mettle – I wanted to feel the worst, to encompass it. The pregnancy made me feel expansive, as if I had grown new ribs, longer ribs, that my chest cavity and not my uterus were expanding. I felt sure that at my next visit, the doctor would ask to measure my wingspan. Something moving inside me made it imperative that I understand it all – not the week-by-week stirring of the speck that had lodged itself like a grain of sand inside an oyster but instead the bold cacophony of the outside world, which, it appeared, was no longer outside, but instead a country of blood and tenderness and terror and chemicals and a strange softness before dying within the scope of my very own body. The country smelled of cardamom, shit, exhaust fumes and a man's scalp, and if I spread my wings wide enough, I could embrace it all, all of it, my wingtips touching, feathers tickling the dust.
*– Wings*

Wings: Whoa! Pregnancy has made you all goth, eh? Which is funny because before I got knocked up I used to listen to a lot of punk and old-school angry hiphop. I loved that shit. Especially NWA. Then, it was so weird, as soon as those hormones got pumping, I was flicking the dial to easy listening. You know who I can't get enough of now? Faith Hill! She's this really nice white Barbie who sings about stuff like heartbreak and tractors and Jesus. WTF! I guess it's true what they say about pregnancy being 'miraculous.' Anyway, the nurse at TeleHealth asked me too many questions, then told me, in a super-solemn voice, that I should go to the hospital. But they always say that, right? I'll check in with you guys when I get back. The bleeding seems to have let up a little, so I'm not too worried ...
– *New Country Girl*

Hey NC – let us know what the docs say, eh? We're rooting for you.
– *Straight Shooter*

Thanks, SS. Can I ask you guys – what does it feel like for you when the baby moves?
– *New Country*

When I was a child, my father packed us all into a van and we headed down to Florida, through Ontario, Ohio, then all those friendly-waitress states with the fat people and big brass belt buckles. We stayed in a pink hotel near the beach and I remember my parents as distant figures prone on beach towels. One evening my father showed me a photograph of a diamond-shaped sea creature in a glossy pamphlet. He told me the creature was a stingray and I should beware of stingrays. I had never been told to beware of anything before and I liked the sound of it – I felt I had entered a dark and brambly thicket, a new and exciting chapter of the quest that was my life. The stingray was silver and translucent, a dangerous sea treasure. It could lie quietly, stealthily on the ocean

floor. A person could step on a stingray and be in mortal danger. How do they move? I asked my father. They flap, he said, and performed the most amazing and strange movement I have ever seen, his arms fluid from his shoulders, pulsing slowly up and down as if the air were water. It was beautiful and dangerous, and so unlike my father, and I understood immediately why I must beware. When I first felt my baby move I was reminded of that stingray, and of my father. It was the most astounding thing, those dangerous wings undulating in my belly. I will never forget it.
– *Wings*

Wings: GOYHH! Women have been giving birth to babies for millennia. What's with all the figurative language and self-importance? What makes you so special? I, for one, could do without it.
– *Straight Shooter*

Dear Wings: You might want to consult your midwife about these mood swings you are experiencing. It's possible there are deep-breathing techniques or yoga postures that may help you feel more grounded and calm. Maybe even talk to your partner about the feelings you are having – and there are some great resources on the internet, agencies you could talk to. You have a new life growing inside you – how *blessed* is that? Congratulations!
– *Spiral Woman*

Spiral: I will not tell my husband about the wings, extra ribs or morbidity of my thoughts – although he, like me, delights in theory and fancy that bucks convention, and it is likely his scalp scent that perfumes my world. As for the internet – we have both been busy with it. The 'facts,' panic mongering and treacly reassurances I could do without, but I have some interest in the lists of baby names from the 1920s. There is a sense of both giddy optimism and hard-won stoicism following the great war that is reflected in the era's monikers. Who could help but admire an

Albert? And could a Ruth be anything but trustworthy? I have told very few people about the pregnancy, which is why I am using this anonymous forum to get some 'feelings' off my fierce and cavernous chest. You sound like a moron.
– *Wings*
PS Grounded? Isn't that what happens when airplanes get stuck on the tarmac?
PPS I don't have a midwife.

I know maybe this is off topic or in the wrong thread or whatever, but I wanted to tell everybody that I finally felt it – the baby – sorry, Country Girl, not to make you feel bad or anything – and it didn't feel at all like they said, like ripples or waves. It felt like something with lots of right angles and willpower. It felt like maybe it was angry. Do you think a baby can be angry in utero?
– *Spiral*

Hello, my sisters! I am a member of another forum for new Christian mothers, but I LOVE the openness of these posts. So welcome and *refreshing.* Don't get me wrong; I still love Jesus, but I love the way all you ladies can *connect*, even when it's through a keyboard. NC – I'm praying for you!
– *Christian Mom!*
PS I have all of Faith Hill's albums!

Wings: Also – I think you are reading too many serious books. They say when you are pregnant you should skip the evening news and just try to watch fun TV shows and read light magazines (like maybe *Cosmo* or that other one that's about shopping). Otherwise it can be overwhelming. Maybe get your husband to run you a bath. But not too hot – you don't want to raise your body temperature. And light some candles – but not too smelly, I know the nose is sensitive! That way you can float away your troubles for a while. (Oh, and I kinda think

Buddhism might be more your thing. Christianity is just so *fraught*, y'know?) *Love Your Bump!*
*– Spiral*

Spiral: *What* can be overwhelming? You sound like you've been watching too many 'fun' shows. I think I hate you.
*– Wings*

Does anybody else think Wings is just a *teensy* bit abusive?
*– Spiral Woman*

Hey gals! Just waiting to be seen by the ob-gyn – they have these nifty heavy-duty laptops attached to the waiting room chairs – très Japanese. Spiral: Wings is just telling it like how she sees it. That's okay. We need to have someplace we can do that. And dissent is healthy, even among pregnant chicks. I mean, there is a level of niceness, generosity and solidarity I can appreciate ... But we need to be honest with each other, because no one else really wants to listen, do they?
*– New Country*

NC: You are so right! We can exclaim all we like about equity and gender equality, but when it comes to it, when it comes to this – being a vessel – we've got a lock on the correct (or unlucky) XY that allows us to ferry another human around while they form bones, bloom lungs and grow soft, downy hair like strange and darling amphibian monkeys, their tiny eyes squeezed shut, their hiccupping bodies gulping down what they know and stuttering it up again. So it seems strange to me that we would not find a bond, but stranger still that what bonds us is the outer trappings – the teensy bonnets and plastic gadgets, the miniature bits and bobs that clutter up aisles in jumbo stores and infringe on dreams by amplifying them. Isn't it enough that we are colonized by our own bodies?
*– Wings*

Wings: *You* are so right! All those products demand sameness instead of discussion, they make us want and want and talk about the same things. It's better, no, that we disagree and tussle with each other once in a while? OTOH, I have them at home: onesies with yellow daisies embroidered on the bum, one of those newfangled carrier wraps it would take an origami expert to master. I am far from immune.
– *New Country*

Oh, NC, I have one of those wraps! I can totally show you how it works! It took me nine hours over three days, but I finally got it! It broke me, though; I cried. I wouldn't want anyone to go through what I went through. I'll email you detailed instructions, some pics and good vibes.
– *Sheila K.*

Hi everybody. NC here. So, the bleeding has let up a bit, but I've been ordered on bed rest. I'm to stay off my feet, lie on my left side and 'do nothing.' I've been doing nothing except thinking for the last six hours, lying here while Devoted Husband is at work keeping himself busy. And I'm pretty sure doing nothing is no good for the soul, even if it helps with the leaky womb. Maybe it's not the time or the place for this, but I can't sleep and I can't help wondering if my troubles today are somehow related to some work I did once ... if a job, duties of the past, can somehow – like asbestos or mould – seep into a person's bloodstream. I keep thinking of that line Hamlet's mother said when she was feeling all guilty – for some reason it sticks in my head, always has. Spots on her heart that will not leave their *tinct.* I feel like maybe I'm tincted – or tainted. Whatever.

Here's why: I spent some time – seven or eight months I guess – as an escort. Not the kind you might be thinking, although that sort would probably be less offensive to some of you ... Oh, gotta go, more later! DH home, phone ringing. Must get vertical, but slooowly.
– *NC*

Girl! I did the escort thing for four months in university. It's the reason I was able to take Anthropology of Sex, Gender and Power and Feminist Perspectives on Pedagogy and Academe. I'll leave you to parse the irony in that. Hey – don't feel tincted! We're humans here; we're allowed to follow our noses, our hearts, our cunts, our convictions. We're even allowed to fuck up. I mean, as long as you're no serial killer, right? Karma doesn't work that way, friend. Actually, I'm not really sure karma works at all.
– *Craving City*

Oh, thanks, Craving, for your response! But I was actually a different kind of escort – sometimes I think it would have been better if I was some kind of high-class ho. But I was no fancy hooker, nope.

I worked at a downtown abortion clinic escorting the 'clients' to their appointments. My woman and I would march from the foot of the path on the sidewalk, through the picketers, up the steps to the clinic's doors. It was a pretty physical job – I kept my elbows cocked like guns at my sides, my strides short and powerful. I had to keep us both steady. Sometimes the path seemed endless, the march forward so relentless. At these times, I looked down at my army boots, with their steel toes and round clown tops, and really felt myself a soldier, disconnected and pure. The enemy was everywhere, lurking in a booby-trapped underbrush. I didn't understand exactly what it was they said as they waved their picket signs. (cc: Funny, but not ha-ha, what you said about serial killers, because a couple of protestors had signs like this: ABORTIONISTS = SERIAL KILLERS.) I could read the signs, but for some reason I could never make out the words they spoke; their shouts came at me in angry staccatos, the machine-gun fire of the righteous. So there was only the march forward, my prisoner and charge at my side. You know, I'm not exactly a physically strong person, but my thighs are big in relation to the rest of my body. I've clipped hundreds of articles from magazines, tips on the camouflage and slimming illusions that should be applied to these things. But in this job my thighs were my secret weapons; my pretty haunches gave me a heft I didn't think was possible. They helped me to push through. I thrust them forward, and they carried me.

Okay, getting sleepy. More later. Why does lying in bed make me so tired?
– *New Country*

New Country: They have done studies that show that unwanted children grow up to be criminals, miscreants, molesters and general fuck-ups. They clog our prison systems; they come into this world unloved, wreak havoc and go out the same way they came in, in a cloud of ambivalence and shame. Do not feel bad about the work you did. Even on a purely practical level, you did the world a favour, saved us all some tax dollars and prevented a small societal seam from bursting.
– *Straight Shooter*

Straight Shooter: I feel sorry for you. Your soul has fled your body, left you all scooped out and sad. What brash arrogance you show, what blatant disregard for human family. It has been proven in numerous studies that in fact the enormous guilt women feel after aborting a precious baby later leads to child neglect and abuse. If you would like more information, you are welcome to join me at a meeting with my brothers and sisters in Love.
– *A Concerned Citizen*

Um, WADR, since when do we care about the opinions of one 'Concerned Citizen' (ahem, and WTF Christian Mom?) with a whole pile of Bibles to thump? When I was fifteen I had an abortion. BFD. Some shithead took advantage when I'd had one too many swigs of peach schnapps. My mom came with me to the clinic, and afterwards we went for Swiss Chalet. I remember how

I cried a little into the special sauce and my mom pretended not to see except she passed me an extra serviette. We never told my dad though. New Country, you're a hero in my books.
– *Craving City*

Ladies, I swear on my pile of Bibles (I really do have a pile, different editions and such ... ) that Concerned Citizen is not me. Really, truly. I mean, I don't approve exactly of, you know, the A-word, but I would never be so mean. That is totally not God's way. Please believe me.
– *Christian Mom!*

Hi y'all! Thank you for your responses, but I feel like I ran out of steam before I reached the end of my story, and being bedridden makes me obsessed with finishing things ... And because I am here, in this unofficial waiting room, on the brink of something, and I consider y'all my family of sorts – my sweet bodiless friends, with nothing to talk about but your bodies – I feel the need to confess.

Once we reached the clinic, I would lead my charge up the stairs and help to check her in. She never looked at me and I never thought this rude. I did get the occasional clinger, whose grip on my arm became claw-like during our approach and whose weepiness I could feel without having to look at her. I allowed this like a man, giving several brisk, open-palmed pats to the back. I was stoic and strong until later I found myself trembling in the parking lot lighting up a cigarette – at least a pack a day during those months. After the procedure was complete, sometimes I was asked to escort the woman from the clinic to her car. The women, as they left, shook off my gallant overtures. They were spent and miserable, or relieved and giddy, but felt they should walk alone with the weight of their decision. I was paid very well for the job and there was only one time when I felt I could be in real danger. I remember the day so well, more vividly even than my wedding day. Is that strange? I think it is strange.

The particulars are all shiny in my mind's eye. It's bizarre I know, but I hold on to those details so tightly. I turn them around to look at them so much that sometimes I think I must change them just by holding them. But here it is, as I remember it: it was an overcast day, and it had rained earlier, a sudden downpour that sent the protestors scurrying to find shelter under a few earnestly planted municipal trees and shop awnings. I was glad to feel the rain; it cleared the way and gave me the opportunity to create an oasis under my big green umbrella. I had perfected the angle that kept us both dry, tilted slightly forward, positioned a foot or so above my companion's head. We were moving forward up the path, keeping a steady pace. She was tall, this client, and it was a challenge keeping the umbrella steady and in place. There were signs the sun might break through the clouds, and I knew this type of light was not a good sign for us. If the protestors were not too soggy they would be more riled up than ever – the sight of light struggling through dark clouds made them bold. I was just about to take the umbrella down so that we could move more quickly when I noticed a young woman break from the crowd and stand underneath a nearby tree. The woman was petite and brunette with corkscrew ringlets that brushed her shoulders – she was like a cherub carved into the top of a church pew. Her eyes were blue and blank. Her certainty made her so beautiful, which is why, I guess, I didn't think of her as a threat.

It wasn't until she was right next to us that I realized her intent. She had a switchblade clutched in one hand, flipped open and at the ready. It glinted like something from a 1950s musical – the moment felt all macho and melodious. I nearly laughed, but then I felt my woman tense and heard her sharp intake of breath. The world slowed down. The sun was still struggling in the sky. I wondered then if I was prepared to die for her, for this, for an idea of freedom and future that gives humans so much agency. I decided I was not, but neither could I allow the cherub to run and slash unchecked. It was too ridiculous. I shoved my woman behind me and squared my shoulders directly in front of my attacker. Then I punched the cherub, quickly and efficiently, in the nose. Odd, but I was thinking of sharks – how best to disorient one if it ever becomes overly aggressive while you are snorkelling in the tropics.

I broke her nose. The tears and the blood mingled on her lovely cheeks and she staggered away. My charge dusted herself off, took my arm again and pulled me towards the clinic. Thanks, she muttered, once I had seated her. No prob, I said. I never saw either of those women again.

And now here I am, leaking blood, confessing to strangers, already tallying all the moments in my life that might have been.
– *NC*

NC: Wings here. Thank you for choosing us to hold your story. To allow these shadowy corners access to the light is perhaps the most meaningful gift we can give each other. I say this with true feeling and conviction and – I hope – courage. You have inspired me to share my own story, you see. The fact is, I could have been one of your companions on your walks from sidewalk to doorstep, from relative innocence to murky knowingness. When I was twenty-three years old, I opted to end a pregnancy. I will not say it was a difficult decision at the time – you could say I saw no other option.

I had been travelling for eight months, backpacking for a few weeks with a childhood friend and then for various segments of time with other friends, who came to seem to me – in clouds of hash smoke, on train station platforms, in the lounges of youth hostels, on stone benches in public squares, sprawled on the grass that surrounded famous monuments – as friends I had known forever, as my soul's true companions.

When, back home in Toronto, I first began to feel queasy, I assumed I had brought back a souvenir, an opportunistic worm or virus simply playing its own role in my body's ecosystem. But then I was Late and Later, and I began to think about all the times in the

last six weeks I had allowed myself to be seduced by the wave of sensation that meant I could gather another human into me. When I peed on that wand and saw that crucifix, it did seem to me just another short-term burden to bear. I had to get rid of it. And if I had not? I don't know. I think I might have married my cousin's ex. He had a wrinkle on his forehead that made him seem kind, and he listened to me when I drank too much Gato Negro. But he was not what I needed. I knew that then, and I know it now. I wish I could say I mourned the loss of life but I could not, not when all I knew of my own past, present and future was the result of my own arrogant spirit tentacling out to touch as much of the world as I could ... Sometimes I think I should be asking someone or something forgiveness, but instead I am overcome by a gut-wrenching gratitude. Who is it I'm thanking? I'm not sure. I'm still not sure.
– *Wings*

Holy crap, Wings! Why don't you give it up and write a novel already?
– *Straight Shooter*

Oh Wings! Thank you so much for sharing. I knew that bristly exterior was hiding something mushy and vulnerable. You don't have to respond to this note – I just wanted you to know I understand and I forgive you for your earlier cranky posts.
– *Spiral*

Spiral: I definitely was not asking *your* forgiveness. And I still think you've been sniffing too much incense.
– *Wings*

Hi Everybody! Sheila K. here. I've been reading your entries like crazy – when I get home from work or running errands I sometimes have to stop myself from running first to the computer before stopping to pee – and believe me, I really have to pee! I guess

I just felt like I had to put my two cents in as far as this whole debate or discussion is concerned. I know there are as many opinions out there as there are birds in the sky, but I feel like maybe I'm different. You see, I don't have a Bible to my name, never mind one I'd like to thump, but I also don't believe abortion is right. I'm not sure I've always felt this way; in fact I don't think I had an opinion, or at least not a fully formed one until very recently. I wonder sometimes if it was the birth of my first child that changed my outlook, but somehow I don't think so. I think instead it is a brand of certainty that comes with maturation, a commitment to a set of views that, when I was younger, I might have attributed to the stubborn rigidity of middle age, but that I now see as a kind of bravery. It's just that I believe that something, once started, should be carried through to the end. Maybe it's because everything in our lives has become so easily disposable. And I think – no, not *this*, you should not be allowed to do *this*. And I understand, I do, that there are issues of freedom, of gender, of a person's parameters being curtailed by others, of desperation and back alleys. But are we not an innovative, creative species that adapts, that finds ways to manage the unexpected? Should we not persist in filling gaps where gaps exist, evolve to take care of what we have created? What I'm trying to say is there must be more than one way to tidy our own chaos, no?
– *Sheila K*

Sheila: I hear you! I try to respect a person's choice, I really do, but I don't think any woman who's ever endured IVF – all that poking and prodding and waiting and wondering – would ever choose to end a pregnancy. It just seems like squandered opportunity, something wanton and wasteful.
– *Spiral*

POST REDACTED BY FORUM MASTER

What does 'redacted' mean? It sounds kind of French.
– *Straight Shooter*

Who is the Forum Master? I didn't know we had a Forum Master.
– *Spiral*

I think it might be God.
– *Craving City*

It's so weird to think of God using a computer!
– *Christian Mom!*

Why would God bother censoring us, anyway? When has he ever cared about women's whinging?
– *Straight Shooter*

Ah, the ghost in the machine. It's actually the perfect place for god to hang out, isn't it?
– *Wings*

I lost the baby.
– *NC*

Oh, New Country, what happened? *What happened?*
– *Spiral*

Apparently my cervix is incompetent – along with my tear ducts. I know I should cry. I should be crying, right? Instead I just feel like someone has stuffed dry straw into the hole where my heart is and I wish like crazy for a word that might burn it up, make me feel something, anything. That so much liquid could gush from me, that my little one could escape me on a tidal wave of blood, and I could be left feeling so arid and artificial … This can't be what it means to be human.
– *NC*

My heart goes out to you, New Country. And Jesus SEES you, He really does. He understands your anguish and loves you and feels your repentance even if you've not yet recognized it. My God is not a punishing God, but there are reasons, there is sense and order in this world, a plan, a structure of sorts that emerges if we take a moment to understand the scaffolding of our lives. It was SINFUL work that you did, helping abortionists to commit abominations. But you are beginning to understand now and that is what is IMPORTANT. You know all too well, I'm sure, considering your CONDITION, that what we carry in our wombs as women is NOT GARBAGE. You know, I am certain, that what stirs within you is LIFE. By eleven weeks a fetus is waking, sleeping, eating, DREAMING. Dreaming of a life outside his mother, but bathed in the light of mother's love, of God's love. Please be strong and understand that although you have made terrible mistakes, there is room for you here in the fold, that we will enfold you and keep you and your baby from harm.
– *On the Side of the Innocents*

Holy mackerel! Who is this nutjob? 'On the Side of the Innocents'? A bit unwieldy as a handle, no? I know we try to respect diversity of opinion here, but I have one word for you, New Country: ignore.
– *Spiral*

To ignore the word of God is to court disaster. *But when Jesus saw it, he was much displeased, and said unto them, Suffer the little children to come unto me, and forbid them not: for of such is the kingdom of God.* The souls you helped banish are with Jesus now. You will not be so lucky. There is a table reserved in a restaurant called Hades for you and your devil spawn. A special place reserved.
– *Concerned Christian*

New Country: Don't listen to these assholes with all their flaming fire and brimming brimstone. I also dreamed about your baby. He was small and dead. I held him in my palm then laid him on the ground. With my wings, I formed a kind of canopy overtop of him. I wove my feathers together to give him shelter. I protected him.
– *Wings*

New Country: Are you still there? Please don't go away because of a couple of kooks with some internet savoir faire and too many holy axes to grind. We're still here. And we love you.
– *Spiral*

Oh NC! I had to have a smoke when I read your news. About six 'ladies with handbags' (you know the type) gave me the dirtiest fucking looks as they passed me on my stoop, knocked up and sucking on a cig like my life depended on it. I'm so sorry, NC. Is someone with you? Where can you go? I hope you have pals there besides us, all stuck in our virtualness.
– *Craving City*

NC: This is probably not the right time to tell you this, but just the fact that you could conceive in the first place, well, that's a good thing. You'll have more chances, you will. Take good care.
– *Straight Shooter*

New Country: You should crank your old music – as loud as possible – until the neighbours make 911 calls. Then you should beat on things – your own breast, tabletops, the fridge door. Do not stop until you are entirely spent. Once you've had a rest, turn up the volume again.
– *Wings*

It is not fair that your baby died. It happens more than people like to admit or talk about, but it is in no way fair. DO NOT let anybody

tell you any differently. Stay away from parks and avoid schoolyards. Maybe take a vacation.
– *Straight Shooter*
PS *Table Reserved?!?*

Thanks, everybody, for all your props and kind words. I know that you are all speaking from your own truth, and that's what's important, even if it is difficult for me to absorb. I am writing to say goodbye as I don't quite fit in around these parts anymore. I wish you all the very best with your challenges, your joys, your wonderful tumult, the times when your faces are not lit by these crass, compelling, miraculous screens. Remember to talk to and touch each other whenever you can. As Faith would sing: 'The secret of life is there ain't no secret/And you don't get your money back.'
Peace and Punk Rock,
– *NC*

New Country – I'm guessing you are in Toronto … If you are, would you like to meet me for tea (or something stronger) one of these days? That is, if you're still listening …
– *Wings*

Wings: I'm still here. I tried but I can't turn off my laptop. I don't want to believe … I just don't want to. So Wings, I want you to keep doing your crazy-assed, lyrical, love-me-or-leave-me thing, I really do, but I don't want to meet you. I don't want to know you. It's just that – even though we're networked, connected, I guess – you're really NOT my family, are you? I don't even know what you look like, or what your voice sounds like or what hair products you use … And, to be honest, I'm just not sure I could deal with it – with you and your, well, your CONDITION, I guess, and by that I mean no offence I really don't –
– *New Country*

New Country: I know I am probably the last person you want to hear from – but I don't judge you, I don't! Gosh, just saying that makes me sound so sanctimonious, doesn't it? I am so sorry for your loss. I've been praying for you. I didn't want to jump into the fray before, with all those loony-tunes giving us God-fearers a bad name. I don't know what God wants us to do, or why He might have chosen your baby, or why He'd want to 'redact' anyone's post. I just believe in Him, and His Great Good Grace is all. I just have to believe in Him. Anyway, I just wanted to tell you, before you left, in case you didn't know, that I am also a Faith Hill fan!!! Especially the songs 'A Baby Changes Everything' which is totally not about what you might think – it's Jesus who is the baby! – and also 'You Bring Out the Elvis in Me' (not sure if you're really into Elvis … ). Take care of yourself, and God Bless.
– *Christian Mom!*

# Drowning Doesn't Look Like Drowning

FOR A LONG TIME MY FATHER refused to talk about the accident. That he considered me at fault was obvious and how to integrate this feeling seemed puzzling to him – although, of course, not to me. I had lost him as surely as I lost my mother, lost him to a recklessness that had been mere frivolity in the past. My mother's risk-taking had always been extravagant but well-ordered, but my father grabbed at dangerous opportunities as if at bullets zinging past him. He had dropped out of the Superior trip because a gig had come up, a friend who needed help moving some 'cargo.' Drugs? Maybe. Not weaponry, that was not his style. But that there was a hard edge, a large possibility of capture or injury, was a given. Sometimes wilderness trekking was too purely animalistic for him. Too distant from the intricacies of human infrastructures. Was my mother angry that he had cancelled – last minute – a trip that was meant to be my initiation into this type of adventuring? If so, she never showed it. In the days leading up to our departure, the expedition became ours alone – we gathered supplies, rolled and cubed clothes and gear into knapsacks built expressly for this purpose. She was a winker, my mother, and in those days she winked at me often, while reaching for a canister of propane, smoothing out a map, pointing out a buckle or clasp. Hugging me, the two of us wearing only our underwear and neon-orange life preservers.

I do not wink at my own children, or at other children, no matter how urgently the gesture seems called for. A slyness, a secret, an apology, an invitation, a harmless salaciousness, an embrace from a distance – I do understand it, its appeal, its charm. I wanted to wink at Nathalie, my first, the moment I laid eyes on her, such was my understanding of the great and serious joke we had shared, but I had broken blood vessels in my cheeks, torn my perineum in two places, my eyes were dry, Bruce was holding my hand too tightly. I could not seem to muster the necessary combination of muscle coordination, will and lightness of spirit required. I felt so sure she would have winked back. And then the moment passed. The little cub was on my chest, her oily face tipped up fiercely towards mine, then latched on to one of my nipples, attached.

If I tell you my mother winked at me while the plane was going down, would you believe me? Could you? It's not real, it's not serious, the wink said. I love and loathe my mother for that wink, a wink I may myself have imagined.

Yesterday was a hot day, the type that can only happen on the edge of the Great Lakes here in Toronto, the humidity a heavy canopy over the city, tamping down energy, smog, aspirations. I took the kids to the indoor pool, frightened of the soaring UV index, and I guess the combination of airborne moisture, nasty pollutants, the fumes from the chlorine – all were too much for James's little bronchioles to bear. I saw it coming: the too-deliberate breaths. A seven-year-old child paying attention to how he breathes is rare and wrong. The slowing of his physical movement and the slow turning inwards, the strange soul-quiet that follows … But before he got in the water he fished his puffer from his bag and sucked on it like a pro, and I thought, The cool water will help. I thought, He can handle this; modern medicine can handle this; I can handle this. It is the mother's pendulum that swings constantly between sheer panic and willed competence. But then he was dog-paddling weakly to the side while Nathalie and Sarah took turns dunking each other, emerging with bangs plastered over eyes like monsters or pop stars, pretending the bubbles they blew were farts, lifting ballerina legs to the sky.

I got an e-mail message the other day; it arrived in my inbox with a happy ping and the subject line *Drowning Doesn't Look Like Drowning.* A forward from a well-meaning fellow mother; the type of dire instructional counsel that circulates amongst us clucking hens. I try not to open them as a rule. I know the gist: Watch out for your kids. There are strangers, spiders, poisons, tornadoes, faulty slides, baddies lurking everywhere. Save them from their own stupid kid selves. But this one I read, eyes skating across the screen without my sanction, the rapid click and the blooming text. *Drowning people are physiologically unable to call out for help. The respiratory system was designed for breathing. Speech is the secondary or overlaid function. Breathing must be fulfilled before speech occurs.*

James could not pull himself out of the pool; I saw him gasp, then lower himself back into the water. I watched his eyes widen and his legs thrash as I scooped him – a fish tired of fighting – up and onto the deck. It's okay, kiddo, I said, it's okay. Let's get your puffer. He nodded, his eyes like leashes hooked on to mine. But the puffer did nothing and once they were all dressed – the girls' hair tangled pelts down their backs, the whining and wheezing from the back seat, the smell of chlorine and kid sweat – I drove him to the clinic at St. Joe's and called Bruce from my cell to come pick up the girls. And then I told James again how okay it really was, as the ER nurse tested his blood for oxygen, and gave me the look that said *Not okay*, and, somehow, *Your fault*, and *Hate this fucking job.* James had stopped wheezing then; his lips were turning blue around the edges, a terrifying resignation growing in his eyes.

I am tired. And I allow myself, through the scrim of my despair, a moment of irritation with James. There is a particular type of work that goes into achieving the harmony we have reached in my household. I remember what Bruce will not: Nathalie's volleyball practice after school, that Sarah will eat green beans only if they are dipped in mayonnaise. This is me, keeper of schedules and child foibles. Bruce is in charge of the jolly in our house: getting us up and out, treating the children like the physical, rough-and-tumble beings they are. Pushing them over, pulling their pigtails – our very own benign schoolyard bully. They adore it, even James, who is treated differently, it's true – gentle!

I have no illusions regarding my relative importance. I am thirty-three years old, a part-time baker, mother to three children. Still, I don't think it is unfair to say that it is the mother's calendar and not money that makes the world go around. I am an ordinary person who does not believe in diesel trains (I have demonstrated), honour killings (I have written letters) or blood diamonds (we wear plain platinum bands and I have signed online petitions). I believe in bread and certain uncalled-for forms of beauty. And I believe in the potential – I do! – of every human to effect a shift, some small change in the world. I volunteer in an after-school program for at-risk youth. The program is designed to teach them real-world coping skills. I bake bread with them, which – who's kidding who? – is nowhere near a survival skill; there *are* these things called supermarkets. So yeah, it's a weird, bourgeois, anachronistic luxury, I know. But, I tell them, it makes your house smell *really fucking good.* That scores me some points mainly because I curse but also because they can tell that I mean it. The smell of bread baking means safety and warmth, a cocoon-like protection they have never known.

It is possible I feel my children's vulnerability more keenly than other mothers, although we all have dark bruised spots on our pasts that never seem to heal. Instead of fading, they pass through the colours of the rainbow, shining dully, differently, on each and every moment in our lives. In my twenties, I searched for and found love everywhere. I was an intimacy junkie, and eventually my drug of choice stopped providing comfort – those sweet, cuddly highs – and my partners, sensing my need, either left or began to hurt me, pressing, pressing, on my bruises. A therapist at the time – wiry frame, wiry glasses, patchouli, geranium scent – explained myself to me. She said I was searching for the love I had lost, a mother's embrace like air or water, a mother's protection that surrounds, versus a father's more belligerent affection – the love that takes on all comers. I've often wondered if this is why I chose to have children, to provide that love that was stolen from me. If I could, I would submerge James in my love, provide healing through benediction, the iron clasp of my embrace.

We call Nathalie, our oldest, The Gnat; it is her nickname, superhero moniker, alter ego. There are times when you want nothing more than to slap her away, forcefully, to make her listen instead of speak, to silence her whine with a quick backhand swoosh. She is persistent, relentless in her demands; she will not go away. And there are times when her very presence, its drone and reliability, brings the most powerful form of reassurance. When Bruce picked the girls up from the hospital, Nathalie lifted the hair away from my ear. Mummy, Mummy, Mummy, she said. James has good lungs, just broken for now and he will breathe better soon, breathe better soon, breathe better soon. She grabbed me around the neck, choked me lightly, then let go, and when I gasped with relief her eyes said, See? Sarah was already clamped into her booster, looking out the window. Crisis embarrassed her, wounded her sense of invincibility and frayed the forcefield she wore like a cloak. I knew that when James pulled through – breathebetter-soonbreathebettersoon – and they were back home, lying like lizards on the floor, head to head, whispering secrets and incantations, Sarah would hurt him deliberately, a discreet pinch or tug at his hair. And when he winced, she would smile – her brother was back. She understands that the vulnerable cannot muster the energy to react to pain or feign indignation.

The hospital room was small and shabby; it had the feel of the Third World, or one of those crowded strip malls at the edge of this city. Something provisional and patched about it. None of the slick sanitization of one of the more monied downtown research facilities. But never mind. The nurses, unlike the harried intake nurse in ER, were bosomy and matter-of-fact. I curbed the urge to follow them to their storage rooms and efficient phones, to somehow absorb the secret of their large proficiency. I wanted to be near James when he woke up. I wanted to answer his questions with my own calm truth. I wanted him to know that although his breath might elude him, I would not.

It got worse before it got better – his lips still blue, an IV in his arm. I watched the tube carefully – for what? – air bubbles, blood, a sign. Then I buzzed the nurses, who were beginning, and rightfully so, to become cross with me. I loved them even for their crossness. James was sleeping fitfully, his breath still laboured. I have always considered my children in light of the age I was when my own mother died. It is the year – the seventh – that stands alone as crucible. Some superstitious part of me believes if they can get through that year unscathed they will make it through the rest – the fevers, the driving tests, the battered hearts, the scabs and shitheads in the playground. And if they survive, somehow I will, somehow I *can* also. But James! It would be a lie – and so inequitable – if I said I loved him best (oh, I love him best!).

And now here we are, steroids pumping into his arm, oxygen mask over his little helpless mug. And I am thinking about my mother and yearning for her and so glad she is not here to see this.

From a young age, I believed God was less Spirit than Sasquatch, a mythical figure very much of this earth – not quite human, although possessed of wise Neanderthal-like qualities. A creature perched alone and unique on its very own evolutionary limb – what it would be to glimpse this creature! Not something you could share widely; who would believe you? And would you really want to share? You didn't share God or trumpet him to the masses, nor did you hoard him – you acknowledged him when He emerged. And if you searched for him you were likely to be endlessly frustrated or attacked by his sham of a likeness around every corner. This was a philosophy I had arrived at mostly through my parents' use of the phrase 'God's country,' which they used to describe remote spaces – uncaring, oblivious spots on the globe where humans had little dominion. I understood that to visit these places was a privilege, that to even breathe God's air, to track him by his prints and scat, was a great and awesome thing. So that when we took off from Thunder Bay in our float plane, Michipicoten Island in our sights, all eleven of us and our various gear, I knew immediately, from that first glance out the window, from the hush that fell over us as we looked down upon the impenetrable forests, their variegated greens, smoky browns, the great sky squeezing up around us, that we were entering God's country and that to acknowledge it was both sacrilege and necessity. My mother nuzzled my head. God's country, she said, and we nodded slowly in solidarity.

Sarah, my youngest, is five now and, strangely, already the one who needs me least. I watch her sometimes while she is playing – building a tower or drawing castles or cats. Her concentration, her focus, would be the envy of most adults. And I think, yes, she would make it fine if I were gone. She would feel the loss as something sudden and violent – a bullet that came out clean – then she would pick herself up and carry on. There is something of the stoic cowgirl to her, in the way she has, already, learned to curse: quietly, authentically. Oh, shit, shit, shit, she mutters when the tower tumbles, when the cat's ears have the look of odd antennae. Then she carries on.

James is finally sleeping soundly, quietly, his breaths less rasp than whisper. We can be forgiven for believing it is angels or fairies – ridiculous, exquisite-winged creatures – who ride on rafts of air composed of children's sleep-sighs. It took me weeks before I could turn my back to Nathalie, even while she slept. I was convinced the very fact of my gaze was keeping her alive – how easy it would be for her, so tiny, so mysterious, to be spirited away.

I have been known to drool on and over my children – when they were infants bundled snugly in my arms, attached to my nipple like barnacles. You're tired, Bruce would say, if he witnessed it, and, yes, the fatigue in those first weeks robs a woman of her sense and dignity, makes vanity a frill in itself. It is the kind of exhaustion that crosses over into a deep, sensual sorrow, everything leaky and askew. When I breastfed, I felt the world's sadness in my throat. I wanted to spit it out and instead I had to swallow it. Still, I can tell you, it was not fatigue or sadness that made me drool over my kids but a slack-jawed adoration, an awe larger and more compelling than love.

My husband is a good man. Still, sometimes in the middle of the night when one of the children has woken us with an earache or outrageous request, he will stare at me, sleep-sodden and merciless, as if I am a stranger who has stolen everything from him. And it is possible I have. *Gentle* is our word, our mantra and slogan and motto. It is our family philosophy and religion. But the way we have sex is the opposite: brusque, silent, its gestures brutal and sharp. Afterwards we laugh and do not speak. And then there is laundry and eavestroughs and crocodile tears and a dishwasher to unload. When we first met, and the moment arrived for me to tell this story, the story of my mother, he listened quietly, then said, Let's not talk about this anymore. You are here. Your mother is not. And he was right; he loves me.

I know I am fortunate. I have taken my place in the world with relative ease. My children are fed, clothed, educated. We hug them all the time. This is not the case for everyone. The school counsellor tells me things about the youth I bake with; I listen and shake my head. They have drawn short straws, it's true. Easy, easy, easy, they say (although everything in their lives is not), high-fiving each other with great tenderness as they come through the door. I love to listen to them; the camaraderie in their shared aggression. *You don't know shit, yo, why not go somewhere like Canada's Wonderland instead of sitting around in that shitty old shed? Oh yeah, why you got a duffel bag and not a knapsack? Low-budget, man, low-budget.* They steal my phone all the time, play games and coax strange images and sounds from it. *Look, turn it sideways, you gots a sexy chick. Whoa, who did that? I did it because I'm king, dawg.* Then, when they notice me watching, they berate me in a way that makes me feel like maybe they like me a little. *Miss, why you always gotta be so in-on? Non? No! In-on! In-on! Like in on every little thing we doin'.* And I think, I am *so* not. In-on. Anything, really. And: What would it feel like to be truly in-on. The 'hood. The world. Your head might just explode. They are the type of kids who are frightening to some people. But for a long time they did not scare me. Then one day I answered a call whose number came up BLOCKED. And someone said *Hello*, conversationally, kindly, even. Then, *I'm gonna kill your fucking babies, bitch.* And it undid me. The next session we baked a large round sourdough loaf. I brought butter and blackberry jam and we slathered it on and ate together like family. But I was watching them in a way that friends should never watch each other. My *children*, I thought. You little shits, you threatened *my children.* Still, the bread smelled really fucking good, and the way those ratty teenagers ate – their eyes surprised and glad – made me forget for a moment, it really did.

Outside the window, I can see the highway, cars crawling along the edge of the lake. It was a room like this where I had my babies, all three of them entering the world as a line of cars streamed past below. The children anchor me, I suppose. Sarah was a Caesarean – they scooped her out of me whole, but the other two were natural, or as natural as these things get. With James I can remember a feeling of impending collapse – I was in the middle of pushing him out when I informed my midwife that I had to sleep. You're having a baby, she said. It was a soft command and a statement of fact. She was telling me to live. Bruce was fetching a cloth for my forehead, and when he walked towards me, cloth outstretched, all concern, I did not, could not recognize him. Why have they let that strange man into my room? I thought. This is what these moments do – they unhinge us from the known, from the familiar, the family. They give us a freedom to let go, to fall asleep, to let it all fall away.

James has regained some of his colour; his forehead is warm, so smooth, when I bring my lips down to kiss him. Soon they will be arriving – the rest of the tribe – and we will strap ourselves into our little metal box and ease onto the highway with the rest of them.

There were eleven of us on the plane and I have always considered this a beautiful and accursed number – I was so obviously an add-on, an extra bead on the abacus. I watched her drown. I have tried to soften or mitigate this fact my whole life, but it remains: it is truth, perhaps the only solid fact I can pull from the whole story. Still, here is how I remember it: a bumpiness, as if the plane were a car going over train tracks – the three modes of transportation suddenly, weirdly, melded – then a sharp drop that made us suck in our breaths and clasp hands, then another, more dramatic drop, the wink, then a clap as terrifying as the fiercest thunder, and a blank. A shooting pain in my shoulder, the cold and the darkness liquid around me and a sick-making need to clamber my way up to surface, to her. And then, once I had seen the sky and breathed the air, a deep unease, a heaviness of limbs. The waves were large, and because of my fatigue I did not fight them, but let the swells carry me; it was if the water were inside me then, cold, so cold, forceful and roiling. I have had the same sensation only once since, standing far from the beach on the shores of Lake Erie, the undertow tugging at my shins, my family safe and sand-speckled on land. That day, I felt the sun on my shoulders and the water around me, inside me, all womb, all soft danger and unrelenting life. I felt my mother that day.

She bobbed up two waves over, her hair slicked neatly back from her face. Did I call out to her? I feel certain that I did, but I have read that within minutes severe cold clouds rational thought. In my memory she is beautiful and strange, comical even, her lips parted in an O of surprise, the face she made when she came upon me in the back of the closet, crouched silently behind the shoe rack, smiling at my cleverness. *Drowning people's mouths alternately sink below and reappear above the surface of the water.* Of course she must have known I was there! I floated, my feet barely fluttering, my clothes ballooning up around me. Afterwards they told me that the air in the jacket and my lack of skill as a swimmer had perhaps saved me. The cold became relaxing to me, I didn't have the sense to panic. I saw another person, maybe two, in the periphery, and it seemed to me they were calling out, to each other and to me. *Physiologically, drowning people who are struggling on the surface of the water cannot stop drowning to perform voluntary movements such as waving for help, moving towards a rescuer or reaching out for a piece of rescue equipment.* I think they were counting, numbering off. Did they assign me a number? If so, I have since forgotten it.

According to legend, Lake Superior seldom gives up her dead. She gave me up because I was not quite dead. My heart had slowed. Children's hearts are more capable of this slowing, this playing dead. The colder the water, the better, the more effective the response. The blood concentrates its attention and its circulation on the important bits – brain, lungs, heart. The lake held tight to my mother – who would not? They never retrieved her body. Normally bodies puff up with the gas generated from decay. Then they rise like bath toys to the surface. And they are found. But, they tell me, the cold water didn't let bacteria grow in my mother. She was allowed to sink.

I am not brave enough to leave them. It is untrue that bravery and love go hand in hand. Love is its own form of cowardice. If I were brave I would rent a car and drive north to the shores of Superior. I would go in the summer, when the water temperatures are not immediately torturous. I am a strong swimmer now and I want time to feel the smooth cold on my skin. I would wade; I would float; I would use my arms and legs to pull me far away from safety. And once the grey waves surrounded me, I would look up into the sky, salute this worn-down world and submerge. I would join my mother.

James wakes up as if he has heard my thoughts; as if now that I have pulled him back, he must pull me back too. Hi, Mum, he says. He smiles. Is it possible for a seven-year-old to be sardonic? Hi James, I say. He looks around. Nice room. Only the best, I tell him, and squeeze his hand. But he means it; he likes this room. He knows it saved him. Still: Can we go home now? Yep, your dad and sisters are on their way. Excellent, he says. He inclines his head towards the TV. Can we watch some shows? I shake my head. I think we have to pay. But when I get up and try the button – the television mounted on its very own space arm – it works. A rerun of *Welcome Back, Kotter*. Is this the only channel we get? He makes a face that makes my heart twitch with irritation and gratitude. Beggars can't be choosers, I say. What does that mean? says James. It means, count yourself lucky. What does that mean? says James. It means, watch the show and I love you. I kiss him on the shoulder. Eww, he says. But he's still too weak to push me away. On the screen, John Travolta's jeans are too tight and everybody looks too old to be in high school, but James gets into it, and after a few minutes, so do I.

# Impossible to Die in Your Dreams

## Eliza: Soup out of Stones

WHEN MY GRANDDAUGHTER Annie was ten, she started talking like a wrestler from a fable. 'I regard you as a nail in the eye and a thorn in my muscle,' she'd say. 'I will trounce you,' she'd shout, with her arms raised, fists clenched. That was after the three-month period when she insisted on watching *As the World Turns* standing on her head with the backs of her knees propped against the recliner. She said it made more sense that way. There's no contesting the wisdom of children. Now, there she is, all dolled up to the nines and tens, ready to wed. And in such a place! I'm not one for religion, but still, a brewery tugs at the old constraints of credulity. And her sister Samantha, always the ornery one, scowling in the corner. Went and got herself a P-H-D and traipsed around the world. Places herself above weddings and other normal human interactions. Thinks tripping through a rice paddy in Vietnam lends her some smarts inaccessible to the likes of me and Bea.

'Why the beanie?' says my friend Bea, nudging.

'Not a beanie, Bea, *yar-mah-kah.* He's Jewish. But not strict or anything. Eats whatever's placed in front of him.'

'Shh,' says Samantha, who has now seated herself behind us. She refused to be a part of the ceremony – said it was antiquated and patriarchal. But now she sits shushing, blinking back tears and choking on love. Guess they never put the term *hypocrisy* on the syllabus at her fancy schools.

Annie's a beautiful girl, wilful and often ill-mannered, but a survivor. It's odd seeing her in white, in a gown, looking like a Cinderella doll with shiny cheeks and teeth. I had them like that – bones and teeth that thrived and gritted and bolstered. Not anymore. But I still got a couple of gnashers, rising proud like tombstones from the gum. I once heard a sprinter on the TV talk about hitting his stride. *I had my legs under me*, he said. I'm the same, legs still under me. And I know some things.

Ah, here they are now, pronouncing the same old promises we go on promising: to be true, to take care, to grow old together.

And the kiss – under the silk huppah, the clean, striving buildings and the blue, blue sky. Perfect. And impossible to fulfill, though we sweat and ache and die trying.

'Jewish, eh?' says Bea as the bride and groom stride past, well-fed youth with years ahead. 'Will she have to wear that scarf?'

Bea's sparky and tough, but crosses wires.

'That's Muslims, Bea,' says Samantha, sighing. 'There are some of those here too. Plus some Gentiles turned Jews, a couple of Catholics with questions, some lapsed Buddhists, or Buddhists ascending.' Samantha scans, then sighs again. 'Some who just do a lot of yoga.'

'Any lesbians?' says Bea.

'That's not a religion.' Samantha gets up to congratulate and circulate.

'Coulda fooled me,' says Bea. 'What with the protests and parades.'

After the snap-snapping of photos, the well-wishers are herded by Samantha through the shipping doors – passageways from a far-off, enchanted land, too tall for mortals – and into the dining hall, with its soaring ceilings and portentous, yeasty smells. Long medieval tables dressed in white have been set up along the walls. But outside there is the CN Tower, that spire of silver and concrete, people being sucked up through its centre as if caught in God's gigantic straw. Bea and I sit out on the patio, watching it all. The rabbi who married the couple – a humanistic feministic Jew with a batik scarf draped around her large bosoms – is mingling with the crowd. I can tell that Bea approves of the woman by the way she followed the ceremony, mouthing along as if at a rock concert.

'Do you remember your own wedding, Eliza?' she asks me, then pauses to reflect and point towards the hustle and bustle of celebration. 'Do you remember this?'

'Yes,' I say. 'Yes, I do.'

And she nods the slow, sad nod of the never married.

A blue jay wings its way across the sky, alights on a scraggly shrub.

'Did I ever tell you about my neighbour's canaries?' Bea is alert again, ready.

*Once, twice, thrice,* goes the refrain in my brain, but I shake my head no.

'The sweetest songs they sang. So peaceful for such bright yellow things. And none of us knew the reason why. Helen would bring them out in their copper cage to the garden, and I'd listen to them while I weeded. Well, it wasn't until years later I learned the reason for their dreamy song. It was cannabis seeds she fed them! Carted the seeds from Greece every time she went back. No one ever blinked an eye or sniffed her out. Picked them from her brother's field. A whole crew of chirpy little drug addicts keeping me company as I plucked dandelions from the soil. Do you believe it? Would you ever have dreamed that one up?'

'No,' I say. 'No, I could not.'

We shift from side to side, heave ourselves up and begin the trek inside. There is a beat or two while we breathe and step. We have it down, our rhythm, our particular intermissions.

'But that's not the whole story when it comes to canaries,' I say. There are times when it is important to come back at Bea with an interesting fact, a tidbit of information. 'My grandfather kept his at the back of the garden – was determined to breed them with the pigeons. Figured if the damn flying rats were to be a nuisance, they could be nuisances with some talent.'

'Yes,' says Bea. 'Right you are.' We shuffle our way past a thin, glowering waiter placing cutlery and napkins just so, last night's libations weighing heavily on his brow. 'Couldn't get them to do it though, could he?' Bea nudges me, something lascivious in her eyes.

'No, he couldn't. They'd screw their own kind silly, but you couldn't get them to give the time of day to a stranger.'

'Too true,' says Bea, sated. 'Too true.'

It's like this with us. We know each other's stories like we know the shapes of our own noses.

Samantha comes over and settles us into the reception area, hands us tall glasses full of fizzy, pink drink.

'Cheers.' She clomps off, too thick-waisted and heavy-footed for her delicate getup. She's an odd duck, that one. As pretty and petal-like as her sister when she wants to be, but het up with notions of a world out of her reach. Out of everybody's reach.

Last week, I had a dream where I flew. But it wasn't the flying you expect from a dream – the soaring freedom of being airborne, carefree. I could fly only a short distance off the ground, and for me, flying was like swimming. I breaststroked my way around town, just over the heads of my friends and family. Not hovering, but floating as if on water, supported and stymied by the thickness of the air. There was my daughter, teenaged and bold, holding a pantsuit aloft, wanting a button stitched, the hem fixed. And my husband, with a teacup outstretched, his Brylcreemed hair flopping sideways, a sly eyebrow in view. The town, which was my world, had gravel paths instead of roads, a pink stop sign at every corner. Bea was there, in an easy chair by the river. And that bastard Bobby, sitting on a bench by the newsstand. Annie was inside buying penny candy, her pigtails straggling free of their fasteners. I swam over to cuddle her, to hold her in my arms, carry her on my back, so we could swim away from Bobby and his groping fingers, his eyes that stroked and cajoled. But it was hard going. I could not reach her, my kick was weak and tadpole-like. She strode out of the store and he called her over – three times her age and one third of her intelligence! *Annie!* I shouted. And she turned to look up at me, her inept angel. But I could only ever say her name. Whatever warning was blossoming in me stuck like a lozenge in my throat. She smiled and waved. She sat next to Bobby and counted out her sweets with him, put them in three piles in his outstretched palms. *Annie*, I said. She smiled up at me again, her cheek bulging with the shape of a jujube. And then I woke up.

'I don't think it's about death,' I say to Bea. Atonement, maybe. Not death.

'No, no, not death,' says Bea. 'Impossible to die in your dreams.'

But this is not what I mean. To die in a dream would be nothing. But to feel it coming down the pipe, to have to do battle with all your willed innocence and slick helplessness. And my daughter, with the same cheery sense of entitlement she wore as a child, a blamelessness she cannot really feel in her core – where is she today while her own daughter twirls and basks?

Bea grunts softly over her supper, concentrating like an animal. My husband, Frank, would make these same noises, little sighs and half-words dedicated to himself as he ate. There were days I could've clocked him for it – a right hook to the jaw – or ended it swiftly, bringing the cast iron down cleanly on the top of his head. Other days, the tiny clicks and deep echoes of his very swallowing filled me with such brutal tenderness it took my breath away. Still, I never begrudge Bea her private sounds and satisfactions. It is one of the luxuries of the elderly – to skirt niceties in the name of infirmity. But now here they are, the couple of the hour, rising to thank us and praise each other.

'Would you look at our Annie,' I say. Bea is licking her index finger to collect crumbs from the table. She looks. We both look.

Who is this young woman – mouth open in declamation, hand over her heart – if not a strange beacon to us all? There was a story – her favourite – I used to read to her when she was a child. In the story a village was starving, hoarding what they little had. And into this village came a hobo with less than nothing. But faith in life's little improvisations – *this* he had. He helped them make soup out of stones.

'He's got a good shape, does he not?' asks Bea of Philip, the groom.

'So he does,' I say. It's true. A birthmark like the boot of Italy down the side of his face, but a good shape, and even better sense.

A pretty girl with chunky arms clears our dishes, the wedding cake is wheeled onto the dance floor. Annie and Philip step forward, sink a knife into the creamy frosting.

Everything speeds up, tightens, then expands inside of me. I am at the park with Annie. Samantha has skulked off to the pool with one of her pals – covetous with her plans and preparations. Annie is wearing dungarees and a sleek hairstyle. She is eleven, with two new soft knobs for nipples. She runs from tree to tree, actually leaps to catch a white and blue butterfly and succeeds. She comes to me, her hands clasped around the creature. 'Gran,' she says. She looks me in the eye. 'Bobby calls me his butterfly.' She opens her hands, exposes her palms like a beggar. We watch it together, the darting, fluttering thing, as it spirals up into the sky like ash. Like confetti. Like the suddenly free, short-lived secret that it is.

Ah, but now she dances. And now she is in the air herself, on her throne, a queen hefted high by friendly drunks. Our Annie, clutching the sides of her chair, terrified, alone, triumphant.

'Earth to Eliza,' says Bea. 'Who's that Samantha's talking to?'

'Couldn't say,' I reply. It is a man carrying himself well, older than Samantha, though not by much. He is taking her hand for the hora, leading her into the fray.

'It's a good dance for the hebes,' says Bea, clapping along. 'For everybody.'

'Yes.' It is a good dance, bodies linked in circles, grapevining around the dance floor, shoulders shifting this way and that, the elation of arms raised.

*'L'chaim,'* I practise softly.

## Samantha: A Room of One's Own

'You're not dancing?' He is tall, this man, his black hair expensively, if modestly, coiffed, and although he does not carry one, Samantha imagines he would suit a cane, a prop of some kind.

'No. Just absorbing it all.'

'From here?' he says. He takes Samantha by the hand and soon she is in it, being swept back and forth, Annie's mother-in-law winking at her from the left, her father waving from the sidelines, his look of perpetual surprise deepened by the sight of her, of her joy. Yes, this must be it. She's drunk and duped into sentiment, into belonging. And her father, so solemn in tone and matte in manner, seems to know something about her she never suspected. How *can* he, when his most fervent interest, for as long as she can remember, or at least since her mother left, has been the building of ships in bottles? She had always dismissed this hobby as an exercise in maddening patience, requiring only the miracle of single-mindedness, a steady hand and overly long pincers. She thought he had shut out the wider world for a fantasy encased in glass, but now here he is acting as though he knows her, as if he can see not into her brain, which is tangled like a briar patch, but into her future, the twisting tunnel that is her very life.

'Your sister is beautiful,' says the man, stooping to her ear. 'Philip told me as much.'

'She is incredible,' says Samantha, watching Annie spinning in the middle of their circle, arms outstretched. When the sisters were twelve and eight, a vast treacherous galaxy stretched between them. Annie was determined to navigate it. Samantha and her friends believed in witchcraft, blue eyeliner and using tongues when you kiss. Annie was their doll and plaything, a floppy, earnest version of themselves. They used her to play séance, to call up the power they felt surging through their bodies like new sap.

There was a blindfold, a purple bandana they rolled and knotted, then tied tightly around Annie's eyes. She was their medium, their conduit. 'One more spin, then stop,' said Samantha, then clasped her sister in a hard hug from behind, pushing her fist into the smaller girl's abdomen to drive out the air. Annie fainted, lay in a heap on the floor while Caroline and Soula conjured love, which meant a boy's hand moving downwards from the small of your back, his hot breath in your ear, which meant a peppery feeling in your extremities, a drowsy warmth in your lower belly, and lower still. Which meant (if you were lucky or cursed) at night, alone, under the covers, something so raw and wracked and already whole that – although it seemed strange to think it – it could not, honestly, ever be shared with anyone else. Annie woke up suddenly, flailing like a fish at the bottom of a boat, fretful with hope. 'Did it work?' she would gasp. 'Will they love you now?' And Samantha and her friends would spit out curt thanks, already weary of the conceit.

But things had been different for Annie. As initiations go, hers should have precipitated a haunting more sustained and damaging than any séance could summon. Why, then, is it Samantha who pitches and yearns, is beset by a desire she can only ever faultily fulfill? When Annie, aged nine, told Samantha what had happened with their cousin Bobby – the clandestine meetings, the candy, the caresses that turned toxic – Samantha had swallowed her sister's shame and turned it into the wrong kind of anger.

'Bobby is a very close friend of mine,' Annie had said, when Samantha recoiled, reproved, denied. 'He said it was just something for us, a love game, you know? Like the say-once game?'

'He is not your friend and this makes you a little, well, this makes you a slut, Annie.'

Samantha releases her mother-in-law's hand, excuses herself to the propless man. 'Just going to the bathroom,' she half-whispers.

'Let me get you another drink. What would you like? I'm Max, by the way, a friend of Philip's from work.' He follows her over to a nearby table.

'Samantha. Nice to meet you. Vodka and cranberry, please. Twist of lime. Two twists of lime.'

'Gotcha. Two twists.' He winks at her.

Smug polished stones cluster next to the sink beside a pile of dried rose petals resting in a shallow pewter dish, and in the mirror: Samantha's own self, flushed from the wine and the dancing. The hairdo seems prepared to rally, but an anxious musk is mingling expertly with her perfume, clouding out from under her arms, between her legs. She touches her cheek, smooths the shininess from the edge of her nose, taps at her emerging crow's feet, considers lip gloss. But no, stall first. Inside the stall is safe and square, the lock slots into place as it should. She swings her skirt up and forward, gathers it in front and works her underwear down with one hand. Once seated, she relaxes into the pee, her panties pulled taut between her knees. Everything, her whole life, shrunk now, to this stall, which is every stall, every seat where she's ever sat to pee. A room of one's own and all the careful deliberation of the drunken: the narrowed eyes, clasping fingers, the slow tear and the slower, conscientious wipe. The light is pleasantly bright, the walls gleaming and graffiti-free. Samantha is not dizzy, although she is experiencing some of the empty-headed euphoria that accompanies dizziness. Her gaze slides easily up the walls to the ceiling, then back down again.

The door to the bathroom opens. A gulp of 'Dancing Queen' before it swings shut. Ivory toenails, strappy black patent leather sandals click over to the sink, then into the stall two over from Samantha. 'Bon voyage!' she calls softly, when she hears a neighbourly flush. Bon voyage! For this is what it has become – the whole affair – watching Annie move slowly away from her, as if on the deck of a cruise liner from the forties. She's fluttering a white handkerchief, pretending, trying on a life that, as children, they could never have conceived.

Marriage: it was a place where dolls lived, stiff-limbed and polite, dry humping on piled-up napkins, a mini Kleenex package for their pillow. And Annie now is stepping into it, as if through a gate in a tall brick wall no one can see past or over. How can this be true? Samantha does not want this to be true. Because the only forts in which she still has faith are those built in the deep days and nights they spent as sisters. If asked *Do you love your sister?* how else could she reply? *Yes. Yes. Yes.* But love is watery thin – impotent! – compared to what she feels. 'Bon voyage,' she says again, to the impassive tile. *Bon voyage.* To the purse rack, with a queen-like wave. The pomp and circumstance, cummerbunds, tulle and pageantry. The solicitous man, gazing over her shoulder into the gaping crevasse of his future. It is not what Samantha wants. Then what is it that eludes her? She braces herself against the wall to work the panties back up into position. A baby, she has been thinking lately. Or not thinking, but feeling in the ache that ripples through the crooks of her arms, the ghost town of her lap. A baby. She washes her hands, dabs them dry with a paper towel, then shakes them gaily under the blower for good measure.

Back at the table, Max is holding a lime slice in each hand, grinning.

'Two twists.' He passes them to her. She squirts the juice into the redness, pokes at the ice cubes with her straw. 'Thanks.'

'So, what do you do, Samantha? I mean, when you're not cutting a rug.' Max laughs as if he's not sure how.

She likes that: *cutting a rug*, the nervousness. 'I've been travelling quite a bit, working wherever I can, trying to get a bit of a handle on the way the world works.' She recoils. *How the world works?*

'Really. Where have you been?' He focuses on a point just above her collarbone.

It is possible she is losing him here, and although she is still not certain he is worthy, she wants him to pay attention, to validate whatever Samantha-style missives she can toss his way. She craves the spotlight but knows she'd feel overly warm in the cheeks, fraudulent, if she managed to get there. Has she always been this way? Crippled by self-conscious righteousness? Oblivious to others in all but the most superficial way? It is likely, she muses, that she will produce a maladjusted, misanthropic child – no matter how much Mozart or Mandarin the baby is privy to in utero.

Max clears his throat.

He likes her. So it is settled then. 'Well, I was working on a farm in Mexico for a while and I've just been teaching in Vietnam – English, to teenagers mostly. Sort of the equivalent of our high school, but more structured and rigid. Which wasn't really a bad thing. I mean, I had some wonderful students, hungry for what I could give them, hungry for what we have. Hard to get them to loosen up though; they've got the weight of the world on their shoulders. So much expectation … '

'Right. That must have been challenging for you.' He is feigning or not feigning admiration. Either way.

'More challenging for them.' She can feel herself being humble and hates it. 'What about you? Are you in marketing with Philip?' Samantha knows next to nothing about marketing and considers this a fault. Enough people seem to do it, all day, for days on end; there must be something molten and mesmeric at its core.

'Well, yeah, more the communication side of things, really. Some graphics and copywriting. Not very interesting. I'm in a band, though, and I do some, well, performance pieces, I guess.'

'Oh.' It doesn't suit him, this revelation. Samantha struggles to match it up with the mannered walk, the missing cane. 'What kind … ?'

'Well, I try to express how the banal, the menial … ' He is dragging his fingers through some spilled red wine on the table, drawing diminutive snouts and asteroids that glow softly up at them. Samantha considers the weave of his linen suit and the slight lean of his nose and finds they please her immensely.

'You know, how the universal, the transcendental, can be encapsulated in the small, seemingly inconsequential occurrences that surround us.' Max lifts his eyes to meet hers, his nostrils aquiver with the power of art explained. It is possible she was wrong about marketing, its central mystery. She smiles like a tired sorceress.

'I mean, I write and sing about whatever happens to me, I guess.' He smiles back at her.

Okay, this is better. 'There's something to be said for paying attention to the everyday, I suppose.' Samantha nods at him, and keeps nodding, as if weighing things up. But what is now dawning on her, like a lazy sunrise, is the fact that she is no longer living the domestic, or even cannily observing it, but instead attempting, clumsily, to ambush it at every turn. She has become unmoored; she is drifting downstream from her very own life. She is saddened by this, then remembers. A baby – *there* was an anchor, an absolute, a tangible. Without meaning to, she has begun to tap her foot in time to the music, is swaying ever so slightly, a happy reed on the shore newly discovered by the wind.

Max nods distractedly in the direction of the dance floor. 'Would you ... ?'

'Yes,' she says, 'why not?'

To talk while dancing seems awkward and prematurely intimate, but the silent alternative more so. The music canters up and around them, creates not so much a mood as an expectation. Samantha struggles to keep the physical distance between their bodies consistent. She knows any type of rapprochement will require careful diagnosis on both their parts.

Max leans towards her, but with a certain sanitized purpose. 'I've done a fair bit of travelling, but really, in the end, it comes down to a kind of day-to-day vigilance, a certain faith in the richness of the domestic sphere. I'm not sure there's much new I can learn through the exotic,' he murmurs past her ear.

'Huh, the domestic. The exotic. What do you mean?' She can't help it; her voice has grown edges. She thinks this Max is trying to put something over on her, and succeeding.

'I mean, well, to put it inelegantly, to use a cliché, I mean Be Here Now, I suppose.' He sighs showily at his own conversational ineptitude, then applies some pressure to the small of her back, leading her into the centre of the cluster of dancers. Why, thinks Samantha, do people always apologize for using clichés, then seem pleased to have used them in the first place? Annie had once told Samantha, by way of comfort and admonishment, that she expected too much of people. 'Yes,' she had shouted in reply, 'yes, I do!'

The song segues into something more rhythmic and cross. Samantha wants to jump up and down, to pump her fist and yell, but she doesn't know how with such an audience. She makes her way back over to the tables and chairs, Max following close behind.

### Eliza: There Are Limits

'Can't say I like this much.' Bea nods towards the dance floor.

The music is hard and bare. A man speaks in nursery rhyme about getting naked over the steady pulse of bass. 'That's rap, Bea. It's the rage.'

'Ridiculous.'

And what can I say? I've tried to pull myself by the seat of the pants into the times of today, to keep up with what is televised, but there are limits. 'Yes,' I reply. 'Ridiculous.'

### Samantha: Mudstick

Somehow – how? – Samantha finds herself dancing again with Philip's mother, a tiny, wiry woman, with dark wiry hair and a quick, wiry mind. 'Welcome,' she says simply to Samantha, who thanks her, twice, wishing this woman were her own mother as they waltz carefully through the crowd.

Why is it, *really*, that Sandra, Samantha and Annie's own flesh-and-blood mother, has not mustered the courage to attend her own daughter's wedding? In her place is a package the size of a small fridge, around which all the other gifts have been clustered like acolytes. The gift is not a small fridge, although it could well have been for all the care Sandra has put into it. Not that Samantha thinks much of the whole gift-giving enterprise to begin with. There is a rule – made up by a posse of matrons and manners mavens (and marketers, no doubt!) – that insists the amount you spend on the wedding gift must equal or exceed the amount the hosts spend to feed you while you make merry. When had the world become so assuredly crass? But perhaps it had not changed much since the days of the obliging milk cow offered with the mild-demeanoured daughter with decent child-bearing hips. Sandra had called Samantha to tell her she had checked the registry and found a corresponding kitchen mixer on sale in Detroit for one third of the price, a scratch on the finish remedied by a daub of similarly hued nail polish.

But if Annie is upset at their mother's absence, she does not show it. She runs like a sleek, white clown – fresh out of finishing school – towards her sister, who is now standing with Max in the far doorway, as if pausing regally before making an entrance. Only it is too late for such things now.

Annie releases Philip's hand to embrace Samantha. 'Married. Do you believe it?' she asks, her breath skimming the underside of her sister's chin.

'Well,' says Samantha. She nods, ducks her head to hide her tears. 'Our Annie,' she mumbles into her sister's perfect hair.

She had a teen magazine she treasured, has it still, squirrelled under grade-school reports and old tax returns at the back of a closet. *To test your breath before a date*, it instructed, *blow softly into a soda bottle, then sniff.* At the age of eleven, she taught Annie and together they misted up the green glass. 'Mine smells … ' Annie always said, so certain and free, even back then. 'My breath smells like yours.'

Max and Samantha return to what has become – within so short a time, in so few exchanges, but life is lived like this, isn't it? – *their* table, to find the ice in their drinks has melted into tiny translucent disks. The serving staff is still loitering around the periphery, wiping down surfaces, scowling with a handsome lack of conviction. Samantha drains her glass in two long pulls. Max places his hand on her knee like a comrade. She watches her sister and Philip on the dance floor, studies their embrace as if from far away, and farther still.

She can feel the weight of Max's hand on her knee, can sense what was once friendly becoming something more, something her body insists she must requite. She shifts her legs to the side, makes to cross them, and Max lifts his hand up and away. Up, up and away, she thinks as a bridal bouquet sails unbidden into her mind's eye. At the next table a baby cries out in hunger or in pain or in anger or in loneliness. The baby's parents stick their heads into the baby's bassinet; they are quicksilver sleuths and the most essential of superintendents. They do not emerge from the baby's lair for a long time. Samantha understands that it is impossible to just sit back and observe a baby. You cannot pass a baby by. A baby has needs, it draws you into its orbit surely and quickly. She looks at Max. He toasts her extravagantly. A person could do worse than a marketer-slash-performance-artist for a father. Samantha lifts her own glass, sips, then excuses herself again. 'Bladder,' she says, 'like walnut.' She holds up her hand in an A-OK sign by means of demonstration.

Max looks elated, then puzzled. 'Okay,' he says.

Samantha walks past her Gran and Bea, huddled together like frail football players with a plan; she steps over her six-year-old cousin Graham tying napkins together in the shape of a lasso; she notices Sebastian Newton in a pile against a wall, his hand gripping the top of a barely upright beer bottle as if it were a ski pole. Was it she or Annie who had kissed him, French-style, after a party at Suzy Ludcombe's? Neither of them can remember, and it strikes her (although not forcefully) that this is perhaps odd. The bathroom looks different this time around. Someone has stacked the stones next to the sink in the shape of a lopsided inukshuk. So we don't get lost! Samantha thinks, thrilled and troubled. She turns towards the mirror, although there is no need, really. She is beautiful from the booze, smart too, thoughts linking up with loud connective clicks. She bends over to check stall vacancy. Ah, shoes she knows. They are her sister's round-toed ivory pumps, size six wide. She reaches under and grabs an ankle. 'Annie?'

'Let go, you stuck-in-mud monster.'

Samantha lets go.

Annie steps out of the stall and bumps her hip against Samantha's. 'Hey,' she says. 'Kidding.' She rinses her hands, glances over at the towel dispenser, then wipes them on her dress.

'That's your dress, Annie.'

'Yes it is. Yes. It. Is.' She grabs Samantha's hand. 'C'mon, Mudstick. Let's play Concentration.' She lifts her palms. Samantha does the same and Annie begins. It is a game less dependent on strategy than memory and association; it is an accounting of sorts. 'Let's play Concentration.' She taps Samantha's hands. 'No repeats, no hesitation.' She taps them again and Samantha taps back. 'You go first, I'll go second.' Another tap. 'Topic is ... Names!'

'Names of what?' Samantha drops her hands and takes a step back.

'Well,' says Annie. 'People we know!' She lifts her hands to tap Samantha's hands again. 'Sebastian!'

Samantha smiles and taps her sister back. 'Dad.'

'Not a name,' says Annie.

'Yes it is.'

'Okay, I'll allow.' Tap. 'Remington Steele.'

'You don't know him, Annie.'

'No,' says Annie sadly. 'Your turn.'

'Maggie.'

'Who's that?'

'Mum's second cousin – she visited from England when we lived in the high-rise on Southam Road. Red hair and those tight dresses with sashes?'

'Oh yeah. Okay. Hands up.' Tap. 'Dominican Republic.'

'That's a country, not a person.'

'Yes, but it should be a person. I think we'd be pals.' Tap. 'Bobby.'

'Don't say his name, Annie.'

'Why not?'

'It's not your turn.'

'Then you go.'

'I can't.'

'Why not, Mudstick?'

'Because I would have killed him.' Samantha leans up against the counter and reaches down to unstrap her shoe, which is rubbing annoyingly against her heel, but finds she cannot undo the buckle. Her hands are trembling. 'I *could* kill him.'

Annie squeezes Samantha's chin and gives a gentle wrench. 'I know that, Mudstick. That's why I never had to.' She smiles. 'Hands up,' she says. Tap. 'Philip.'

'Yes,' says Samantha. 'He's a good one.'

## Eliza: In the Dark

When Annie was twelve I gave her my autograph book. It was only partway full, the inscription on the first page still fierce, intact, a message from my own mother. On the first line, in careful cursive: *Above all to thine.* And on the second: *Own self be true!* I remember what I felt when she gave it to me, a thrill like eating ice cream too fast and a guilt that settled cloudily in my chest. I thought I knew what the message meant: that I must be true and never lie. And I knew the reason she had written this – it had something to do with a missing saucer and one of my unlikely falsehoods involving the cat. Still, I treasured that book, and even felt a twinge of regret when I handed it over to Annie. 'Own self,' she said, patting her chest. Then, 'Be true!' as if signing to a caveman.

Samantha is still talking to the tall man, her eyebrows meeting in the middle of her forehead like something from a political cartoon. Smile, I will her. Look into his eyes. There is softness in her, I've seen it. Post-Bobby, for an entire year, Annie refused to dress in anything but purple. When her mother lost patience, what little she had, it was Samantha who emerged in a lavender pantsuit and mauve eyeshadow to intercede. Softness and loyalty the girl has – it's a certain spontaneity that's missing. Always skidding around inside her own damn head. Still, I will give her this: there is no one Samantha despises more pointedly than her cousin Bobby Mason. But our Annie forgave. Annie invited him to the wedding. It was me and Samantha who burned the sealed envelope – queenly stamp and all – over the gas flame of my stove, relished the flames licking and flickering, then feigned puzzlement when the bastard never replied.

I have arrived at many conclusions in my life whilst wrapped in the charm and force of the moment, only to cast my certainty away when the next challenge foils me. Still, here is what I know: there is a brand of betrayal that cannot ever be forgiven, but it is unique to each and every person. There is a night I will always remember. Frank had left us for a while – found something sweet and comfortable with a secretary or some such. Annie and Samantha's mother – my daughter, Sandra – was young when he left, three years old. She got up the night he came home and stood at the top of the stairs in her nightie, staring at him through veils of sleep. He held out his arms, then reached into his pocket for the trinket he had bought in the hopes of being welcomed, reborn. She blinked and remained suspended in her place. Then she raced into her daddy's arms and I understood in a flash how – with a child's certainty, the most certain of certainties – I had been blamed, and how much, how absolutely I had lost.

I look around me at the leftovers of celebration. Napkins wadded like sad ghosts on the tables. Sleek, silver cameras abandoned next to bread baskets, delicate fringed swaths of cloth used to keep out the cold tossed casually over the backs of chairs. Glasses – half-full and half-empty – everywhere. The couple of the hour on the dance floor, swinging each other round, holding tight to hands as their friends watch and cheer. The city night through the window, the tower – that desperate beacon – standing straight up to the stars none of us can see, here in the company of streetlights and skyscrapers.

It scares me still, how bright we keep things, how hard it is to preserve the dark. Even now I believe that darkness is where we are most safe. In the dark they cannot see you. Bea – only seventeen! – came to us in the dark in June of 1944, her wide eyes made whiter, more round, by the gloom. We found her mother in the morning, crushed under a wardrobe that had worked itself free, shaken loose when a bomb hit blocks away. Six days later her father came home with one arm and three bars of chocolate. He hugged Bea lopsidedly, then left her to her own devices. We shared the chocolate, and my fiancé booked us a passage to Canada.

'Annie, she deserves this,' sighs Bea, her plate heaped high with tarts and confections.

'Yes.'

I give Bea a little squeeze and she turns to me, surprised, then smiles.

'You're not getting any of this coconut pie, if that's what you're thinking,' she says.

Samantha: We Fail?

'You know,' says Samantha, 'I had this one student in Vietnam who cycled for an hour and a half each morning to get to school. He wasn't bright – average, I'd say, or just above – but my God, he tried his nuts off in every single subject. I've never met anyone so young and so dedicated. I helped him fill out a university application for a school in the States. Some business school whose name escapes me – associated with one of the Ivy Leaguers. Princeton, I think. I want to go to a world-famous university, he kept telling me. I want to make my father proud. I must come back and get a very good job. Yes, I said, and thought, How terrible for him, to be carrying so much, to wake each morning and step, unthinkingly, into that fierce forward motion. He was one of three, the middle child, living in a house with dirt floors. His favourite book was *Who Moved My Cheese?* Samantha stops talking to take a sip of her drink. She knows she is drunk and holding forth. Max is making a listening-type face, his eyebrows raised generously, but she's pretty sure he is also sneaking discreet peeks at her cleavage. She doesn't care; a message is burning inside her, it begs telling.

'This boy's father told the children, when they were very young, that there would be money for only one of them to go to school.' Although it is a hackneyed, possibly ethnocentric image, Samantha cannot help picturing the family huddled around the central cooking fire of their ragged home. She places the aspiring boy at the edge of the circle, clothes him in a Nike football jersey, some cut-off jeans and a pair of worn leather thongs. She smooths his brow with one open hand, then steps back, into the shadows. 'This man set up a scholarship fund for the child who earned the highest marks, then he worked like a dog in the rice fields to make the funds grow.'

Samantha pauses. She is telling this story for herself more than Max. Why? Because there is a lesson to be learned. If you want something, you must not waver. If you need something, you must try your damnedest, always, to get it. While in Vietnam, she had explained to her students the difference some marks on a page could make.

> *Macbeth: If we should fail –*
> *Lady Macbeth: We fail?*

You had a choice between indecision and imperiousness when it came to the relative success of your plans. Like all of life, it was only a matter of intonation. Samantha leans forward and places her hand lightly on Max's forearm.

'Did he get in?' says Max.

'What?'

'Did he get in to the school?'

'Oh,' she says. 'Yes.'

'Well, then, you did a good thing helping him the way you did. His father must be so proud.' Max announces this matter-of-factly, almost curtly, so that it resonates with truth.

'Yes,' she says, beginning to like the way he makes her unsure of the point of things.

They go out together into the night, into the courtyard and the grassy stretch of park, over a small knoll, to a spot under a maple buttressed by chicken wire near the chain-link fence. The city surrounds them, blocks and blocks of blinking, squared-off ambition. Standing there under the ozone – tattered, as it is, like a child's security blanket – Samantha tips up her face to kiss Max.

### Eliza: Forget-Me-Nots

Frank begged off with seasickness on the journey from Carlisle. Bea and I spent most of our time on deck playing games with the wind, watching it work our hair into strange birds of prey, boisterous bouffants. The ship felt luxurious and large to us, despite the crowds, and I still get shivers thinking about the red velvet ropes in the stairwells.

I found them lapping at each other on his narrow bunk, Bea's eyes squinched shut in love or concentration – who can really tell the difference when it comes right down to it? Frank's eyes fluttered at the sound of my step. He could always, in all our years, hear me coming. Our gazes met, magnetized, mid-air.

Up on deck the spray had real spunk, and I hated the fact that the ship was my home.

Bea's mother had embroidered her handkerchiefs for her sixteenth birthday – tiny blue forget-me-nots with black staring centres sewn along the scalloped edges. I brought Bea to tears halfway across the Atlantic by snatching one from her sleeve and waving it over the churning grey of the waves. She was on her knees with nausea and frustration before long, and stayed there, sobbing, until I placed the hanky daintily, royally, on her bowed head. In this way we forgave.

Annie's dress has been trampled at the back – the dusty spirits of footprints on the dragging train. The flowers that were worked so finely into her hair (rolled and twisted like hamentaschen, she told me, a pastry representing the hat of a Hebrew hero) are gone, and wisps have sprung free around her temples. Her nose is slick with sweat. She signals to the DJ to stop the music with a slicing motion across her fine neck, and the silence is confusing; it slows us all down and sharpens our vision. The guests trip back to their tables, await instructions. Annie has collected her bouquet from the head table: gardenias, marigolds and dahlias, their stems wound round with a wide hot pink ribbon whose ends trail and flap. She lifts the bouquet in the air – up, up and up – towards the bright disco ball. There are sighs and deficient giggles, and Samantha to my left, averting her gaze. Annie turns towards us; she knows how to find and hold her sister steady. They stare at each other. What is it about a room full of people waiting on love to be declared that plugs up the throat? Annie stops in front of Samantha, salutes her with her eyes. Then she turns in my direction, scoots alongside my chair, crouches close – ah! the smell of her hair, the smell of her sweet baby head! – and lays the bouquet in my lap.

People talk about opposite points of your life like the tail ends of a measuring tape that will meet only when you've travelled and tallied that last quarter inch. But Frank once brought me a set of Russian dolls after he'd been out all night. He smelled of pipe smoke and a single woman's soap when he handed them over – round-faced, brightly swaddled women nestling right down into themselves to a tiny, solid core. Sometimes my wedding – Frank's smart, purposeful army uniform, the joy and terror doing caged battle in my chest – fits tightly around his deathbed, a too-low ceiling, and how it felt to hold the hand of a husk. Other times, a small moment or image will grow, harden like lacquer and click into place over my entire self. The way Frank allowed his tented book to fall to the floor as we dreamt our way to the ends of our stories and away from each other. My daughter's face as she pulled on her socks for the first time, the smell of my father's shirts at the end of the day, Bea's red golf umbrella snapping open above us, a certain shade of sky.

### Samantha: Muddling

Out in the night, with Max's arms around her, her dangerous heels sinking into the moist earth, Samantha realizes something. It is a bracketed understanding that settles outside and slightly to the left of her head, and will eventually drift into her blind spot. She remembers how she and Annie saved the Kleenexes they snotted into at their granddad's funeral, balled them in their pockets, then deposited them in a cookie tin and wedged the lid tightly down. She remembers bestowing cast-offs on Annie – three-limbed Barbies and too-short sweaters. Her sister's face receiving these poor gifts was terrifying in its anxious bliss. 'For keeps?' she'd query softly. '*For keeps?*

'It's all about muddling, isn't it?' Samantha mutters drunkenly, good-naturedly, into Max's shoulder. Lady Macbeth thought it wise to unsex herself; she gave demons leave to drink from her breasts so she could get on with it, the business of power, but today, Samantha thinks, well, today people go to great lengths to procure offspring, seeking out test tubes and turkey basters, or rescuing tiny foreign tykes left behind by mothers themselves overlooked and overwhelmed. All over the world, blazing bombs in the shapes of planes or pointy fingers zoom down from the sky. The future breakdances madly on cardboard boxes laid over the earth's mismatched plates and lava – and still we stake a claim on it!

Max kisses Samantha's collarbone; his hands find purchase under her bum.

She keeps thinking she's found it, the answer, and then it morphs, all sci-fi, into something alien and unclassifiable. *For keeps*, Samantha chants silently, as she guides Max's fingers, unbuckles his belt, offers up important corners and foldings of herself.

'Are you sure,' he says kindly, but only partway means it.

## Eliza: Good Luck to You

'She didn't have to do that,' I say, cradling the bouquet in my lap, saltwater squeezing out from under my eyelids.

'But she did,' says Bea, putting her arm around me.

'She did,' says Samantha, teetering strangely on her heels, legs pressed together, ankles crossed as if gathering herself together, holding something in. She shakes her head and kisses the top of mine.

I reach up to grab on to her smart self. (You know, I once asked Samantha why she couldn't find herself a fella. Can't stay up on the shelf too much longer, I advised. She told me she was deeply involved with books. On the shelf, she said, was fine. Well, I said, good luck to you when it comes to reproducing.)

'She did,' Samantha says again, and takes hold of my hand, squeezing oh-so-tight.

Bea, who is in her cups, has begun asking questions. 'A dove brings white babies, right?'

I do not answer.

'Nothing but bleached-out pigeons, doves.' Bea is slurring, but happy. I take her hand, but she pulls it away.

'And a crow brings black babies,' she says.

A caution is kicking inside me. I look over at Samantha, who is frowning down at Bea. Bea knocks her knife off the table, then bends, gruntingly, to retrieve it. From under the tablecloth comes a new question, more pointed. 'What, then … ' This is muffled by the thick linen of the tablecloth's overhang. She straightens up, places the knife in the centre of the table, far from the edge of the known world. 'What brings *no* babies?'

I shake my head while Bea smiles into her chest. Always, always, there is Bea, hurrying up the joke, harrumphing to herself.

'Two swallows,' she manages, between gasps. She slaps the table, overcome with the hilarity.

Samantha, for all her prudery and politics, is laughing along with Bea.

And I laugh too, knowing, in my heart of hearts, that, timing or no, this is good.

## Notes and Acknowledgements

Some stories in the collection have been previously published (in slightly different form) in the following books and periodicals: 'BriannaSusannaAlana' in *The New Quarterly* 94 and *Journey Prize Stories 18*; 'My Friend Taisie' in *Hobart # 8*; 'Dominoes' as 'White Bread Fiction' in *PRISM International* 41:4; 'Dingbat' in *The New Quarterly* 85; 'Bye Bye Flangle Nuts' in *The New Quarterly* 99; 'Wanted Children,' in *Toronto Noir*; 'Impossible to Die in Your Dreams' on bookninja.com and in *The New Quarterly* 107.

Writing and publishing a book is sometimes a bit like raising a child – it takes a village. Many thanks to: *The New Quarterly*, the Toronto Arts Council, the Ontario Arts Council, the Canada Council for the Arts and the Writers' Trust of Canada for monetary and moral support; Kathryn Kuitenbrouwer, steadfast friend and supporter of my writing habit; Jennifer Birrell, for impromptu childcare; Simona Opris for help with Romanian history and language; Amber Wilson, Kim Jernigan, Carrie Snyder, Julie Birrell and Hilary McMahon for early readings of the manuscript; Alana Wilcox, who handled these stories with true care and integrity; and all the good folk at Coach House, who gave the book a home and called it their own.

My family bolster and sustain me always; this book wouldn't exist without their help. As ever, love and thanks to the exceptional Charles Checketts, who keeps me in good grub and good spirits.

## About the Author

**Heather Birrell** is the author of the previous story collection *I know you are but what am I?* (Coach House, 2004). Her work has been honoured with the Journey Prize for short fiction and the Edna Staebler Award for creative non-fiction, and has been shortlisted for both National and Western Magazine Awards. Birrell's stories have appeared in many North American journals and anthologies, including *The New Quarterly* and *Toronto Noir*. She lives with her husband and two daughters in Toronto, where she teaches high school English.

Typeset in Bell and Agency.

Printed in February 2012 at the old Coach House on bpNichol Lane in Toronto, Ontario, on Zephyr Antique Laid paper, which was manufactured, acid-free, in Saint-Jérôme, Quebec, from second-growth forests. This book was printed with vegetable-based ink on a 1965 Heidelberg kord offset litho press. Its pages were folded on a Baumfolder, gathered by hand, bound on a Sulby Auto-Minabinda and trimmed on a Polar single-knife cutter.

Edited and designed by Alana Wilcox
Cover design by Ingrid Paulson
Author photo by Charles Checketts

Coach House Books
80 bpNichol Lane
Toronto ON M5S 3J4
Canada

416 979 2217
800 367 6360

mail@chbooks.com
www.chbooks.com